# The Measure of Everything

## A Novel by Ed Davis

Plain View Press
P. O. 42255
Austin, TX 78704

plainviewpress.net
sbright1@austin.rr.com
1-512-441-2452

Photos for cover and title page are by Patricia Perry.

# Dedication

For Al Denman, Julia Cady, Dave and Sharen Neuhardt, and all the other earth-minded angels who worked to save Whitehall Farm in the winter of 1999.

# August, The New Millenium

*The road to Meredith's Pond dips down beneath an old railroad bridge, now bike trail. Billy passes into its shadow and emerges into a new, white world. It even sounds different in the fog, water from yesterday's rain spilling down the dam into Shawnee Springs Creek. Through mist he sees puffs of brighter white on the banks, duckbills buried in feathers.*

*His heart rises, a fish flashing into light. How can you have hope, so rare is the thing you seek?*

*You just do, that's all.*

*The day will be a scorcher, but not yet. Approaching slowly, he swims through cool air beading on his bare arms and face. You never look before it's time. Even thinking can make it fly. You circle toward it, let go of need. Become clean, open, empty.*

*And there it stands in the spillway: unlikely, awesome, almost invisible. Stunning in flight, the great blue god, grounded and fishing, looks small and compact. As always, it takes his breath, leaves his heart beating fast.*

*Motionless, his heron searches the water, fragile and fierce. It knows he's here. So softly and gradually Billy doesn't notice at first, the August air fills with wintry flakes, and memory and presence collide at the edge of all that happened eons ago, only yesterday . . .*

# Chapter One

Putnam County, West Virginia
Sunday, March 12, 1999


Had Billy known all along where he'd go – or had the road chosen him? Well, Route 35 East (and eventually south) only led one place in his mind. And right now, with Neil Young singing "Heart of Gold" on the Dakota's stereo and two pieces of paper burning a hole in the pocket of his flannel shirt, he thought West Virginia had never looked so good. Or bad.

He'd had to wait until the Shawnee Springs Credit Union opened this morning to leave. And last night he'd hardly slept in the rest area on Ohio State Route 86, going into the bathroom every hour or so to change the bandage on his hand. (It was hardly bleeding at all now.) So after a two-hour nap behind a K-Mart, he was finally crossing the bridge at Gallipolis, the river blinding white in the afternoon sun. It seared the edges of his memory as well as vision, blanking out all that lay behind him. That was the thing about the road: made you look ahead, not behind.

Welcome to Wild, Wonderful West Virginia.

The land here in Putnam County struck him, as it always did, as awesome in its raw beauty. Farming country. He admired the old leaning barns, the silos, muddy cattle standing in greenish-brown puddles of snow-melt. Billy rolled down the window and inhaled. Mud and manure. A thaw seemed in progress here, although winter still had a chokehold back home in southwestern Ohio, though it was only four hours away.

Home. Had Shawnee Springs ever really been home or just a temporary oasis?

The barn ahead on the left bellowed its slogan about Mail Pouch chewing tobacco. He considered the ads folk art compared to the interstate billboards peddling booze, broads and no-tell motels. The silky Kanawha River serpentined beside the two-lane. No traffic whatsoever on Sunday morning, everybody at church. And he'd passed several high-steepled country churches looking straight out of a Norman Rockwell painting, their parking lots overflowing. Billy smiled. God's country.

Which took his thoughts right to Grand-dad. After Ma's death, visits had tapered off and finally Billy's dad hadn't wanted to see his father at all. "He doesn't like my occupation, my women or my lifestyle," Dad had told him the last time Billy begged him to go see Grand-dad. "He can go to hell."

So they hadn't even gone to Grand-dad's funeral, and Dad had finally stopped going back even for a once-yearly visit to other relatives. Now Billy had to see his father's homeplace.

The glittering river, high from the snow-melt, gleamed as if lit from fires within. Occasional dead deer littered the roadside, but the pavement had straightened out. He reached over, clicked off the stereo. He knew how the others would see his leaving, with only a week till the auction. *Traitor, thief.* The pocket above his heart tingled. Could he really cash that check?

He was pretty sure it was all over with CitFarm now. The headlines, the photos. Irreparable damage. He wouldn't be surprised if someone had even gotten hurt. Schuyler would see it as the perfect chance to obliterate the violent radicals. Couldn't've designed it for better media exposure himself! Thanks a lot, Mark.

Still, he found himself grinning and gaping like a five-year-old at every picturesque barn and farmhouse, his heart rising as he watched a kestrel leap into the air from a fence post ten feet from the truck. Movin' on. They'd never find him, though he was less than two hundred miles away. Maybe it had taken a farm fight to revive the existence of Grand-dad's farm for him. Now he had to see the place, get some perspective, decide his next move. It was a destination, maybe a launching pad. He didn't know yet, or need to know.

For now, he was doing his best not to think about where he'd come from. About Seth. But he couldn't stop the images . . .

○

Only three weeks ago, he'd watched her walk through the door of the Bean Tree, its jangling bells announcing a newcomer. Outside it was snowy mid-February, but inside the coffee shop, with soft jazz playing in the background, it felt snug. She stepped toward the burners, lifted the hot water carafe and poured, approached the register, paid for a teabag and headed for a table in the rear.

Beside him, Bonnie snorted. Across from her, Ira grinned.

"Come on, Billy, the farm's zoned agricultural and residential with a three-hundred-foot frontage. It ain't gonna happen."

"Zoning can be changed," he replied. "As a matter of fact, our wise township trustees are discussing it as we speak."

He had smiled past Bonnie, right at the stranger (who, he discovered to his delight, was staring right at him). "So I guess you won't sign my petition?"

Bonnie glared for ten seconds, then suddenly rose.

"Bonnie." Ira placed a hand on her arm. But she knocked it away and huffed out the door, leaving an explosion of bells in her wake.

Ira sighed. "Billy, there's been pressure on Ray ever since November to get something done about affordable housing."

Billy shook his head. "She's got a blind spot for her big brother. I think he'll vote with the pro-developers when the time comes."

"Maybe, maybe not. I'm outta here. Got math tests to grade."

"Tonight then, Citizens to Save the Farm: Conference Room Three?"

"I guess. Not that it's gonna do any good."

As soon as Ira was out the door, Billy turned toward the rear. Sure enough, she was looking right at him. He cupped his hands around his mouth:

"So maybe *you'll* sign my petition, lovely lady?"

Before she could respond, he was on his feet, walking toward her table.

"I'm Billy Acorn."

"Acorn?" she repeated.

"Yeh, when great-granddaddy Achor showed up at Ellis Island . . . well, you know the rest." He shrugged, trying for boyishness. "It's kinda mythic, like Johnny Appleseed."

When she just continued to stare, he spoke again softly. "And you are?"

"Oh, I'm sorry. Eliza- . . . Seth Abel," she got out.

He laughed. "Hello, Eliza-*seth* Abel. You sure have a unique first name."

When she brushed back her blonde hair, he found himself loving the gesture.

"My daddy wanted a boy. And I guess for awhile I wanted to be that boy. Anyhow." She gave a little wave of her fingers. "I decided to quit being Beth and chose Seth. I haven't used Elizabeth or Beth in years."

"How come I don't know you?"

"I just moved back last August."

"No way. I'd've noticed you."

She smiled, not taking the bait. *Damn.* Had she seen him scrutinizing her fingers for a ring.

"I mostly work – the retirement community south of town?"

"Comfort Manor. Great place, I hear."

"And I take care of my son."

"How old is he?

"Paul's twelve. Sixth grade."

He nodded, storing it for later use. Before she could open her mouth, he spoke again.

"Where'd you move back from?"

"New Mexico . . . Taos."

He nodded. "I crashed there with a friend of mine once, on the way to 'Frisco. We even saw a rain dance at the Pueblo." He laughed. "And I swear to God, it rained!"

She smiled. After a brief moment, he sobered. "I'll bet you're an artist."

"My husband is . . . was. He's an art dealer now . . . very successful."

"Oh." He affected great sadness. "You're married."

"Separated."

He brightened. "Well, welcome to the Buckeye state, Seth. Shawnee Springs isn't exactly Ohio, even though it's *in* Ohio. We like to think it's sort of a country all by itself."

She folded her arms. "How about you? Lived in town long?"

"Going on ten years."

"Burke grad?" She had her fingers stuck in her armpits, shivering.

He shook his head. "I came, I crammed, I departed without degree."

"Me, too."

He looked shocked. "When?"

She smiled tightly. "Before you."

"But not much before." Too late he sensed flattery wouldn't work on her.

"So . . . this petition."

"Oh, yeh. May I sit down?" She nodded at the empty chair across from her. After sitting, he laid the document between them on the table.

"Wood Thrush Farm. It's in danger of being sold at auction within a month to developers who will most likely turn it into Crackerbox City – who knows? – maybe even a Wal-Mart. A bunch of us think that Township Trustees should refuse to support re-zoning and purchase Wood Thrush Farm outright, re-selling it to farmers with easements. That's added to the deed, signed and recorded at the courthouse. It means the land can't be used for any other purpose besides the one stipulated. Forever. We want that purpose to be farming."

She was reading the petition, hunkered forward, her lovely hair falling forward around her cheeks. Without looking up, she spoke.

"Is it free?"

Billy smiled broadly. "Not hardly. If a developer would pay $1500 an acre, and the going rate for farmland in the area is a thou – then the cost of the easement would be the $500 difference."

"Whoa," she breathed. "Per acre?"

Billy nodded.

"Where *is* this farm?"

"It surrounds the village on the north, south and east, bordering Route 69 and Springville Road."

"You mean . . . " He watched it dawn slowly. " . . . all those fields I see all the way to Oldham's Dairy . . . ?" He nodded, knowing she was converting words into images of corn, trees, sunsets. "And . . . along Springville road?"

"Yep."

"That's *all* Wood Thrush Farm?"

They listened to the last gasp of steam leave the latest just-brewed pot.

"And it could be sold to developers?" Her voice was growing tinier and tinier. "They could put in . . . shopping centers?"

Billy nodded sadly. The machine made one final shudder before it ceased.

"I'll sign."

"I knew you would."

"What's this meeting tonight about?" She blushed. "I . . . overheard . . . "

"Strategy. With only a month till the auction, we've got to get people off their butts, get organized and . . . "

"You need an event," she said, "something for the media." Her voice had firmed up, her gaze direct.

"Aha: you've done this before." He stroked his beard. "You were at Burke in the mid-eighties, right?"

"That's right."

He sat forward eagerly. "Did you know Lloyd Kieron?"

"He was my history professor. " Her voice had begun shrinking again.

"And the leader of one of the most successful no-nukes movements in the U.S." He shook his head. "Dr. Keiron's gotten weird, some say crazy. Lives in the old Fletcher mansion on the south end of town – his late wife, the chicken heiress, left it to him. Alexandra's dad owned half the chickens in southeastern Ohio." He wagged his head. "Since her death, they say he won't see anybody."

She shrugged. "Idealists get bitter, too."

"Not Lloyd Kieron – not the brightest mind against corporate the-way-things-are that Burke has ever seen."

She'd begun putting on her coat.

"Maybe you'll come to the flagship meeting of CitFarm – Citizens to Save the Farm – tonight," Billy said, "village building, Conference Room Three, seven o'clock."

"Maybe."

As she turned and headed for the door, Billy called behind her, "Maybe you can tell us what kind of event we need."

"Something dazzling," she threw behind her. "Unearthly. With angels, trumpets and a celestial choir."

"Hey, and there's a rally tomorrow morning in front of the village building."

But she was gone.

○

He came back with a start, yanking the steering wheel hard to avoid a dead skunk. He'd totally spaced out for a few minutes. Now he realized he should be getting to the intersection with Marsden Valley Road. A mile or so back, the two lanes had widened to four, and he'd begun to see blue interstate signs. An interstate out here? Sure enough, as he slowed to forty-five, then thirty-five, he read a sign saying Charleston was just twenty-five miles via I-275. Damn – a fucking beltway over to I-64 at Charleston. And this used to be the boonies.

When he saw he was on a fast-food strip, his heart sputtered. True, it had been fifteen years since he'd come this way, but he was sure this was all farmland before. But he also knew: build an interstate and they will come. And build. And come.

Stores were getting larger: Lowe's, Kroger, K-Mart. He knew it was only a matter of time, and, sure enough, the inevitable loomed into view: A Wal-Mart Super Store. Damned if they hadn't paved paradise while he wasn't looking. Grand-dad's farm was now part of Charleston's 'burbs. Billy slammed his fist against the steering wheel.

Sitting at the light, Billy turned the stereo back on. When Neil began singing "Everybody Knows This Is Nowhere," he cranked it, despite the glare from two suits in the BMW beside him. As soon as the light changed, the yuppie driving gunned it and was halfway to the next light before Billy got the Dakota into gear. The sky, luminous blue before, had turned dark. After three more lights and still no Marsden Valley Road, Billy was seriously considering turning around and heading back to Ohio. At the next gas station he turned in. A perky blond kid wearing the red Speedway vest lounged at the counter.

"Help you, man?"

He didn't look old enough to work. Maybe it was his zitless, baby-soft face. But, no, it was probably the circa-1968 hair: parted in the middle, flower-child style, dangling well past his collar.

"Yeh." He leaned heavily on the counter. "You can direct me the way out of hell."

The kid giggled. "Yeh, West Virginia sucks."

Billy straightened. "My grand-dad has a farm someplace around here. This used to be the prettiest farm country in the world." He looked back over his shoulder. "Till they asphalted it."

The kid blushed. "Sorry, dude. Didn't mean to, like, diss your people. But for me this state is such a drag."

"I'm looking for Marsden Valley Road."

"Beck's Dairy?"

"Yeh, that's Grand-dad's neighbor."

"Beck's rules, man! I been trying to, like, get hired out there for years. Man, they even got insurance benefits. You wanna go back two lights and hang a louie at Wally World."

Billy's face must've registered blank.

"Go left at Wal-Mart."

"Thanks," Billy said, heading for the door.

"Hope you brought your clubs," the kid hollered but Billy hardly registered the nonsense syllables.

# Chapter Two

Shawnee Springs, Ohio
Saturday, February 18, 1999


As soon as he stepped outside his apartment building, Billy was
blinded by piled-up snow, glinting in the mid-morning sunshine.
Shading his eyes, he almost went back upstairs. It had snowed several
inches on top of last Monday's storm. Nobody'd show – not for this,
maybe not for any rally to save an endangered farm. Certainly not the
lovely lady he'd met in the Bean yesterday.

He quickly buttoned his dad's old navy-blue pea coat, the one he'd
found hanging in the closet when he was packing for college. ("Take
it," the old man said, waving in dismissal.) It still smelled faintly of
mothballs and Aqua Velva.

Damn, how could he oversleep today of all days? And he had the
beginnings of a headache.

The grinning teenager shoveling snow in front of the Trout Tavern
must've heard him mumbling to himself. He whirled around, nearly
knocking the shovel out of the kid's hands.

"You writing a book?" Billy yelled. "Leave out the chapter on me,
okay?"

The kid just grinned wider. "Hangover, Billy?"

"I quit drinking my last birthday."

"Ri-ight."

He walked on. It was beneath his dignity to tell the little prick that
the abuse of substances had never been his thing. Acorns had other
addictions – to self, mostly. So when his buddy Ira gave up pot, strongly
encouraged by the gendarmes, his employer and soon-to-be-ex-wife,
Billy did, too. If Ira didn't burn it, Billy couldn't bum it, simple as that.

Maybe he *was* hungover, though. On Seth Abel. Yesterday at the
Bean Tree, she'd left in a hurry after signing his petition. But he'd told
her about the rally. Fat chance that she'd come.

The clock above Knott's Clock Shoppe read nine-forty-five. Late to
his own rally. *Damn.*

When he reached the edge of the Village Center parking lot, Billy
couldn't believe his eyes. A crowd was gathering, and, against the
yellow-brick building, catching the growing morning light, was spread
a huge colorful banner. Stretched between two broomsticks, it was
being held up by two Burke students while Channel Twenty-Five's crew
videotaped it.

FARMS ARE FOR FARMERS.

Holy Mother. Had Burkers done all this? Mark?

He crunched up to the crowd, looking for the S.O.B., raising his hand to shield his eyes, snow-blinded. He cringed to remember how Mark had saved the day last night in the student union (his fellow CitFarmers had convinced him to go recruit). After Billy had pulled the plug on the juke box and finally gotten their attention, it was Mark who, recognizing him from the cement company protest two years ago, got his fellow students to pay attention to "the guy who'd brought the capitalist pigs to their knees."

Billy shook his head, trying to see. The blazing sun had turned all outdoors into a spangled sheen of light. His headache was worsening. Mark Zamora conjured memories Billy didn't want to revisit. He still saw flames in his dreams.

He almost walked into a table with a sign saying:
GIVE TILL IT HURTS.

Behind it, Woody Freeman beamed his million-kilowatt grin in every direction like a mirror ball. So it was he that had put all this together – in less than twelve hours. If it had been left up to Billy, they'd have a handful of Burke students. He doused warm tendrils of shame fingering upward into his chest. Thank God the old man was talking to *Shawnee Springs News* editor Cyrus Harmon and hadn't seen Billy. He didn't want to have to congratulate him just yet.

Billy turned, and, lo – there she was, Seth Abel walking toward him, hatless, long, golden hair gleaming, eyes wide with wonder, looking for all the world like an elven queen. His headache vanished.

She strode right up to him. "You're not pleased with the turnout?"

"Oh, sure, but . . . "

"You were frowning."

"It's out of control."

So lame. But he couldn't exactly say *It's not mine.* He studied the crowd with her: a group of townies was setting up a plywood platform to keep a small P.A. system dry; five or six Burke students were tuning guitars, banjos and mandolins; a guy at the contributions table stood raking in cash and checks; Wendy Small and Jim Jonas from Channel Twenty-Five walked around thrusting microphones into the faces of anyone who'd talk to them. The response to his (okay: Woody's) call to arms had been phenomenal. Best of all, there was no sign of Mark.

"Who's that?"

He followed her gaze. Woody, also hatless, with a wondrous shock of white hair glowing in the light, was flickering like a squirrel between trees as he moved from one group to another, folks inclining their heads toward him as if he were imparting secrets of the universe.

"He's sure got charisma," she said, looking up at Billy with rain-grey eyes.

"He's Haywood Freeman. Retired Burke prof. He's the land trust president. Great organizer – but kinda pushy."

"Now I remember him."

"You had him for a class?"

"Nah." It was beginning to bother Billy that she wouldn't look at him, just kept staring at the old man. "My advisor never let me sign up for any of his philosophy classes."

"Dr. Kieron, right?"

She nodded. "So what's a land trust?"

As he explained, he was thinking how she'd reacted to Dr. Kieron's name similarly yesterday afternoon in the Bean. He had a sudden inspiration.

"I'll bet you were at the Pitney protest in the eighties, weren't you?"

She nodded. Why were her lovely lips so tightly closed?

"So you knew Dr. Kieron well?"

She shrugged. "Kinda."

"A great, great man." *Damn.* He sounded too reverent. But he sensed that Seth did not share that reverence. A topic to be probed later. He retracted both hands from beneath his armpits where he'd been trying to warm them.

"Christ in a crock, Seth, I haven't even said good morning." And before she could dodge, he hugged her, and though she didn't return it, she didn't shrug him off, either. He let the hug linger a bit beyond polite-social length. It felt good, very good, and last night's dream of her rose unbidden before it was squelched by the sudden appearance of the boy by her side.

"Hey! Mom!"

She turned around. "Paul!"

She'd said her son was a twelve-year-old sixth-grader. Small as a fourth-grader, though, and his skin was as dark as Seth's was pale.

"Matt invited me to go with him and his dad to ice-skate in Cedarton."

Shading her eyes, she looked toward the parking lot entrance. Billy followed her gaze to a beige Mercedes with its motor running. A spikey-blonde-haired kid peeked out the back window. A man sat at the wheel, a woman beside him, though he could only see the backs of their heads.

"Matt Plummer, right?" Billy said.

Paul looked up.

"I know Matt's father, Ben. Owns the stained-glass shop." He winked at Seth. "Always makes a large contribution to the Widows and Orphans fund."

"Oh, yeh," she said. "You're the money man, aren't you?"

Billy grinned. "I guess you could say that."

"So, Mom, can I go?"

She was wavering. With the kid gone to Cedarton, maybe he could wrangle an invite to Mom's abode. A strategic planning session, perhaps.

"Paul, I'd like you to meet my friend, Billy Acorn."

The kid grinned. "Is he nuts?"

Billy laughed, repeated the immigration story he'd told Seth at the Bean. "We've been nuts ever since."

Paul looked back at his mom. "We'll be home by dinner, okay?"

"Well, all right, but . . . "

The boy was gone, waving behind him, half-falling in the barely-plowed parking lot.

"Plummers are a great family," Billy offered, but she ignored him, frowning.

"But you don't know how to ice-skate," she wailed as if Paul hadn't already gone, "and you're not dressed warmly enough, and I'll bet you didn't eat breakfast, and do you have any money for lunch and . . ?"

Clearly, she kept the boy on a short leash. Billy kept his trap shut, though he longed to touch her forehead and uncrease her brow. For several moments, she stood looking after her son, as if she'd forgotten Billy was there. He waited as long as he could. Then he patted her shoulder. "Good-looking boy."

At last she seemed to remember who he was. "So. What's happening?"

Billy rubbed his hands together furiously. "Freeman got out the vote. He musta stayed up all night. Every townie who's ever showed the slightest sign of activism decided to jump on the hay-wagon, looks like."

"Maybe all they wanted was to be asked."

"Yeh. By the right person."

"Oh, come on – it's still great, even if it isn't your baby."

He lifted a hand to protest, but suddenly the Burke musicians erupted into song, a cacophony of strings and drums coming from the vicinity of the banner. Freeman stood waving his arms, conducting.

Billy touched her arm, whispering conspiratorially. "The developers are inside."

"Who?"

"Today John Schuyler and all his development cronies come and look at the parcel descriptions and hatch their nefarious plots. Maybe after they see and hear us, they'll wonder if Shawnee Springs is such a great place for development after all."

Her eyes lit up and she squeezed his arm. "Brilliant," she whispered.

Before he could pull her into another hug, she was walking toward the side of the building where they'd set up the speakers. "It's starting," she said. "Let's go!"

The crowd was yelling: "We like farms! We like cows! Developers, developers, go home now!"

This part of the game he loved. Stroking a crowd was like eating donuts: fat and calories and a mega-sugar rush. Catching up with Seth, Billy heard a voice beside them.

"Hey, would one of you mind holding the sign a while so I can get a cup of joe?"

A female Burke student with straight, chopped-off, dyed-black hair stood against the wall behind the microphone with her denim jacket open, displaying an amazing dragon tattoo across her upper chest. Seth grabbed the broomstick holding the banner.

"Give 'em hell, Billy. I'll be right here."

He turned to look at the crowd, which had grown to about fifty, a fairly good cross-section of the village: liberal and conservative; young, old; white, black. Not bad. A gaggle of demonstrating Burke students could be dismissed, but villagers coming out on a brass monkey morning – *this* was something.

Woody stood at the mic, working the crowd. Billy waited a few more seconds, then walked up beside him, making sure the old man saw him in his peripheral vision.

"I yield the floor now, my friends, to the voice of youth."

Billy nudged Woody away in his impatience, feeling a small pang – there would be no crowd at all if it weren't for his old prof.

"Thanks so much, folks, for coming. Is it cold or what?"

"NO," somebody roared. "IT'S HOT AS HELL OUT HERE!"

He lowered his eyes, tented his fingers prayerfully, gave the cameraman time to find him in his lens.

"Well, like John Patrick Burke, first president of Burke College said, 'The measure of a man's life is what he's done for others.' And all of you have come out this morning to preserve farmland for 'the others' that will follow us."

"FOR THE OTHERS," they roared. He waited till they subsided.

"I grew up over on Sunset Drive," he began, "right across from the farm. And though Mom and Dad are dead now, they left me their house . . . in this place. I remember summer mornings, hearing roosters crow, the smell of hay wafting across the field. I've been all over the world, from the Australian outback to the mountains of Nepal. I loved Tibet and Jerusalem, but . . . when it comes to holy places, I'll take Wood Thrush Farm any day of the week."

When they started to yell, he raised his arms for quiet. "It's about home, everybody. My mom and dad might be gone, but my home isn't – not yet. Home is right here for me, and, I'll bet, for lots of you." He opened his arms now, inclusive. He was trying not to turn around and see the effect on Seth. "Villages and farms might seem to some to be relics of the past. But if we're to have a future – if this country is gonna survive, it needs to fight for them. It's the Wal-Martizing of America, people, and it's our choice whether we're gonna just roll over and let 'em asphalt our asses or show 'em what Ohio, what America needs." He paused. "America needs Wood Thrush Farm."

`He dropped his arms, and they cheered, the sound lifting across the parking lot to bounce off the stand of small cedars and back to the village building behind him. As the sea of sound ebbed and the tide went back out, he knew what he needed to do next, to keep the cameras rolling.

Billy waited till they settled a bit. "But somebody cares about Wood Thrush Farm staying farmland. *I* care, and apparently all of you do, too, so I'd like you to hear from someone who, even though she's new to our town, already cares about it as much as we do."

Too late he remembered her at the Bean's back table, frowning, judgmental and silent, while he tried to sell his petition to Bonnie and Ira. But it was too late. They were waiting. He could practically hear Channel Twenty-Five's film being exposed.

"Give a listen to your new fellow villager and Burke alumna . . . Seth Abel."

He stepped backwards and peeled the broomstick out of her hands, avoiding her eyes. She walked, dream-like, toward the mic. He did his best to keep his eyes off her bluejeaned butt. The crowd quieted and she stood there for hours, it seemed. *Come on, Seth.* A baby cried and seemed to awaken her.

"When I went to Burke in the eighties, I got involved in a couple of causes back then. But . . . I got scared."

Her voice sounded high and shaky. And no one wanted to hear about fear; they wanted to hear about kicking ass. But they stayed quiet, even the baby. Stronger now: "I ran from responsibility, but I found out you can't run forever. Sooner or later, you've got to take a stand for what you believe in."

Approving murmurs from the crowd comforted Billy a little. But so far she wasn't exactly Mother Jones. Had he misjudged her?

"I went out *there* – into the world." She pointed vaguely toward Dayton Street. "And I had a child." She paused – what was she saying? By now, Billy felt himself slipping away, could barely make out her words.

"I was glad I had a son, but it's hard raising a boy in a home where your partner's decided money is more important than anything else. So when I chose to come back to Shawnee Springs, I chose a sacred space. I chose a place where I'd been to a college that isn't like any other school anywhere else. A school that educates not just the mind but the soul."

It was instant – it could happen that swiftly, the moment when you had them. As he watched the audience's energy enter her, she stood up straighter, brushed her gorgeous hair back.

"I chose this place where, long ago, the Shawnee came to the healing waters right here on the edge of Glenora Wood and healed themselves. They probably mostly healed the wounds the white man had given them, the same old wounds of greed and aggression that sicken us to death today. Well, we need water and we need grass and we need trees and we sure need farmland and farmers if we're to be complete human beings."

The baby suddenly cried, long and loud. People spontaneously laughed. *Good, good, laughter was useful, laughter was good.*

"HERE, HERE: FARMERS!" someone hollered before the crowd grew quiet.

"I came here from a land of desert and sage and mountains. But you've got something that New Mexico lacks. Green. Lots and lots of green: green trees, fields, lawns. The color of growth. Of life. And where better to have green than surrounding our town – a deep green sea around us. To be able to breathe in the sweet scent of green. I want that for my son and for your children, too. For this baby down front here."

A ripple ran through the crowd. Upturned, expectant faces. Approval.

"Oh, I know – I grew up in rural Kentucky – that not all farm smells are green. Some are brown. Yellow. Black!"

The laughter was hearty, not just polite.

"But let's have all the colors as long as they're natural. Let's have the full palette of corn, cows and pigs for our kids. I want my son – and this baby right here – to grow up seeing, smelling, knowing Wood Thrush Farm. They'll be better people for it. So I want to do whatever I can do to save this farm. And I hope – "

Her voice abruptly ceased, as if the tape had broken. And raising his eyes from where they had again drifted to Seth's ass, he saw her shoulders lift tensely as if she were recoiling from an explosion. *What the hell?* Had someone thrown something? He panned the crowd furiously, but they bent toward her like flowers toward the light, mouths open.

When she turned, he did a double-take. Her cheeks were flaming red, her head bowed as she stumbled backward away from the microphone, nearly tripping over the cord.

"Rot in hell, you son of a bitch," she muttered.

"What's wrong?" Billy said, reaching toward her with his free hand.

But she was gone. And though he wanted to follow her, there was nobody to give his end of the damn banner to, so he was stuck holding the short end of the stick, as usual.

# Chapter Three



Much later, after the final word of the final speech had been spoken, the last chant chanted, the last "We Shall Overcome" sung, Billy finally managed to get to the Bean Tree to see if Seth might be there, sipping herbal tea as she had yesterday.

Walking in, he set the bells a-jingle. In the darkness, the place appeared empty. Early morning coffee-and-newspaper crowd was long gone, lunchers not yet arrived. Billy inhaled the thick, braided smells of coffee beans from Colombia, Kenya and Guatemala rising like steam from the scarred wooden floor. The huge jars lining the wall to his right – everything from dark Italian roast to light toasted almond – buoyed his mood. After stomping snow off his boots, he walked toward the coffeepot, lifted and began to pour. Mexican, Sumatran, he didn't care as long as it was black as damp earth and hot enough to thaw February out of his bones.

*Green*, she'd said. By the time the first crocuses opened, they'd know the farm's fate – for good or ill. Better to stay cold and dark for a while longer.

Carrying his steaming mug before him like a chalice, he threw a buck on the counter under the bored teenager's nose, and headed for the tables in the rear beside the bean tree, a weeping fig in a huge ceramic vase. Somebody had glued a million black and brown coffee beans to its limbs. Tiny white Christmas tree lights completed the travesty. Though tree-huggers hated it, Billy loved the joke.

"Hey, Dildo, I mean Bilbo."

Squinting into the darkness, Billy picked out Bonnie smiling mock-sweetly from the table in the rear where she sat cooling her coffee. *Damn*. Ira, beside her, waved two fingers. Not for the first time, Billy noticed how Bonnie had aged. God, only two years older than he, but at thirty-two, she looked a decade older. Her long red hair still curled wildly around her flawless white face. She was damn good-looking when she wasn't scowling. But that wasn't often since That Night

"Hey, guys." Caught off-balance, part of him still at the rally, he couldn't think of a single outrageous thing to say. He weaved his way back to where they sat.

Ira snorted. "I liked to shit my pants when you said you've lived here all your life."

Bonnie sputtered, spraying coffee. "God, and when you talked about dear ol' Mom and Dad! But, hey, all the media want is sound bites anyhow. They don't care about the truth." She pointed. "For instance, that you, my dear dickhead, are a goddamn carpetbagger from Toledo."

So they *had* been at the rally! Lurking in the bushes, no doubt. As Billy sat, he saw how red Bonnie's hands were with clay. No doubt she'd been up at dawn throwing pots. Many's the time she'd leave him in bed while she went to her studio. She spoke again. "So you got the local donkeys to come bray with you."

"Yeh, but if Schuyler gets his way, all the songs and speeches won't mean piss in the ocean. You know what'll happen after the farm's sold." He sat while they looked at him, Bonnie, her upper lip curled, Ira, half-grinning. He broke into song: "Little pink houses for you and me."

Bonnie snorted. "Maybe they'll build something affordable. Right now I pay Sid Godwin $675 a month. *One* fucking bedroom!"

Billy couldn't stop himself. "I don't think you'll want one of the pieces of crap they'll throw up and call a house: Bovine Estates, Cow-Turd Trace. . ."

"Goat-Cheese Landing," Ira said in his high, nasal tenor.

Billy laughed with him while Bonnie glared. "And it could be even worse. Wendy's, McDonald's, Long John Silver's." He paused dramatically before stage-whispering the twin syllables: "*Wallll-Mart.*"

Bonnie exploded, "Come on, Shit-For-Brains, the land's zoned agriculture and residential. Yes, John Schuyler is a builder. Yes, he'd like to responsibly develop affordable housing for Shawnee Springs, but he's got to work within the law, y'know."

Billy sat forward. "We knew this might happen once a couple of pro-developers got on the board. They'd sell their mothers into prostitution. They don't give a damn about preserving farmland."

"You know Ray would never let them do that behind our backs," Bonnie hissed. "And I resent like hell you suggesting it." She glared at Billy. "What do you think's gonna be done with it if you and your fellow rabble-rousers get it, Bilbo?"

"Farming, of course."

Her hazel eyes narrowed. "*You're* not going to farm. You probably never got your hands dirty in your life."

Billy sat back, stuck his thumbs in imaginary suspenders. "Guess I never told y'all about helping out Grand-daddy Acorn on his farm in West Virginia." He grinned at Ira, who saluted him with his mug.

"Guess you never told us you'd recruited some blonde bimbo to be your back-to-the-land poster child," Bonnie shot back.

Billy returned her stare. Two years, and she still hadn't gotten over him. *Move on*, he wanted to say. Instead, he took a deep breath before he leaned toward Ira.

"I've met someone who might epitomize what this farm fight stands for."

"You epitomize it," Bonnie put in. "Naïve idealism and stupidity."

He ignored her. Ira was looking at him now. "Someone experienced to meet the media, help get our cause front and center. Seth Abel, who you apparently heard today, worked with Lloyd Kieron in the eighties on the Pitney project. She's back here with her son after living out West."

"Oh, yeh?" Bonnie said. "And where's hubby?"

He was determined not to look Bonnie's way. "She might be willing to front the fight."

"Screw that action!" Bonnie shouted. "We don't need some *outsider* to come in and speak for us."

Billy half-turned her way. "Excuse me, but last time I checked, you were with the opposition."

She grinned, folding her arms. "I'm keeping my options open."

Billy mentally groped for patience – then he had it: an image of Bonnie, her body slick with sweat, after they'd made love in the pine forest that June night. She smelled and tasted as bittersweet as the pine needles they lay on.

Ira was nodding. "A single mother saving the land for the next generation. It's powerful. And she talked a good game today. Plus, she's photogenic."

"Well, I didn't think I was interested in this little lost cause," Bonnie said. "Now I'm sure of it."

"Wait." Ira had his hand on her arm. "If she knows Lloyd, maybe she can bring him back."

She shook her head. "Kieron's dead, as far as this town goes. When Alexandra died, he was through with us."

"But, my God, Bonnie – chicken factories, thousands of birds housed in one tiny shed! And when she decided to quit funding the outdoor education center in favor of Cedarton's 4-H camp . . ." Ira shook his head. "Folks were hurt."

Bonnie crossed her arms. "We should be ashamed of ourselves for judging her. Why is one town's nature stuff more important than another's? She decided to spread the money around, is all. I went to the funeral, okay? Know how many Shallow Springers bothered to attend?"

Ira stared at the table.

"I was the only one. He was crushed."

"Poor Lloyd," Ira muttered.

"So don't depend on King Kieron the Giant-Slayer to come fight your battles for you because some fresh-faced babe shows up and declares herself his successor."

Billy waited several heartbeats. "So, Ira: you think it's a good idea to bring Seth on board?"

"What have you got to lose?"

Bonnie stood, wearily, shoulders sagging. "You guys are such suckers for a pretty face." She was out the door, bells erupting behind her.

Her departure, Billy found, left him feeling even more deflated than Seth's an hour ago. If he weren't careful, he'd be back to feeling sorry for himself. Right now his attention focused on the letter from his father in his shirt pocket. Why in the hell was he carrying it around? Oh, yeh: he was supposed to be doing something about it.

Ira looked at his watch. "I'm history. Play practice at two." When Ira stood, Billy let his eyes measure Ira's full six feet, two. His hunching took off maybe an inch. Turkey buzzard, Billy thought, not for the first time. He couldn't resist one more jab.

"Are you with us?"

Ira grinned. "Can't say yet. Like our friend there, I'm keeping my options open."

He made it out the door without even disturbing the bells.

○

Just about to put his key in the lock, Billy noticed a folded white sheet protruding from the crack between door and frame. The door opened, and it fluttered to the floor. For a second, he considered leaving it there. Then he bent and scooped it up.

Inside, he sat carefully on the ragged green butt-eater of a couch he'd gleaned during the village's annual Spring Clean. The cushion gave, dropping him within inches of the scarred hardwood floor. The coffee table looked like a cutting board, huge gashes criss-crossing its surface amid dark brown stains. And when the horrible green and gold La-Z-Boy was fully extended in horizontal position, it listed to one side like a car with two flats. He loved it; all you had to do was tuck a couple of pillows beside you so your body didn't ooze into the downward lean. He'd taken many a good nap there, though his hip sometimes ached afterward.

The stereo was the one thing he hadn't gleaned. Older'n hell – Dad's gift to him when he left for college. Before sitting he caught a glimpse of the photo on the windowsill. He walked over, grabbed it, returned to the couch and eased onto it (too fast and your ass slipped between the cushions and landed on an iron bar).

He stared at the eight by ten, the only photo in the apartment. High school graduation. His second step-mom, Dorothy, had taken the picture. The old man, fat-jowled from way too many Whoppers with cheese on his lunch "minute," had his arm around his son, who, pre-beard and long hair, looked about fifteen. "Dopey Opie," Billy said aloud and grimaced. But it was the old man drawing his attention. "Go for your dream, son," he'd said, and as if to convince Billy he meant it, he grabbed his son's hand and placed a check in his palm. Only later did Billy realize it was for ten grand: severance pay. Stay away, it said. Don't be a problem.

Well, he hadn't been, and, true to the bargain, the old man had bank-rolled his year of college – as much of it as Billy could stand – and what came after until last December when, days before he turned thirty, the fateful letter had come. He glanced toward the mysterious new epistle lying on the coffee table. That couldn't be good news, either.

Dad's letter sizzled to life in his shirt pocket above his heart. He tweezed it out with two fingers and read for the fortieth time.

"Dear Son, I've waited for you to 'find yourself' down there. But I realize now that I've been aiding and abetting. It is with sadness and love that I regret to inform you that this is the last check. If you seek education likely to land you a job, I'll reconsider. Happy Birthday. Dad."

He laughed out loud.

Happy Birthday!!

His father had zero sense of irony, born lacking the ability to be anything but absolutely sincere. Al Acorn even believed it himself when he told customers the warranty covered everything (until the dupe actually came back wanting a new transmission). It's what made him the top-ranked Toyota dealer in a mid-sized market: he believed his own bullshit. But he never laughed. Ever.

Billy let his eyes rove around the room. He'd brought Bonnie here only once. She'd stood a few feet inside looking like she'd just smelled a fart. Then she threw her purse down on the floor, grabbed him with hands still red with clay and kissed him hard. Looking around now, he saw the place through her eyes. She must've thought it was worth it. She'd stayed the night.

His eyes roamed to the table. The sheet of paper seemed to stare right back. *Shit.* He leaned forward and reached for it, his weight making him sink even lower into the cushions, until, rocking a bit, he gathered enough momentum to spring forward off the couch, plucking up the paper before falling back into the chair. He opened it and read:

"Mr. Acorn, your rent is in arrears in the amount of $1400. Please vacate premises by 2-20-99. Thank you. Yours truly, Sidney G. Ellis."

He sprang out of the chair, took three steps to the stereo and began ripping out wires. In, out, fast.

# Chapter Four

Putnam County, West Virginia
Sunday, March 12, 1999

Billy decided to continue driving south before retracing his route
back to Grand-dad's, to know the worst. Sure enough, the four-lane
south was nothing but fast food, home improvement stores and gas
stations for the next twelve miles. Once he reached Charleston's
outskirts, he turned around. At least he had a blazing sunset to comfort
him, but it only reminded him of the one he'd seen over Wood Thrush
last night. That made him see Seth, her jaw set angrily. He cranked the
volume higher, glad he'd stuck in *Comes A Time* after the gas station.
Neil was whining "Four Strong Winds" as if he meant it. If Billy'd
had one of Ira's high-test doobies, he might've smoked it. Then he
remembered the fifth of Jim Beam he'd bought at a party store outside
Chillicothe – that'd help him sleep tonight, if he needed it.

By the time he reached the intersection at "Wally World," it was
dusk. However, he couldn't miss the billboard on the right: a cow in
granny glasses reclined in Easter basket green pasture pointing to the
left with one hoof: Beck's Jersey Dairy: six miles. The cow was blue.
How could he have missed it before? And why would a dairy need
such an advertisement? Then he grinned. They'd built a four-lane for
yuppies in Beamers. Farmers might as well make a buck, too. He took
the left slowly, and the world began to change.

At the foot of a small hill, large oaks, willows and walnuts rose
beside the two-lane. Billy wondered why they hadn't logged it, but
maybe developers had been too busy up on the main highway. They'd
get around to it sooner or later.

In the pink glow of sunset, Billy made out modest homes with huge,
well-kept lawns, even an occasional house-trailer. And fields – by God,
there was still farming going on out here, family farming. For the first
time in twenty or so hours, Billy's heart rose. Maybe this *was* the road
home after all.

He thought of his grandfather, dead all these years, and his own dad
– how come those two hadn't gotten along? But they'd been so different
– or maybe so alike? In each other's presence, they'd never looked at
each other when they'd talked, and they'd never said much to each
other, Al Acorn sitting at the table in his pin-stripes, Grand-dad at the
other end in his bibs. What a loss. If his dad had gone into farming,
Billy might be living here, might . . . Then he got a quick image of the

kid up at Speedway. Would he hate it, would he want out? Was the crop always greener on the mountain's other side?

Billy found himself relaxing. The snow was so patchy you could see through it to last fall's leaf-cover, glowing in the sunset-fire, whole trees back-lit so their bare branches looked like huge-racked bucks. He'd seen a group of about a dozen deer standing down near the creek grazing a barren cornfield. Tucked away in a corner of the world like this, what else besides the land would a person need? But he knew the answer to that one.

Only the right woman to make it all perfect.

A couple days ago he'd thought that would be Seth Abel. Now he laughed aloud to think of it. But when he got a flash of her face as she'd told him about her and Kieron, he sobered. Screwed, blued and tattooed. Man, what a bastard. And her thinking she could make her old prof see the light.

Coming to himself, he realized the sun was gone, leaving him driving through a swath of blackness, hard to navigate with his eyes beginning to blur. Cresting a hill, he saw the sky shimmering weirdly above the trees ahead, as if from a small city. His heart jangled in his chest. This couldn't be good. He was within three, four miles of Grand-dad's place now.

The road suddenly widened – the first sign something was wrong. Then, he rounded a curve and saw the huge field off to the right lit by humongous stadium lights. An athletic stadium? Out here? But, slowing, Billy saw no bleachers, only netting at the end of the July-mid-day brightness. Then he saw the lone golfer, resplendent in white sweater, cap and pants. A driving range! In the back of the boonies, in winter, in God's country! Billy knew he must look like some moon-mad drunk with his jaw hanging to his belt-buckle, but surely that asshole out there in his golf cart was the real idiot, wasn't he?

Billy slowed to a crawl. He felt like he'd followed the yellow brick road straight to hell. Hadn't anyone fought those wanting to build a driving range on prime farmland? But as Billy eased on past the blazing carnival lights, he saw another sign: Udder Duffers. It was that damn blue cow again, only this time it was wearing a golf cap and wielding a club, squinting his eyes in bovine concentration. It was the slogan that made Billy's head sizzle: "Another country pleasure brought to you by Beck's Dairy." Miniature golf. At least no one was playing, though it seemed open for business.

Tears burned the back of Billy's throat. He knew now this *was* Beck's, all of it; he knew that hard-working German Gerhard Beck

– or, more likely, his heirs – had sold out, had turned a modest farm operation into a theme park.

What else could you call it? By now, Billy was passing the Hoof and Tooth, Fine Dining and Gift Shop, the restaurant topped by that desecration of a cow, standing on all fours above a red-roofed structure as big as a bowling alley. But what made Billy pull off to the side quickly to do a real take was the parking lot: six, eight, maybe even ten acres of asphalt over what used to be the cow lot – and it was nearly full. (Where were the huge barns he remembered? Had they been torn down, or were they simply obscured by blue cows?) Half of Charleston must be inside gulping down cow shakes and bull weenies.

A howling sound tore up out of his chest, nothing like he'd ever heard issue from his throat (or maybe anyone else's) before. He imagined himself crawling up the restaurant's drainpipe, wrecking bar strapped on his back, to see if he could topple that cow from the roof. He howled again, louder, for Beck's barns and cows, for Wood Thrush, for Grand-dad, for Seth and Paul, for Ira and Bonnie . . . for himself.

Then he shut up and sat there for some time in the unearthly glow from all the lights, watched smiling families with skipping children leave in their vans and SUVs, burning five or six gallons of refined crude to come to the country for a cone and a foot-long. Surely Old Man Beck hadn't lived to see what they had done. The frosty-haired, thigh-slapping old German would've killed himself.

Billy leaned over, snatched the bourbon out of his knapsack, broke the seal and took a long pull, not giving a shit if a statie came roaring from behind the sign to slap him in cuffs. It would serve him right for abandoning Seth and the others. (He imagined Oldham's Dairy, its tiny shop which sold only milk, fudge, home-made bread and ice cream. A driving range? Never.)

He put the bottle back into his sack, wiped his eyes on his bandage and pulled back onto the road. Might as well go on. Forward or backward didn't seem to make much difference.

The turnoff to Grand-dad's was only a half-mile past Beck's, not enough to get beyond the driving range's glow. The old mailbox still stood at the head of the red-clay-rutted road. Somehow seeing the black-lettered name ACORN undid some of the damage done by all he'd seen in the last hour. No blue cows here. Just brown and black and white ones. He knew the land was still being farmed as recently as four-five years ago, by a couple named Janikowski – he'd had trouble imagining people coming all the way from Poland to rent a farm in West Virginia, but his father had assured him it was happening more and more often, as Americans pulled out of a profession seen as not only undesirable but doomed.

Billy crawled up the rutted road to protect the Dakota's transmission. He'd meant to arrive in daylight. The Big House, as his dad called it, rose into view in the glow of his headlights. He dreaded having to bother the Janikowskis this late – well, not that late, but how many visitors did they get after dark? He only wanted to use the little remodeled coal house out back, hoping it still had its functioning buck stove and a few sticks of firewood. It was Grand-dad's little library in his sunset years, where he devoured everything from *War and Peace* to *The Rise and Fall of the Third Reich*. Now, Billy was dreading the prospect of knocking on the door, arousing the dogs, if there were any, and having to refuse if they insisted that the grand-son of the deceased owner take a bed inside the house. (Maybe it was all he'd been through lately – his bandaged hand was suddenly sizzling – but he longed for solitude above all else this night. Seth and Ira loomed like shadows at his mind's periphery – there were decisions that still needed making – it wasn't too late. Yet). He'd fight to stay in the coalhouse, if he had to.

Pulling up and dousing his headlights, he saw only the glow from a small lamp in the little parlor off the formal living room. Billy glanced at his watch: seven-ten. Surely they weren't already in bed. If he had to return to Sprawlville and take a room . . . He'd go to Charleston first. Quickly he got out and stood, his legs stiff with disuse. Thank God: no barking dogs. Blessed silence and moonlight. Tilting his head to see the stars, not totally obscured by Beck's light pollution, he recalled the pond, the geese back home. It all seemed more than a world away.

On the porch, he paused, ambushed by memory. Grand-daddy at the door, pipe in his teeth, greeting them, with his shy, aproned wife behind him, the thick quilt of fried chicken wrapping itself around them as soon as they stepped inside. Billy racing to meet cousins and start the endless game of hide and seek in the huge house with its cluttered closets, scary attic and basement. He smiled grimly in the light from the moon. It was one of those moments – he'd had maybe three of them in his adult life – when he asked himself: How did I get here? (And the question he dismissed as soon as it unfurled on his mental screen: Where next?)

He knocked. Nothing. Just when he was considering getting back in the truck and heading back out to the road, the porch light came on and the door opened wide.

"What in the living name of Jehovah . . ?"

Billy stared into the hazy glare. "Aunt Della?"

"Yayess . . . ?"

"It's Billy, your . . ."

"Mercy God." The tall woman flung open the screen and hugged him so hard they both almost reeled backward off the porch. Her muscled body had not an ounce of fat anywhere. She'd always been the strongest woman physically he'd ever known, and apparently age had not changed that.

"What in the dickens are you doing here, Billy Mike?" she asked after finally turning him loose.

He grinned. No one had called him by both names since he was twelve. "I could ask you the same thing, Della Mar*ie*. Like where are the Janikowskis?"

"Up the road a piece. They bought the Pickford place after the old man died, and the boys didn't want to farm it – same old story. But they still farm your grand-daddy's land, too." Her smile melted, and she instantly looked her sixty-some years. "You need so much more than you used to, to make ends meet. But come on in. It's colder'n the devil's thoughts out here."

"Actually, I was wondering if I might stay in the coal house?"

She glared. "Get in here and let me fix you a snack."

Sighing, Billy let himself be dragged inside, let himself contemplate the fried chicken, mashed potatoes and gravy, green beans and slaw that would probably constitute a snack in Dad's oldest sister's mind. He inhaled the bitter scent of more than a century of Acorn cooking mixed with woodsmoke and mildew, bleach and grease, the smell of his childhood. It dizzied him.

"Look at you, Billy Mike," his aunt said after turning on the overhead light. "You look like a summer breeze would plumb knock you down." Coming closer, she reached out and gently took his bandaged hand. Then she stroked his forehead, fingering the scabbed wound above his eye. "What in heaven's name happened to you, honey?"

"I fell."

"You're not gonna tell me. All right then. Come on. We'll look at that hand later. Your belly's gonna come first."

He followed her into the entryway's darkness. She was right: he was almost hungry enough to eat a blue cow.

○

After the feast she'd prepared, it took Della ten minutes to rebandage Billy's hand. She'd only clucked when she saw the cut; she

knew a knife wound when she saw one, but they seemed to've agreed
not to ask each other hard questions. The room she gave him was at the
end of the long hall upstairs. More smells: of old, worn oriental rugs,
potpourri in dresser drawers, cedar-lined closets and under all, the faint
hint of mothballs. His chest tightened with more memories: he'd slept
in this room once, before he was in school, he and his mother, a time
when Dad must've been hunting. Standing in the doorway, he almost
told Della no, he couldn't sleep here, but he couldn't put her out any
more than he already had. Plus, he couldn't wait to get to the bourbon,
knock himself out.

"Honey, towels are in the bathroom, extra quilts in the closet. You
need anything, you just holler."

She kissed his cheek and was gone, squeaking back downstairs. And
she had asked him nothing about what he was running from.

He flopped down heavily on the bed, fully clothed. He hadn't asked
her either: where was Uncle Don? What about Claudia and Little Don
(God, her daughter and son would be in their forties, he guessed, the
cousins who, so much older, had still played with him when he came to
visit)? Was Della living here permanent or temporary?

He sighed, unscrewed the bottle and swallowed the first hit, leaning
back against the cherry headboard, feeling warm tendrils stroke his
brain. And for the first time what he had done smacked him between
the eyes. Reaching into his breast pocket, he pulled out the check. Five
grand. Wouldn't take him far, but it would take him somewhere.

Resisting the impulse to take another drink, he closed his eyes. His
entire body felt paralyzed, except for his heart, which was slamming
so hard inside him, it hurt. He envisioned it engorged with blood,
filled to bursting. He could die, have a heart attack right here, right in
this room where he and Ma, God bless her, slept in this bed in a room
where countless other Acorns had slept, fucked, birthed, died.

He glanced around the room, his gaze lasering across the oak wash
stand, the ornate chest of drawers atop which a white lace-crocheted
doily (his grandma's work, he knew) gleamed like purity, like truth.

Grandma. Quiet, smiling – but not always; her mouth-corners
turned down as she worked in the kitchen, kneading, kneading the
endless biscuits her husband demanded at every meal, beautiful, fluffy
white, golden-butter-burnished. She must've made zillions. An entire
life spent baking bread (with everything else she had to do).

The thought took him to his own mother. He saw himself in those
old photos with his mom – after he was born, there were no pictures
of Ma, it seemed, without Billy Mike – her name for him – beside her,

clinging, then later on, laughing with her at each of his birthday parties (his twelfth the last one), splashing him with a hose in his kiddy pool, sitting beside him in her pink robe on Christmas morning. Her life's work: caretaker of an ambitious, workaholic husband. And a little boy. Then he received the image he dreaded: holding his mom's hand as she lay in the hospital bed in a pool of sunlight. Her freckled arm, purple from needle-pricks, had an IV stuck in it. And happy though he was to see her – they were both laughing – she didn't smell like her usual sweet lotion and soap. She smelled . . . yellow. It was the last time he saw her alive.

He still couldn't move, knew he didn't have the voice to call out. He couldn't even lift the bottle to his lips. For the first time in his life that he could remember, he just lay there and felt the pain. At one point, every nerve and cell said, *Go*, and he tried to will himself up off this bed, down the stairs, into the truck, back to Ohio to . . . to what?

And those goddamned flames again. During the cement company fight, he'd let Mark talk him into an "event." Accompanied by the punk and his drunken cronies, they'd gone over the fence. A few flat tires and fucked-up gas tanks and maybe the company would get the message to stop burning toxic wastes. Behind his back, they'd set the guardhouse on fire. After the dipshits had fled, he'd discovered the guard inside, unconscious and pulled him to safety while the sirens howled. Somehow he'd gotten away.

*Never again*, he'd sworn. And now this.

When Billy opened his eyes, dying flames wavered on the fleur de lis wallpaper. But they were only shadows thrown by branches of the sugar maple beside the house.

"Ma."

His voice was a croak, but his heart had slowed down. His armpits felt swampy, and he found he could lift his arm, though it was as heavy as if it had a cast on it. A little blood had seeped through the new white bandage Della had wrapped around it. The color was soothing, dark red on white.

And just like that, he was numb. He lifted the bourbon, but now the smell made him nauseous, his body and mind falling toward darkness. He capped the bottle, stood up and emptied the contents of his pockets on the dresser. He carefully laid the check he had drawn this morning against Blue Jacket Land Trust alongside his Dad's letter on the dresser. Then he fell back onto the bed and slept in his clothes.

# Chapter Five

Shawnee Springs, Ohio
Sunday, February 19, 1999


Billy was parked in front of Ira's cottage on the edge of Glenora Wood. He tilted his head backward and closed his eyes. So he'd finally come to this. Better get it over with quick before he changed his mind. Again.

He threw the notebook on the passenger's seat. As treasurer of Blue Jacket Land Trust, he tried to keep some sort of running tally. Woody had just smiled and shook his head when Billy'd suggested the "elder statesman" handle the money.

"You're the money man. Widows and Orphans – go get 'em, Bilbo!"

He winced, regretting how, years ago, on the first day of Freeman's class, Billy had said his favorite philosophical work was *The Lord of the Rings*, branding him Bilbo forever. But fund-raising for the village foundation, so-called Widows and Orphans, was his proudest accomplishment. He loved looking local business people in the eye and asking for a thousand bucks. They always gave less, but they always gave.

So Billy was glad to be treasurer. He sensed certain as-yet-unarticulated advantages down the road. He shook his head. The few thousand dollars they'd collected so far in donations was hardly enough to justify skipping to Brazil.

It wasn't too late to save his pride, what little was left. But where else was there to go? He looked behind him at the mounds of snow, glanced guiltily at the Dakota's bed, everything he owned crammed into it. Groaning with stiffness, he got out.

The door opened, and there Ira stood, wearing the raggediest green-striped purple robe Billy had ever seen. A relic from the seventies, maybe even the sixties.

"Jesus Christ, Billy, it's Sunday!"

Billy couldn't hold back a giggle. Ira had the funniest knees. He was so tall the robe only came to mid-thigh.

"Come inside. It's colder'n a witch's tit standing here."

After Ira closed the door, Billy saw that it was one large room. A rough table stood against one wall with books and papers as well as bread, apples and oranges on top of it. A circa 1960s refrigerator hummed against the opposite wall. A filing cabinet and rocking chair

– musta been John Kennedy's, it was so old – pretty much completed the furniture.

"Jesus, Ira, where do you sleep?"

The tall man pointed behind him to the pile of blankets in the corner.

"On the goddamn floor?"

"Good for my back, Bilbo. I never met a mattress I liked."

"I got something to ask you," Billy said.

Ira had flopped into the rocking chair. Now he pointed to the desk chair. Billy decided he'd rather stand for what he had to say. Before he could speak, he noticed something on the desk-kitchen table he hadn't seen before.

"Who gave you Valentine candy, you old buzzard?"

Ira sighed. "One of the kids."

"You're lying. Bet it was some good-looking mama."

Ira ignored it, and Billy regretted saying it. He knew there hadn't been anyone since Gretchen took Amber and fled to Florida two years ago.

Suddenly Ira stopped rocking, reached out, grabbed the heart-shaped box and thrust it toward Billy. "I hate chocolate."

Billy was tempted to tear the wrapping off right then – he hadn't eaten since yesterday afternoon. But something said *wait*. Plus, he was tireder than he was hungry at the moment, so he sat down at the desk.

"So how old was this young wench with the hots for you?"

"Eight."

"Amber's age."

Ira nodded, and Billy could practically see the weight settle onto him. It was hard to remember how alive Ira had been, carrying his blue-eyed, blonde, giggling daughter up and down Dayton Street on his tall shoulders every Saturday, walking beside her as she marched with the rest of her Burke School classmates in the semi-annual street fair parade. If ever a man had withered and died over a loss, it was Ira.

"She'll be nine next time I see her. If I get to see her."

"Didn't the divorce declare you the summertime dad?"

He shook his head. "Seems my ex doesn't want me in the picture at all – she's suing for sole custody. And Amber's changed, Billy. You should've seen her at the courthouse. Gretch had her all dolled up, her hair professionally done, wearing adult-looking clothes."

Billy recalled the dirty-faced wild-child cart-wheeling in the schoolyard while he and Ira shot the shit on the benches. "Gretchen brought her to court with her?"

"I asked her to. Didn't know when I might get another chance to see her. I was right. Haven't seen her since October."

"So she's getting custody, even though they don't have a damn thing on you."

Ira nodded. "Except one, Bilbo. One thing."

"But, man, you weren't convicted. And you haven't touched a joint in three years."

"Once you've been arrested, nobody forgets."

"Just an itty-bitty bunch of Mary Jane?"

"Possession with intent to sell was the exact charge, my friend."

It was hard to believe now, Ira had been clean for so long. Billy'd been damn glad his buddy had once taught Senator Irving McLevitch's daughter. The Senator had gotten the charge reduced to simple possession, but now he saw they'd taken away the thing more important than Ira's freedom.

"Well, hey, it's a good thing that Shawnee Springs forgives a man for smoking a little weed. How many communities would let you teach kids after being arrested for that?"

Ira nodded and began rocking again, the chair squeaking. Billy was stalling, and he knew Ira knew it. He couldn't do it – not yet.

"You make up your mind on the farm issue?" he finally asked.

"You talk to the farmers yet?"

Billy sighed. "No. I don't have corn tasseling out of my ears like you."

"You're not gonna get anywhere without them, Bilbo. If you do raise enough money for the easement, what are you gonna do with the land after the auction if the farmers don't buy it?"

"What do you mean 'you?' Aren't you with me, old man?"

Ira tented his fingers and gazed off toward the single front window that was letting in very little light.

"I see both sides. Bonnie's right: we do need affordable housing. Maybe the trustees won't sell us down the river."

"Dammit, Ira. Ray Gershowitz . . ."

"Ray ain't in nobody's pocket. And the farmers aren't too crazy about deeds that tell them how to use farmland, even if it does mean they'll get it for a thousand an acre cheaper."

Mere mention of the farmers made Billy's heart beat faster. He could talk all night to Burkers, but he knew he couldn't sell farmers free rain.

"So, Ira: will you talk to them?"

"Is that why you disturbed my Sabbath beauty rest?"

It was Billy's turn to gaze toward the grimy window. "I came to ask if I could crash here for a while."

"What happened?"

"As you may remember, I turned thirty last Thanksgiving."

"Do indeed. Don't want to remember how many pitchers we drank at the Trout." Ira smiled.

"Neither does my old man – who, unbeknownst to him – was paying for them. Ira, old buddy, I didn't tell you, but he wrote me a special birthday letter. It's over."

He steeled himself for what was to come – Ira'd given him hell often enough about still sucking the tit. But Ira was pulling at his beard.

"He cut you off the dole, huh?"

Billy nodded. "And Sid threw me out. Got my eviction notice yesterday."

Ira smiled, showing perfect teeth beneath his mustache. "Where will you bed Ms. Abel without the penthouse?"

For one-point-five seconds, Billy was furious. It was hard enough groveling without being mocked. Plus, he was going on about three hours' sleep, no food and two cups of sludge. But then it hit him: Ira was envious. *He* would be, if Ira had made an inroad with a gorgeous woman.

"Looks like celibacy along with poverty. Call me a fucking monk. But it'll only be until after the auction, okay? After that, I don't know . . . I can't see beyond that yet. It could be time to move on."

"And enter the world of briefcases and traffic jams?"

"If we save Wood Thrush, I think I'll become a farmer."

Ira guffawed. His whoop usually made Billy laugh, too, but this time he felt the faintest simmer of shame – was it that ridiculous to imagine him on a tractor?

"Better watch it, Bilbo," he said when he got his breath back. "I just might hold you to it."

So what if he'd never held a paying job since he'd left Burke? He'd done a ton of work for free. Burke gave him a voice – a voice to raise hell for humanity. His dad, of course, had said he'd learned only too well how to work at non-paying jobs, maintaining that working in his car dealership would give him plenty of chances to help humanity. For big bucks. Okay, maybe he was stupid to think he, a city boy, could take up shovel and hoe. But, by God, he could at least make it so that others could.

Ira had started rocking again. Billy was shivering inside his pea coat, but it was probably nerves. Just when he was about ready to invite Ira to go out for breakfast – Blue Jacket wouldn't miss twenty bucks – his friend suddenly stopped in mid-squeak.

"Have you ever considered apologizing to Bonnie?"

"What for?"

Ira's stare hung fire. "For what she's become since you were with her."

"Which is?" Billy couldn't keep sarcasm out of his voice, but he found himself shivering. Wasn't there any heat in this place? A woodstove stood in the corner, but it probably hadn't been stoked since last night.

"Bitter. Cruel. Self-loathing."

"That's *my* fault?"

"No. But you acted like you never noticed she was crazy about you."

Billy shook his head. "I should never have come out here."

Ira ran his hand through his thin, shaggy hair. "I ain't saying she didn't fuck up, too, but *you* shoulda known better. She'd never been with the likes of you, stud-boy."

"She wasn't a virgin, Ira."

"Ain't what I mean, Bilbo."

"Then what . . . ?" He spread his hands.

"It's the loving and leaving part."

"I never told her I'd marry her!"

Ira stopped rocking, sat forward. "Then you should've never laid a hand on her."

He leaned back. "You didn't see her growing up. I've lived in this town all my life. Bonnie was sweet and shy. Wouldn't say moo to a coon. She even had a crush on me in seventh grade. I never knew it until ninth. I knew when she fell, really fell, for a guy, it was gonna be murder."

"Are you saying I'm the first guy she fell for?"

"Teefuckingtotally."

"That she didn't have other boyfriends before me?"

"Meaningless."

"Aw, Ira, she was a grown-up. Look at me. Do I look, act or sound like a marriage type of guy?"

Ira frowned. "A whore is what you are."

"Damn right. And I'm staying that way."

"Want some help gettin' your stuff?"

"I think you should dress first."

"No shit, Sherlock."

○

An hour later, Billy stood knocking on his second door of the day. When Seth opened it, he thrust the heart-shaped red box at her.

"It's okay if you don't want to see me, but I got a really great deal on these, so I'd like you to have them."

Seth frowned at the package as if it were a cold turd.

"God, Billy, how bourgeois. And Valentine's Day was Tuesday."

"I didn't know you on Tuesday."

Her scowl lifted.

"Billy, yesterday, when I seemed to be calling you those names, I . . ."

He saw his chance. "I deserved every one of them. I put you on stage without your permission. I should be hog-tied, drawn and quartered, hung up to bleed till Christmas. Even though you were fabulous."

"You stink. What is that stuff?"

"It's called Lumberjack. Ira said you'd love it."

She stepped back. "I prefer woodsmoke and cow manure. I'm from Piney, Kentucky."

"You are!"

She blushed. So beautiful when she did that. "I'll never learn not to say the name of my hometown. People always look at me like I just said Dogpatch."

"Well, it is . . . rustic."

"Would you like to come in? I'm freezing." She pulled her robe tightly around her flannel p.j.'s.

"Does this mean my apology's accepted?"

"No. You've got a lot of explaining to do."

"Anything, as long as you take these off my hands."

Hesitantly, she accepted the box, the cellophane blinking gold in the light.

They were hardly seated on opposite chairs when she lit in.

"So why'd you say that you were born and raised in Shawnee Springs when you're from Toledo?" Her eyes flashed. "Don't look innocent. My sources say you lied."

"It makes better press."

"And your parents: you said they're dead when they're not. God, Billy . . ."

"My mom is dead – when I was twelve. Old man's remarried for the third time. But, hey, Machiavelli said the ends justify. . ."

"I hate Machiavelli, and anybody who wants my vote of confidence will not lean on that cruel excuse for a political philosopher."

"Okay, Seth. I'm not as good a person as you are. But the farm is worth saving. I think we can work together. And if you decide you agree, then you'll call the shots. No more lying, no more deceit. I'll play it as straight as you want me to."

She looked amazed. "Why should I believe you? And even if I did, maybe it's not up to us. What about Professor Freeman, the students, all the villagers who came out yesterday? We're not alone in this, Billy."

He took a deep breath. "The students can be a powerful force, but if a new issue comes up, they're gone. And villagers? What they do best is bitch." He paused to smile, but her expression said she wasn't having any of it.

"The townspeople were fantastic. So were the students. I want them in on this. And Professor Freeman."

He felt the words forming on his lips – it would be so easy to defame his old professor – but those eyes . . . He changed course.

"Woody is a good man. People respect and listen to him."

"Then he'll make a great leader."

"He's a loose cannon, Seth. He's used to students hanging on his every word and writing them down."

"But he's retired."

"And needs the spotlight even more than he used to."

She smiled. "He's got pizzazz."

"Well, people outside Shawnee Springs won't be so generous. We need to broaden our base immediately. The land trust needs more money. Most people in the Miami Valley think Shawnee Springs is full of wild-eyed liberals and dope-smokers."

"They're just stereotyping Burke students."

He shook his head. "They dismiss us too easily. We couldn't even get Cedartonians to help us close down the cement company's toxic burning scam, and it's closer to them than us. I think maybe two people from the whole town showed up to demonstrate. Our first job is to make this look like a caring, unified community coming together to fight evil developers who don't give a damn about the environment or human values. And set an example for the area, the county" – he was rolling now – "the whole goddamn country!"

"That's what we are, Billy – a unified, caring community."

"Not if Freeman's out front."

"Billy."

He leaned forward. "You think I'm jealous of him, right?"

"Of course you're jealous. You're a man."

He absorbed the hit. "Did you hear about Burke's big sexual policy brouhaha last year?"

"It was all over the alumni magazine, and I for one approve!"

"Did you read *Time, Newsweek, U.S. News & World Report?* The media descended on the campus for two weeks and made it look absolutely ridiculous that these liberal-as-hell kids had decided that there must be well-defined, documented 'stages' in a sexual relationship. And that's not all. They made fun of the co-ed bathrooms and showers, the 'substance abuse dorm,' the fact that being gay is not only accepted but encouraged . . . "

"They exaggerated. What's this got to do with Woody?"

Billy looked away. He'd only lie a little.

"Woody was the faculty honcho for the whole thing. The sex policy itself was the brainchild of some senior women, but Woody's the one who ran with it, so he's widely seen – at least in the Miami Valley – as the lead loony. He even gave a TV interview in which he said the stages leading to mutual bliss – his words – should be codified in writing with signatures affixed, as frivolities – his word – proceed. The Dayton papers had a field day with that." He felt a rush of adrenaline. Okay, frivolities was some Burke kid speaking, but the rest was true.

"All right, so he's one spokesman, maybe not the spokesman. But I trust him and sense that everyone in town does, too. We must follow his lead."

He liked the sound of that we. "I agree. We can keep him away from reporters and play to his real strength: behind-the-scenes organization and negotiation. As land trust president, he's dynamite. At the auction, we'll want him front and center, crunching the numbers. But not till then."

Billy watched, waiting for the paint to dry on his masterpiece. At last he seemed to have gotten through. He was even thinking about asking Seth to unwrap the chocolates. By God, if she didn't want them, he sure did: sugar on top of a sleep-deprived adrenaline rush might be better than three beers. Something suddenly occurred to him. "Yesterday, at the rally, after you

spoke . . ."

She cut her eyes away. Before he could say anything else, they both heard footsteps on the stairs. Paul wandered in, wearing frayed pajamas, and slumped on the couch, sitting as far away from them as he could get, yet still be present. He was petting something that looked like a mouse in his palm. Billy looked at Seth. The time for asking personal questions had passed. He turned in his chair.

"What you got there?"

"Data. He's a hamster. What are you doing here?"

Billy flashed the old Acorn trademark smile designed to win the hearts of women and children. "Discussing strategy."

"Oh-h, ye-es: to save THE FARM."

Whoa – it wasn't just Mom who was blunt. Billy snuck a glance at Seth. She looked pained.

"So when do you expect to go back to New Mexico?" It was out of Billy's mouth before he thought about it. He could've done worse. He could've cracked on the kid's kiddy p.j.'s. or his little mousie.

Paul's eyes narrowed as he turned toward his mother, deflecting the question to her.

Seth answered quickly. "We don't have any plans just yet."

"Yes, we do." Paul glared at his mother. "To stay here in Shitty Springs forever."

"Watch your mouth."

"Then can we go home?"

"Shawnee Springs *is* home now."

The kid bowed his head, getting on eye level with his rodent. Seth's jaw relaxed a little. She reached out to touch her son, but before her fingers could graze his arm, she retracted them. Abruptly, Paul got up and padded into the kitchen. The refrigerator door opened and closed, bottles clinked.

Billy let out a breath. If he ever got into this woman's heart, it would be through the boy. It certainly would never be *around* him.

"He saw me on TV – the clip they showed on the news last night." Her face looked grey. "It upset him."

"The part about having a baby . . . money being more important?"

"The part about needing grass and trees and farmland."

Billy heard it all over again, the baby crying in the background, the hush of the crowd. "Great sound bite."

"It set him off." She lowered her voice. "He thinks it means we'll stay here forever. Sometimes I think we should go back." She gazed toward the kitchen. "I've gotta go make breakfast. Care to join us for a waffle?"

Billy's stomach practically screamed – he still hadn't eaten today – but politics won out. With the kid so recently pissed at him, his presence could only grate.

"Nah, I better go. Got some calls to make."

She followed him to the door. He stopped when he got there, turned around.

"By the way, we raised nearly five grand yesterday."

"Wow. How much do you think we need?"

"A million for the easement alone."

Her face fell.

"Woody speculates the farm'll sell for three, though it could go as high as four million, if the trustees vote to re-zone the land residential." He shook his head. "We'll never get enough for the land trust to buy it all – we want the farmers to buy it if we spring for the easement."

It was all he could do not to take her in his arms, but he only said, "You know any wealthy angels?"

"Not by name."

"Wait a minute." He was on the stoop now. "You know Lloyd Kieron. His wife – she died last year – was a chicken heiress. She must've left Lloyd zillions. You think you could ask . . . ?"

She shook her head furiously. "I knew him. I don't *know* him."

The door was closing fast. "I'll contact Woody. By Sunday, we could be ready for a town meeting, get this thing organized. Will you come?"

"Shouldn't you talk to the farmers?"

"You want to help me with that?"

"You'd better speak to them before Sunday." Then she closed the door.

# Chapter Six



He left Ira's mid-morning. Not only was the cottage lonesome after Ira left around eight, but it was cold, and although Ira said to keep the stove wood-stoked, that there were plenty of downed trees in the surrounding woods awaiting his chainsaw, Billy felt too guilty at staying there to use his pal's precious fuel.

He hated being a parasite to a friend. With Dad, it was different; the old man could afford it, plus he needed to pay for running his son off just to get him out of his and his new wife's hair. Billy had never lived like a king while "on the dole," as Ira had put it, but he'd never had to worry about buying groceries and paying rent, either. When he realized Ira lived on oatmeal, tofu and tempeh, he knew he'd need cash to eat. Even factoring in ego, he decided that getting a minimum-wage job was a waste of the skills Dr. Kieron had taught him, and there wasn't much time to save the farm.

So this morning he'd decided that Blue Jacket was going to pay him twenty dollars a day. It was an eating allowance only – okay, and an occasional cup of good sludge – and he didn't have to tell a soul. He was an employee, and the fact that he would be the only paid employee didn't matter; his circumstances differed from other volunteers, that was all. Lots of nonprofits had salaried people. Besides, it was only until the auction on March 20. Twenty bucks a day for twenty-six days. He'd stick to it, come hell or high water.

And money was trickling into the box at the post office whose number was on all the flyers and the website. All he had to do was walk to the p.o., open an envelope and make a withdrawal. Though they'd requested checks and money orders, many sent cash. Piece of cake. In, out, fast.

○

An hour later, Billy stood at the pay phone on Dayton Street. "The farmers are ready to talk to us, Seth." Despite the cold, he felt cheered. A single call to Fred Pennington, the one farmer he knew, who'd served with him on Widows and Orphans, had done the deed.

"That's good," she answered, a bit breathless. Catching her on her mid-morning break at Comfort Manor had been a lucky stroke.

"They'll be a tough sell, and even though my grand-daddy was a farmer, I sure as hell ain't one. At least not yet."

"Your grand-daddy?" She laughed. "You sure he wasn't mayor of Toledo?"

He bristled. "Grand-dad farmed two hundred acres in Putnam County, West Virginia – we went down every summer till Ma died. There's good dirt in my genes. I even worked for him one whole summer: plowing, planting, haying, the whole nine yards. Maybe what little experience I had, I can use to connect . . . ."

"Nah, I'd better talk to them. Better to have no experience than pretend."

"What will you tell them, Ms. Piney, Kentucky?"

"About how their trustees are about to sell the farm down the river."

"I see. You're going to tell them about their friends and neighbors who haven't publicly declared themselves one way or the other. *You're* going to blow the whistle on *them?*"

"If necessary . . . to save the farm."

Stung though he was, he saw she might be right.

"Okay. You do it. I'll explain the technical stuff."

"Billy, I need your opinion on something else."

"Sure. I'm much better at giving opinions than farming."

"It's Paul. At school Monday, there was . . . an incident."

His legs froze. What kind of trouble could such a scrawny rodent-lover get into?

"He said he wasn't going back." She sighed deeply. "In the cafeteria, two boys in Paul's class abused him while the teacher was at another table talking to parent visitors. The boys had apparently been to the rally last Saturday, heard my speech, and . . . "

Her voice fragmented. He waited.

"Remember what I said about raising a son in a home where children aren't valued? Well, these two boys were trying to buy Paul all day from each other, saying, 'I'll give you a buck-fifty for that little baby boy,' and 'Nah, he's a *used* baby boy, and, besides, he doesn't have a daddy, and his mama's a radical. How about a nickel?'"

Before he caught himself, Billy chuckled, relieved it wasn't worse. "Well, his mama *is* a radical. Did Paul tell you all this?"

"No, his friend Matt told me most of it when I called him."

She paused to blow her nose, and when she continued, her voice sounded muffled. "They kept saying what Paul needed was soul food. I don't know what that had to do with anything, but they made a big deal of it."

"Remember?" he said gently, "You said, 'Burke educates not just the mind but the soul.'"

"Well, at lunch in the cafeteria . . . " Her voice threatened to choke off again. "That was the worst. Paul was with Matt at the end of his table when those boys, Shawn and Lucas, brought their trays over to his and sat down. They'd mixed up macaroni and cheese and beans and greens and they tried to make Paul eat it." Seth was crying now. "Billy, Lucas *twisted* Paul's ear till his head was against the table, and Shawn put the spoon up to Paul's mouth and told him to eat it. When Paul told him no and shoved him away, Shawn held Paul's hands behind his back while Lucas made him eat some of it."

He let her cry for a few seconds. It was bad but could've been worse. No blood, at least.

"So I let Paul stay home today. And I'm leaving at lunch to go over to that school and . . . "

"Don't, Seth," he interrupted. "Tattling would just make it a lot worse."

"So I just let him suffer?"

"It'll get worse if you go. Teachers and principals just make everybody shake hands, and the moment their backs are turned – POW – somebody gets hurt. Paul will learn his own methods to handle it quietly. I did." He remembered Chuck Dunlop and what his dad had told him: just walk away. It *had* worked, even if it had cost him friends. But Paul had Matt.

"You mean it'll just go away?"

"Nine times out of ten."

He waited, realizing he was freezing, and his stomach was rumbling like distant thunder. As Paul went, so went Seth, he thought. He needed this lady – CitFarm needed this lady – too much to lose her to the kid's troubles. Billy had been bullied, too. Hadn't every kid? There were only two choices, really, and he couldn't see a kid Paul's size standing up to two bullies. Paul had to ride it out.

Seth's voice was stronger. "I'll wait a little while. I don't want to screw this up."

He exhaled slowly. "He hasn't asked you to get involved, has he?" She was silent. "I didn't think so," he said. "I'd wait a really long time." When there was no response he spoke again: "So: farmers at eight in the village building gym, okay?"

"Okay."

"By the way, I'm staying with Ira Flint. If anything comes up, here's his number."

He paused to let her write it down. When she came back, her voice was small. "Billy?"

"Yo."

"Thanks a lot . . . for the advice."

It felt even better than the twenty-dollar bill in his shirt pocket. He'd filched it from the envelope of Sherman Edgington III of Seattle, Washington. Breakfast was way overdue.

○

As Billy stood before the bleachers in the gym waiting for Seth, he studied the farmers in the bright light. Mostly male, they didn't look as he'd expected – which, when he thought about it, was a cliché. They weren't all wearing bib overalls and sheepskin jackets. Clad mostly in corduroys, khakis and flannel shirts, they looked like church deacons or a group of Jaycees. Until you got up close. Then you saw the deep, sun- and-wind-carved lines, red splotches and even scabbed gashes on their faces. Their hands looked hard, as if they still gripped tools.

And not a soul in the room, except for him, was younger than fifty.

Finally he saw Seth come through the fire-doors and start up the three steps. By the time he got to her, her eyes were wide and glittery.

"I told you a media event would help," she said. "Bet they saw the news after the rally."

Billy shook his head. "Farmers only watch the weather channel. Fred got a phone tree going."

When she looked puzzled, he pointed to a largish man in a green John Deere cap talking quietly just in front of the bleachers. "Fred Pennington. A good man. We won't do this without him. And I purposely did *not* invite the media. In case we bomb."

"Thanks a lot for your confidence."

"This ain't gonna be a cakewalk."

"Let's get the show on the road." When she gripped his forearm, he felt her trembling fingers. He was full of electricity, too, damn glad he hadn't eaten since his late breakfast.

"I'll warm them up for you with a review of the essential facts," he whispered to her, "then turn them over to you for heartfelt, okay?"

Her nod wavered, and she suddenly looked grim.

"Ladies and gentlemen," hollered Billy, his bright voice bouncing around the gym's walls," please take a seat and let us get started."

They obeyed instantly, except a burly white-haired, bib-overalled guy with bushy black eyebrows above icy blue eyes who glared as he passed. Billy turned to see if Seth had seen him, but she'd already seated herself on the bleachers' empty first row.

Then he saw Ira sitting on the second row, wearing his denim jacket and floppy-eared hunting cap. The lights brightened. Billy walked right over and bent toward his buddy.

"I thought you were still among the uncommitted."

"Maybe I am." Ira had put on his poker face, which could mean anything. "And if you didn't want me to come, you shouldn't've left me the note."

"'Course I want you here. Depending on whose side you're on."

"The right side, of course," Ira replied solemnly, then winked.

Billy stood back up. He was able to return Seth's panicked-substitute-teacher smile with an unshaky grin.

"Thank you all very much for coming," Billy said. "We know what we're all here for, and that's saving Wood Thrush Farm for farming, keeping it zoned agricultural, any way that we can."

They were silent. He was right: they didn't believe for a minute that their precious trustees were going to sell them out – after all, none of the trustees had yet declared themselves publicly for development. Why take the heat? They'd probably delay until right before the auction. What could he and Seth say to convince them otherwise? Well, establish credibility first. He'd studied all day, even memorizing some facts on note cards in his breast pocket. Now he reviewed the process of easement, warning them how developers could raise the prices. Seth, whenever he'd glance at her, looked blank, staring into the middle distance.

"Twenty-six days till the auction, folks," he concluded. "I probably don't need to tell you that time's running out. As a matter of fact, if there's anyone else who'd like to speak, now's the time."

When he glanced at Seth, her mouth gaped open. He could almost hear her thoughts: *Damn, Billy. Never yield your pulpit.* But before he could quickly introduce Seth, the bushy-browed guy in bibs came bouncing down from the third row to stand towering over Billy. When Billy muttered, "Keep it under three minutes," the man didn't even let on he'd heard. Billy sat beside Seth, shrugging when she glared.

"I'm Garth Erickson." The big man's voice boomed among the gym's rafters. "I'm a farmer."

They applauded. *Oh shit.* He couldn't look at Seth. How could Mr. Machiavelli have thrown it all away so easily?

"You know," Erickson said, scowling fiercely, "it's not bad enough that farmers have every Tom, Dick and Harvey tellin' 'em what to do with their land. It's not bad enough that farmland here in Simon Kenton County is being lost at a rate of 1,000 acres a year because old-timers can't get their sons – or daughters – to stay on the land, so that they have to sell to strangers for the highest possible bid if they're gonna have any retirement. Now we got . . . "

When the guy clapped eyes on him, Billy still had enough balls to stare right back.

" . . . other people comin' in and tellin' us what we ought to do with our land."

Billy resisted the urge to holler back at him. Just what were the trustees about to do except tell them how their land was going to be used? But trustees were *insiders*, while he, on the other hand . . .

"Now, look," Erickson continued. "There's plenty wrong with farmers selling off little parcels here and there, four and five acres, and if you look at land sale records, that nickel and dime stuff is mostly responsible for the loss of 70 acres of farmland a day in Ohio. *That* eats us up more than the sale of big farms like Wood Thrush." He paused dramatically. "Money talks; the farmer walks."

The muttering assent behind him made Billy's heart shrink to the size of a raisin. Who, if not the farmers, would buy the land even if Blue Jacket did prevail at the auction? The idea was to re-sell it to them after the land trust bought the development rights.

"And if Wood Thrush gets sold and cut up, some of you will lose big-time. Tommy, how much land you rent there now, three-hundred and fifty?"

Tommy answered affirmatively.

"Me, I'm sixty-four. I'm about done. But you younger guys, if you keep at it, you're gonna have a tougher and tougher time getting enough land to make ends meet. God knows, we all need at least a thousand acres."

When the man's eyes fell on him, Billy knew he was preaching not so much to the choir but to him and Seth, letting them know that they weren't fit to lead them, that no non-farmer could understand. The folks assembled here had no idea what was about to happen, that they could lose it *all* at auction.

"So now this prime acreage is for sale. Now, at last, Tommy, you and a lot of other folks in this room can have a chance to own, not just rent, and somebody's trying to tell you what you can and can't do with the land before you even get a chance to buy it!"

Now Billy heard a low, ominous rumble of voices behind him. *Wait'll the trustees tell you. Wait'll the developers take the price into the stratosphere*, he longed to holler.

"Well, the bottom line is every one of you must have the right to do whatever you want to do with your land, always. It's either yours when you buy it, or it ain't. That's the way it's always been since this country was settled, and that's the way it must always be. So am I right when I say not all of us look at this easement thing as entirely good? Here's probably the prettiest piece of farmland in the county that could be tied up forever if this here – " He looked disdainfully at Seth and Billy – "CitFarm tells us what to do."

The rumble became louder, and Billy envisioned his insides as the rain-soaked ruin of a burnt-down barn. Erickson mopped his brow. "So hell, yes, we agree with the tree-huggers that farms ought to be preserved – by *us*."

The gym's rafters rocked with their thunderous applause. And as defeated as Billy felt, when Erickson brushed by, his legs were already tingling to move him up before them, to answer him as best he could, then get Seth up to sing her passion song. But before he could reach his feet, a familiar voice behind him spoke up loudly.

"Well, I don't know if I'm *us*," the high nasal voice said as soon as the crowd's buzz gave way to taut silence. "I sure as hell ain't a farmer."

Billy felt his legs go slack. It was Ira. Glancing at Seth, he shook his head, but smiled. Turning, he saw his stoop-shouldered friend standing, scanning the faces of the seated farmers around him. Though a few had laughed, it was nervous, edgy.

"I respect what Garth said about making a living. But there's more, and it's gotta get said, too, though you may not want to hear it, especially from a failed farmer. I mean, one who'll *admit* he's a failure."

More laughter, this time real.

"I don't know about this renting and owning. There's more to land than making a living."

They grew deathly quiet. Billy wouldn't have stood in Ira's boots right now for a million bucks.

"Most of y'all know I'm a teacher, so if you'd put up with me lecturing for just a minute, I'll shut up and never try to tell farmers about land again, I promise."

They shut up.

"I know how important it is to make a living – I've worked since I was fourteen – but livelihood is not everything. Land, if used properly – and most small-operation farmers avoid all the destructive practices of agribusiness with over-planting, over-spraying, over-everything – *will* provide a living. It's when people get greedy that everything goes haywire. Well, the land was here before any of us were, and face it: we're just one of many, many species passing through earth's long life. The earth was here long before us, and it'll hopefully still be here after we're long gone. What I'm saying is the land has a right to *be*, independent of what humans think it should be used for. And why is that?"

Billy was incredulous. Ira was doing what Billy had been silently telling himself that he must not do: romanticize. Sentimental city-boy bullshit, they'd say. Yet here was Ira telling them. And unlike Erickson, he didn't look like he was even sweating.

"Because land has intrinsic value in and of itself. In your most private heart of hearts, you know – you who toil in that soil every day, sunup, sundown, over and over again, boiling in the sun, freezing in the wind, howling and cursing and, yes, praying and singing to that fallow ground that both helps and hurts you – that you might need the land, but the land doesn't need you. And that's a beautiful thing. Why? Because it's the most simultaneously humbling and ennobling experience to realize that man is not the measure of everything, that the earth is. You only have to work on land as little as I did, to know that it's bigger than you are, to know that, if there is a god – capital G – it ain't you. What man or woman among you hasn't felt that at some time?"

Though the room remained silent, it had a different quality this time. Like in Grand-daddy's Baptist church right before they sipped the grape-juice at communion.

"Okay, if you agree that the land is worth preserving just for itself – not necessarily for the living we do or do not make on it – then you'll no doubt feel it's better with trees on it, better left uncovered so you can smell it when it rains, better without asphalt, without chem-lawn and cookie-cutter houses, without the huge imprint of man's muddy boot on it. In other words . . . " He now raised his voice, startling Billy, who now realized how softly Ira had been talking. "In other words, the land is a repository of souls. Even God must be touched when we put people back in the ground when they're dead, though he probably laughs at the fancy packaging some of us insist on."

A smattering of laughter.

"For all our obsession to master everything we come into contact with, we can't master nature – you farmers know that. So let's live with it. Putting an easement on Wood Thrush Farm would do that. It would be our witness to the world that land is worth preserving because *it just is.*"

He sat down. No applause; no murmuring, just a weary, more-or-less accepting silence. When he started to rise, Seth placed a hand on his thigh. It felt hot as a branding iron, and her eyes were emerald.

She stood up and faced them solemnly. "If you're interested in saving the land from development and preserving it for farming" – she stared behind him to the right, exactly where Garth Erickson sat – "then please come to the town meeting this Sunday. We need to find out all the facts, and make our presence known." Her lips moved soundlessly as if she'd forgotten what else she wanted to say. Billy almost rose to rescue her, when she seemed to remember. "Consider saving Wood Thrush for your sons and daughters." A hushed pause. "Or *someone's* sons and daughters."

Brilliant. Fucking brilliant. God, he wished he'd called in TV. Standing beside her at last, he grinned, scanned the crowd as fearlessly as if they were mere Burkers.

"Seth's right. Come and express your will. We want Citizens to Save the Farm to function as your voice and Blue Jacket Land Trust as your agent, and if you decide making the land available for farming forever is the best idea, we'll do *our* best to make that happen. It's going to take money as well as strategy, but we've already started raising it. People in this town are digging deep. Plus there are other sources we're investigating – I'll discuss them at the town meeting, two o'clock on Sunday at the Presbyterian Church. But at the very least, we'll purchase as much of the farm as we can. With your help, should you choose to give it. Yes, question?"

It was the man Erickson had called Tommy. "What's the chances of buying the whole shebang?"

Billy's heart leapt. They'd gotten through. "Pretty slim at this point, since we're still without obvious angels. But it could happen. Anything's possible. The truth is: we have no idea what will happen between now and March 20. One more reason to be at the meeting Sunday. We'll get organized."

People began putting their coats on. With incredible relief, he realized the meeting was over. Now he did take Seth's arm and gently squeeze. But before either could speak, Erickson loomed before them, stabbing his large finger in Billy's chest.

"When this is over, you want a job?"

Billy stood dumbfounded looking at Seth. She just shook her head.

"I could have your ass on a tractor in twenty minutes." He reached out and lifted one of Billy's arms. "Ha, look at that." He let it fall. "You shovel shit for a month and you'll have arms like steel cable."

Billy flushed hot all over. "Listen, my friend, I've shoveled shit before – lots of it on my Grand-dad's West Virginia farm. And I've hayed all day, every day, till every last bale was in the barn – and it wasn't any itty-bitty piece of dirt, either. Five hundred prime acres, and there were ten of us. So I just may take you up on that offer."

Erickson guffawed. "Son, if you can shovel the way you talk, you'll fill my manure pit in a day!"

Billy felt a hand clap his back.

"That's a big-time compliment coming from Garth Erickson."

He turned to see Fred Pennington smiling his gap-toothed grin. "Call his bluff, Billy."

Erickson had his sour face back on. "I've been wrong before," he said, turning his palms up. "Once."

Then both men howled and slapped each others' arms. Glancing around, Billy noticed that Seth had left his side. Scanning the gym, he saw her talking to Ira near the door. *Shit.* That's where he wanted to be, celebrating with his buds. But something kept him rooted.

As Erickson strode away, he yelled, "I mean it, City-Boy. When this is over, if you wanna try that tractor . . . "

Billy resisted the urge to flip him off and waved, instead.

"Garth's a good man," said Fred. "Too bad his sons found better things to do than farm."

"Oh, yeh?" He was still stinging from the big man's seeming insults. "Like what?"

Fred screwed up his mouth. "Oh, one's in insurance down in Cincinnati. The other one's a teacher up in Troy." By the time he and Fred parted with a hand-shake, he looked toward the door. Alone, Seth was walking toward him.

"So," he said when she reached him, "I guess ol' Henry Ira Thoreau saved the day."

She was smiling so broadly that a thin knife-blade of jealousy jabbed him between his lower two ribs. Seth spoke in a high nasal voice: "'I guess I just decided y'all are more right than wrong.'"

It was so Ira, they both laughed.

"I gotta get home to Paul." She unwound her arm from his and, waving behind her, disappeared through the door.

He felt instantly deflated. Him a farmer? When pigs became pilots.

# Chapter Seven

Putnam County, West Virginia
Monday, March 13, 1999

Billy felt as if he'd been back in the Mountain State for days. Everything felt normal, natural, comfortable as his aunt cooked a breakfast of ham and eggs, biscuits and milk gravy – real milk – plus her specialty: fried yellow squash with onions. Hung-over from bad dreams as much as the booze, he'd thought, as soon as he smelled it, he couldn't eat a thing.

But that was before he staggered downstairs and saw the table, set with his grandmother's china and silver. Huge bowls and platters held enough food for a crowd of threshers. Immediately Billy was starving. Turning from the stove, Della apparently liked what she read on his face.

"I thought maybe you hadn't had country cooking in a while, Billy Mike."

"A while?" he murmured. "Try ten years."

He ate for almost an hour.

He'd so far managed to deflect her questions with his own. And while he ached to ask the obvious – what are you doing living here and where's Uncle Don? – he sensed she wanted to talk about that as much as he wanted to talk about Seth Abel. But she was plenty willing to tell him all that had happened to the land.

"It wasn't old Beck but his boys that sold out. After the four-lane was put in five years ago, they saw their chance to go big-time, so they started building things up in a hurry. I guess you saw that golf course?"

Billy nodded. "Straight out of *Apocalypse Now*."

She just looked at him from across the table. She said she'd eaten earlier, though he didn't believe her. "Well, it's a disgrace."

"Nobody fought it?"

She sighed. "I did. But, honey, the local religion's changed around here. Used to be Baptist. Now it's jobs."

That set Billy off, and, while he continued to guzzle her sludge (freeze-dried but the food improved its taste), she sat and listened attentively while he described CitFarm's fight. Her blue eyes alternately blazed up, simmered, sizzled and embered to coals, as CitFarm's fortunes waxed and waned.

"Do you think when you get finished up there, you could come down and make it so the farm'll stay a farm after me and your daddy are gone?" she said.

His heart sputtered, misfired. The sweet taste of gravy soured. "Aunt Della, from what I've seen." He cut his eyes in the direction of Beck's. "The war's over and y'all lost."

"No." She sat forward, her tanned arms taut as leather on the table in front of her. "It's not over. Sure it is up on the highway. And over there" – she closed her eyes against the pain – "but for your grand-daddy's land it's only begun. They want it bad, Beck's does. They've done about as much as they can with that little old dairy farm, and they need a real farm for what they have up their sleeve."

"What else do they want, a fucking amusement park?" He blushed deeply. "Pardon my french." It didn't faze her, though Billy remembered her as a twice-a-week church-goer.

"That's right. Like Camden Park. You know, in Huntington."

"But . . . zoning?"

"The Beck brothers do whatever they want. Nobody can stop 'em. At least nobody down here."

'And the other farmers?"

"Not many left. And they're all in trouble. I could tell you stories. Beckwood they been calling it – you know, like Dollywood? I call it Peckerwood. They even already got a name for the rolly-coaster: 'Hills and Hollers.'"

Billy was glad he'd eaten already; he couldn't have eaten a bite now.

She sighed. "Cain't really blame the farmers who're left. Kids don't want a thing to do with the farm, and all of 'em are getting old and want to retire. I've been out to talk to 'em all, and got the same message ever' time: 'Della, you just don't understand.'"

Her eyes shone. He thought of Seth, how she'd taken him and the farm movement so seriously that first day in the Bean. More seriously than he himself had. He wouldn't have done a damn thing without her on board. Della needed a Seth. An Ira. A Woody.

"Have you ever heard of easements, Aunt Della?"

"Isn't it kinda like a lease?"

As he explained, Della's dark eyebrows began lifting. Sitting forward in her chair, she put her arms back on the table.

"You say it's forever?" Her voice was a raspy whisper. "Nobody can touch it even after the owner dies?"

"Only to farm it, or whatever use that's specified in the deed."

"Well, mercy God, that's exactly what we need, Billy Mike. It would keep the buzzards away. Do you think . . ?"

"Well, it takes a lot of money. A lot of people have to buy into it, make big donations or it doesn't work. Sometimes there's an organization that does it, a land trust. There are state-run, even national organizations that buy easements on land to preserve it . . . if they consider it important enough . . . and feasible."

He hated that last word, hated that he'd pumped her up only to watch her deflate, her shoulders sinking.

"West Virginia's not important enough for national people to take an interest, Billy Mike."

Gloom reigned over the kitchen that only moments ago had been bright.

"I'm so sorry, Aunt Della."

There were large slabs beneath her eyes now. Since arriving, he'd had trouble believing she was much past fifty, but now she looked seventy-five, if a day.

"So there's not a thing we can do?"

"Not without an easement, not without . . . " He thought of Woody, who'd probably have his hand on Della's shoulder by now. " . . . an angel."

"Well. I better do these dishes up." She stood.

"Let me, Della. It's something I can maybe do right."

"Psht. Won't take me but a minute."

Maybe, though, there was something he could do. It would require a trip to Charleston.

# Chapter Eight

Shawnee Springs, Ohio
Thursday, February 23, 1999


While Ira was at play practice, Billy set up his stereo – at least the place had electricity – and was listening to a very stoned Neil Young sing *Tonight's The Night* at full volume while he showered – who was gonna complain, the trees? During "Roll Another Number," the phone rang, sending a chill up his spine. It had that middle-of-the-night-somebody-died quaver to it. He pulled on a pair of Ira's gym shorts and the holey Grateful Dead tee-shirt that he slept in and ran for it, dripping, got it on the fifth ring.

"Yo."

"Billy, Paul's locked himself in his room upstairs and won't let me in. He . . . he just killed his hamster and I'm afraid of what he might do. I think he's banging his head – he did it once before when he was much younger – and" – her voice shredded.

"Be there in three minutes."


○


Without knocking, he strode through the door and found her in the kitchen looking like someone who'd just found the body. Poised to say something – God knew what – he heard the sound, like a bass drum with a loose head.

Bomp.

She closed her eyes and shuddered before speaking.

"The boys were working on a science project – and Matt suggested it be about Data. Paul somehow got the idea that the only reason Matt had hung with him was to use his hamster, so . . . he squeezed it . . . too hard."

Bomp. Bomp.

"You think he did it on purpose?"

She nodded, eyes closed. She was beyond pale, her skin translucent, blue veins visible in her neck. If the kid wanted to kill his mom, he'd sure found the perfect way. "Stay here," he said. "I'll holler if I need you."

"But I know what . . . "

"He knows you'll react. Let me try."

She nodded.

By the time Billy reached the door, reality set in and he allowed himself to admit he had no clue what he was doing. He had only the dimmest idea of what he'd find in the kid's room. On the way over, he'd let himself fantasize this as a way to get into her good graces. But the instant he'd heard that sound of head hitting wall, this had become something else. Even though he knew what being a screwed-up kid felt like, he'd never resorted to head-banging.

As soon as he reached the top, the pounding started again, almost as if the boy knew he were coming. Messed-up kids did magic sometimes. He used to swear he could make the old man stop arguing with Noreen, his second wife, if he concentrated hard enough. Sometimes counting backward did it. By the time he stood in front of the door, the banging echoed through the upstairs.

"Hey, Paul," he yelled, rapping lightly, then louder: "PAUL." But he'd known all along he'd have to bust in. Though there wasn't much room on the narrow landing to get any momentum, he popped the cheap lock on his second try. The door flung open, hitting the wall, and Billy practically fell into the room. He waited. Silence. Looking around him, he saw the empty hamster cage sitting on top of a beat-up desk. Did he have the hamster in the closet with him? Sudden chill gripped him to the bone. When the next bang came – nearby and loud – he was glad no one was around to see him start. Looking to his right, he saw the open closet door. He cut on the light and stepped inside.

Paul sat in the corner, his knees nearly to his chin, facing forward, eyes red from crying, lips parted, slamming the back of his head against the wall every two or three seconds. In his open right hand lay the hamster, fur matted from the boy's sweaty clutch. *Just stay present,* Billy told himself, breathing deeply.

On his knees, he reached out to grasp Paul's ankles, but the boy let go an amazingly hard kick that caught him in the chest. Pulling back, he blinked away stars and waited to get his breath back. As his breathing normalized, he watched Paul watch him as the boy continued slamming his head every few seconds. He could wrestle the kid out of here, but he didn't want to carry a kicking, screaming twelve-year-old down those stairs to hand over to his stricken mother. If only there was a way to get with him somehow, calm him down. Tears were a good sign. They might give him an opening.

On his hands and knees, Billy entered the small closet. He closed his eyes, and it came to him. If Noreen weren't around, he'd been able to get nine-year-old Nerissa to quit doing almost anything, even singing constantly in her screechy voice, by imitating her. Lowering his head,

Billy bashed it into the drywall, only a couple of feet away from the boy. He timed his blows to be between the boy's, and just as hard but no harder. It took about a minute and a half and about a dozen bashes, but finally Paul stopped. Billy bashed twice more, then, easing back on his haunches, he returned the boy's blank stare.

"Wanna get out of here?"

After about five seconds, Paul nodded.

Billy stood stiffly, extended his hand. The boy's eyes shot upward, then back down to the dead fur-ball in his lap. Then, as carefully as if the creature were still alive, Paul placed it on the floor and reached up, let Billy pull him to his feet and guide him out of the closet. Billy was pleased to see that, although the door stood open, Seth had stayed downstairs as he'd told her. Even ol' Noreen had known enough to stay the hell out of the way when Dad administered the belt to "the boy." Billy hadn't minded all that much – whatever he'd done to Nerissa was worth it, plus after only a couple strokes, Dad usually lost his nerve. And at least he had his old man's attention. Looking at Paul, he couldn't remotely imagine what it would be like to whip him, what the blows would feel like in his hand, in his mind. He shivered. No wonder his dad couldn't do it, not really.

The kid seemed wobbly. Billy fought the urge to tackle the boy, throw him over his shoulder, scream Geronimo and storm downstairs – something his father would've done.

"You're the head farm-saver," the boy said finally, his lip curling.

"Nope. Just the treasurer."

The kid shook his head, eyes smoldering. "You want *her* to be on your side, to get what you want. Well, watch this."

And bending down suddenly, he began intaking huge gulps of air.

Billy couldn't hold back a grin. He knew this game! Jim Bob Bailey, the high school dropout next door, had taught him to "put himself out" by hyperventilating.

When the kid stood up suddenly, Billy was ready. The kid's face grew paler than his big front teeth, and if Billy had not reached out immediately with both arms, Paul would've fallen on his face. Billy laid him, limp as wet laundry, across the space-ship sheets. It wouldn't take long for him to come to. He looked around. On the wall above the bed hung a huge poster of the galaxy, complete with planets and constellations. On the other wall were taped photos: Picard, Worf, Data, Geordi . . . the whole crew.

He shook his head. *He's way too old for this space crap. Needs bands and babes. First chance, I'll bring him some CDs.*

Sitting beside Paul on the bed, he had just felt the boy's hot forehead for fever, when he heard her behind him.

"Should we take him to the emergency room?"

"Nah," he said without turning. "He just hyperventilated is all." So she'd been standing outside in the hall the whole time. She'd probably been right behind him on the stairs. Of course. World's Best Mom – not Noreen hiding downstairs sipping Chardonnay while the guys "worked things out" (her favorite phrase) upstairs. He snuck a look at her standing in the doorway, arms crossed. Wisps of golden hair hung wildly from the bun atop her head. Her eyes were grey again, her cheeks flushed. Damn, she was beautiful – even with one foot in hell. "He's fine. He was talking before he put himself out." He tried for a reassuring grin. "I did it all the time at his age."

Her voice wavered: "We can take him to the hospital."

"It's an old trick, Seth. Don't fall for it. Please." He realized his headache had disappeared, and he had a huge erection. Why hadn't he worn something besides these shorts? When she walked over and touched his temple, he grew even more excited. When her fingers came away, they were bloody.

"Must've hit a nail. Don't sweat it. Head's harder than granite. Look – not a mark on Paul."

As she knelt on the floor and began stroking the heavily-breathing boy's cheek, Billy felt a little embarrassed, not only because of his hard-on, but the mother-and-child reunion made him feel an outsider. Also, he sensed some change in Seth. She seemed *fragile*, like if he touched her, she'd break into a million pieces or burst like a balloon. Guess that's how *real* parents respond in a crisis. Thinking about the contrast between his step-mom and *this* mom helped bring his body back under control. In a few moments he'd be able to stand without embarrassment.

She finally looked at him. "I'll take care of him now," she whispered. She was dismissing him, and she was right. His presence now would hinder, not help, but could he be blamed for wanting to stay where it felt so warm and cozy? Rising, she stood, bent toward him.

"Thank you, Billy. Thank you so much," she whispered, kissing his cheek lightly. "I'll call you later." When she stepped back, he saw that at last the tears fell from both eyes, catching the light, leaving silver traces on her cheeks. Standing, he resisted embracing her, instead reached, dabbed at her tears with one finger and held it to his lips.

"No ER?" he said.

"No ER. Go now." She knelt again beside her son.

And he went back down the strangely uncreaking stairs, a shadow of his former headache throbbing lightly, licking his lips, tasting this strong woman's salt, bright and sharp as the sea.

# Chapter Nine

Shawnee Springs, Ohio
Friday, February 24, 1999


Billy was sitting, feet kicked up on Ira's desk, twisting the phone cord around his finger. He was watching the brown spider walking the web between lightshade and window glimmering in morning sunshine. It was so cold in the cabin, he could see his breath.

"So Paul's not going to school today?"

"I'm staying home with him."

Her voice weighed a ton. He could imagine the gravity in those eyes. They'd be deep, serious grey.

"You know what he told me last night, Billy? After you were gone?"

"That he wanted to grow up to have a head as hard as mine?"

"That it wasn't Data he'd wanted to hurt."

"Then who?"

Silence for several seconds. "He wouldn't say, and I wasn't about to bully it out of him."

"Good move." Though he'd called her – he'd hardly slept at all thinking about the two of them – he longed now to hang up. The emotional footing felt slippery as hell.

Billy waited a few respectful seconds. "I think you should go to work, Seth."

"I can't leave him alone today after what happened."

"He won't be alone. I'm coming over."


○


When she answered the door, Billy couldn't believe she was the same person as the woman who'd greeted him last night. Her newly-washed hair smelled like a spring garden, and her lips shone with silvery gloss. She didn't look like a suffering mother; she looked delectable. Then it occurred to him why she was wearing makeup.

"Long night, huh?"

She just stared. "What's with the stereo equipment?"

He insinuated himself between the storm door, then past her, his arms full. His once-over of the downstairs last night had highlighted a big part of their problem: no tunes. He hadn't even seen a radio.

"Audio therapy. Now you just go on to work and let the Tune Meister go to work."

She wrinkled her nose, tried to peer into the canvas bag of CDs dangling over his shoulder. "Classical, I hope?"

"Oh, definitely." He smiled his best widows and orphans smile.

She looked skeptical but his heart high-fived itself when she began putting on her coat. "Well, if anything happens, here's the number at the Manor. I'll be back at noon."

He air-kissed her goodbye and headed for the stairs. Four hours to administer a shot of rhythm and blues. He offered a silent prayer he'd brought the right drugs.

○

Periscoping his neck from his position on the floor, he saw Paul's eyes were open as he stared at the ceiling. All this time the kid hadn't said a single word, though Billy had kept the tunes coming, choosing tracks for their vein-unclogging ability: "Mystery Train," "Great Balls of Fire," "Long Tall Sally," "My Generation," "Helter Skelter," "Piece of My Heart." When Billy thought he detected movement during "Purple Haze," he quickly increased the dosage with "Fire" and "All Along the Watchtower," but Hendrix might've been too strong. Apparently the kid only needed a triple by-pass rather than a transplant. Since then, he'd slowed the IV drip to introduce the antitoxins more gradually into the kid's system.

Following the Hendrix overdose, he sampled side one of *Sgt. Pepper* (he thought he heard sighing during "Getting Better"), two cuts from *Madman Across the Water*, then, in a fit of what-the-hell inspiration: *Aqualung*. Now he thought he distinctly heard a murmur from the vicinity of the bed. From his position on the floor, his fingers reached for, found volume and cut it way down.

"Whadja say?" Billy's tongue was dry from disuse.

"Who is this?"

"Jethro Tull."

The kid giggled. Billy sat up straighter, tried to see the boy's face. Was that a smile?

"He sounds like a cartoon character – I can see him twirling his mustache as he ties a girl to the tracks. And . . . and that last song's words . . . " Now the bed shook with Paul's laughter. "You know, about snot running down his nose."

The room brightened. A sixth-grader's take on Tull! He'd probably love some fart references, too. The drugs had kicked in. He was seriously considering cutting to the chase – *Rust Never Sleeps* – when a shadow fell across the floor, onto the bed, obscuring the boy's face.

"Would you metalheads like some lunch?" Seth asked.

He hadn't heard her car in the driveway. Music must've been too loud. Since she'd entered, gravity oozed from the ceiling, weighting everything. Billy could barely keep his head up. And things had been so weightless and bright for one shining moment. *Damn*. Fifteen more minutes and he'd had the kid strumming air.

"Yeh," Paul said. "Peanut butter and pickle."

"Pickle?" Billy made a face.

Paul had his feet dangling off the bed. His pink toes reminded Billy of the pads on a kitten.

"Come on."

And the boy was out of the bed, racing down the stairs in his Star Wars pajamas. Seth smiled.

"So, Dr. Rock, is the patient cured?"

"Downgraded from critical to serious."

"Classical, ha." But her frown was a fake, as she sought to suppress mouth corners from lifting into a grin.

"I meant 'classic.' Sorry."

He stood but almost fell back down, his lower legs and feet numb as rocks. She stood on tiptoes in stocking feet and kissed him in the middle of his forehead. No kiss from any woman anywhere, anytime, had ever felt better. She smelled like clean sheets hanging in the sunny breeze. With a hint of lemon. Her lips glistened; she'd freshened her gloss and maybe even changed clothes. For him?

"So." He made his voice barely audible. "Who does Paul want to kill?" She studied her feet – gorgeous, sexy feet. "And, more importantly: why?"

Now she looked back up, miserably. He longed to retract the question. He waited until they heard Paul hollering downstairs.

"I better go do some real work," he finally said. He hoped like hell she wouldn't ask what that work was, exactly. A nap at the library, probably, though what he most wanted was to lie down on those Star Trek sheets with her and put on Santana's *Abraxus*. But that wasn't going to happen today.

"You want to stay for peanut butter and pickle?"

"Nope. Gotta run." He tried one step, but his legs collapsed. She caught him or he would've been down with the dust bunnies.

He regained his footing. "Sorry. Lost feeling in my feet."

Her face had gone grey.

"I think I should get . . . professional help for him."

He remembered the family counselor they'd gone to after his dad's remarriage and the resulting disasters. The woman was like a game show host on speed. "Own those feelings!" "Share that pain!" "Gratitude is an attitude!" Billy wanted to puke on her Persian rug. Thank God, the old man felt the same way, and they'd never gone back.

Before Billy could respond, sound exploded from downstairs. The kid was singing the guitar riff from "Aqualung." Had it down pretty good, too. Billy grinned.

"Why not give the audio therapy a little time to work."

She squeezed his arm. "Man therapy." When she kissed him on the cheek, her breath was very warm and sweet. With a hint of vanilla. For the first time he appreciated that herbal tea she drank. "Acorn therapy."

"PEANUT BUTTER! PICKLE!" Paul roared up the stairs, followed immediately by the riff again.

"Got your feeling back now?" she asked with an impish grin.

He smiled and put his arm around her waist, pulling her from the room before he did something he'd regret. Like lick the silver from her shining lips.

At the door, Billy was saying goodbye when, at the table where he was eating, Paul yelled.

"Billy, wanna help me bury Data?"

With her back to her son, Seth raised her eyebrows, her mouth opening but emitting no sound.

"Sure, when?"

"Tomorrow?"

"All right. If the weather's good. Better put him on ice or something in case it warms up."

"Okay." Head down, Paul returned to his sandwich.

Seth's face had returned to normal. She was almost smiling. "Data's in the garage," she whispered. "In a plastic butter tub." She giggled, her cheeks flushed. "I think he's staying fresh."

It was all he could do not to take her in his arms. But instead he lifted the brow of his cap.

"Mornin' to you, ma'am. Now you and the boy have a good day, hear?" His John Wayne was lousy.

"What about your stereo, your CDs?"

"Put him on the IV again as soon as possible. Nothing stronger than Stones this afternoon, increasing to Led Zep by evening, then Neil Young and Crazy Horse all day tomorrow."

She touched his arm, but he was already pulling away. Let it build. The fever, when it broke, might save them all.

# Chapter Ten



Inside the church, the flea market was humming. Looking around, Billy saw that the givers had done their share: on long folding tables lay clothes, tapes, albums and videos, toys, even original art. In its own little corner on an easel sat a large water color of – what else? – a Wood Thrush Farm sunset. Perfect item for a sale to benefit the farm.

He fingered the wad of greenbacks in his pocket, the latest batch of contributions. He'd already had to increase his expense account. The country farmer breakfast at the Sunset was fifteen bucks, with tip. He realized how silly his original estimate had been. Nobody lived on twenty bucks a day; he required thirty, minimum.

But where was Seth? She'd said she'd meet him here to get their act together for tomorrow's town meeting. When he'd called her last night, she'd said Paul had played CDs till bedtime. Billy just grinned. It had worked for him lo those many years ago.

Strolling over to look at the painting's price tag, he turned toward the door and laid eyes on the last person in the world he'd've expected to see at a church flea market. Standing barely inside the room, as if facing contagion, the dignified white-haired man was talking to a woman in a knit hat. His eyes focused. It was Seth. Talking to Dr. Lloyd Kieron!

Kieron was speaking.

"I thought I might find you here, Elizabeth. On neutral ground, so to speak."

Something in his former professor's tone stopped Billy from going over. A few feet behind Seth, he paused to finger some old albums: *Wayne Newton Sings Lennon and McCartney.* Billy shuddered.

"I heard your speech last Saturday," Kieron said. "Very interesting."

When she finally spoke, it was in the small voice he'd heard on the phone the other night. "Lloyd, I'm so sorry for your loss."

Billy snuck a peek. Kieron leaned on a silver-tipped cane, his face so drained of color that he half-expected his old professor to tumble forward into her arms. But the older man recovered quickly.

"No one in this town knew Alexandra – or accepted her. They called her the rich bitch."

Billy wasn't about to get involved in this conversation. At least not yet. He approached to within ten feet of them, hidden behind a hanging display of garish jewelry, feathers and dream catchers – cool stuff if you were going to a Woodstock reunion. He realized he was still holding the Newton album, so he appeared to study it while listening. Good God – what business did Wayne Newton have singing "Lucy In The Sky With Diamonds?!"

"Well," she said, "I know what that's like. I've been an outsider ever since I got back last summer."

*Not true*, Billy wanted to scream. He snuck a peek. Kieron was smiling, apparently oblivious to eavesdroppers.

"So you've come back to save us from burgeoning capitalism."

"I came back to find a good home for my son."

While Billy glanced through his dangling shield of beads and Hawaiian leis, Kieron's smile didn't falter, though his eyes gleamed a little madly. "I would've thought home is where your husband is."

"What're you afraid of, Lloyd? I'm not going to ask you for anything."

Things were getting interesting.

At first, Kieron stared impassively as if he hadn't heard – or, like Billy, had no idea what she was talking about. But then Kieron looked past her – right into Billy's eyes. Billy lifted the record closer as if the liner notes contained mystical secrets. Kieron's eyes had betrayed emotion – fear? – before returning to steely blue. What the hell? Billy's former hero seemed less the steely opponent of all things bourgeois than the mustachioed tormentor of single moms.

Now Seth stepped closer to the man and said something Billy didn't catch. Kieron's face suddenly reddened, as if he were preparing a salvo – and Billy knew what those torpedoes were like. His hull had been damaged a few times by their fury for not knowing something his professor thought he should have. Just when he was considering rescuing Seth from certain destruction, a nasal voice intruded.

"I'll be damned! If it isn't Professor Kieron out trawling for bargains."

Billy peered above his album cover to see Ira towering above the pair, holding in both hands, as if an offering, an electric screwdriver and a gilt-edged old book – *Life in the Maine Woods* (yeh, he *was* Thoreau, all right). His floppy-eared hat tilted rakishly, one flap up, one down, Ira grinned as if they were all best friends. *Damn*. If Ira only knew, he would've kept the hell away. As Billy was doing (feeling rather chicken-hearted as the tableau unfolded).

"Ah, Herr Flint!" Kieron pumped the ends of Ira's fingers holding his purchases as if Ira had come to award him the Nobel. "Long time no see."

Billy tried to telepath *Watch out*, but he could tell his friend was oblivious to what he'd interrupted.

Kieron was stroking his chin. "Have I seen you since your trial?" It was his loudest public conversational voice. It meant Trouble. "No, I believe the last time we chatted, that ignominious business still lay ahead of you." He turned back to Seth. "Herr Flint has collided head-on with our judicial system." Then, speaking even louder (for the benefit of eavesdroppers, Billy guiltily acknowledged), the professor struck an orator's pose, Antony at Caesar's coffin, MacArthur at Corregidor, Lincoln at Gettysburg – Billy had seen 'em all. "But, fortunately, a man can be charged with serious crimes by our hypocritical drug-war-obsessed judiciary yet remain innocent in the eyes of the denizens of this liberal enclave. And perhaps in his own eyes as well."

Billy's heart felt blood-drained. He'd often felt powerless against Kieron's onslaughts, the one man who could truly cow him, but that was different; if you showed up to class prepared, if you engaged him honestly, you could earn Kieron's respect, even approval and the tiny smile that glimmered before his mouth tightened again. What was happening now before Billy's eyes was different; this was assault with a deadly weapon – a gilt-edged tongue – and the intent was clearly to kill.

Now Kieron spoke at full classroom volume, rewarding the rubberneckers (Billy noticed he wasn't the only one listening).

"Unfortunately, Shawnee Springs isn't the world, and selling a substance even as inconsequential as cannabis is frowned upon by society at large." Ira was pale. Billy fully expected him to drop the screwdriver. Or gouge out Kieron's eyes with it.

The Great Man turned back to Seth. "So praise be to those powers whose intercession spared a good man – teacher and father – the indignity of incarceration."

Billy found his fists clenching at the word father. It was the thing in life his buddy took most seriously. Kieron better watch it.

"Well, I hope it's all over," Kieron boomed. "To defend one's innocence must be a terrible inconvenience, wouldn't you think, Elizabeth?"

If she said anything, Billy couldn't hear it. Maybe she'd been turned to stone. But now Billy saw his old prof without benefit of undergraduate awe. Kieron was merely a bully, and there was no way you could win against a guy who was a pro at turning your words against you – *oh, I see, in Hitler's place, you would simply wait until the Western powers gave you some real estate? You wouldn't actually use the world's best military machine to win the world.* Best to turn the other cheek, even though it wasn't Billy's style, and he longed to say or do something in Ira's defense.

"And there are children to consider, too, just as you said in your peroration the other day, Elizabeth – yes, I was there. I'm sure Herr Flint, an astute social scientist before turning his talents to teaching, would agree that the effect of an arrest on parenthood is nothing less than devastating."

While he watched Ira's face turn from biscuit dough to strawberry, Billy marveled. This honest, principled man who'd earned the respect of farmers ought to deck this windbag. Instead his friend wore the sad veil Billy had seen all too often since the divorce. It was too much. Billy strode around the counter and entered the triangle.

"So," Billy said cheerily, "can CitFarm count on you for a donation, Dr. Kieron?"

The professor cocked his head slightly, his lip curling. "Who are you?"

It stung for one point three seconds. Billy had taken three of the man's classes, accompanied him on numerous field trips, stood by his side at more than one protest and even drunk beer with him in the faculty club – at Kieron's invitation.

"I'm a guy who believes in a cause," he said, imitating the professor's classroom voice. "I'm a guy who has the audacity – some might say stupidity – to think that principles can sometimes win out over greed, who believes that, despite the all-too-often negative lessons of history, that bumbling humanity can sometimes do the right thing. I'm a guy who's trying, along with his fellow citizens, to raise a million dollars to fight capitalist bourgeoisie and the almighty Way-Things-Are."

Billy's heart was racing, his stomach stuck halfway in his gorge. His neck was getting hot, so there was only one thing to do. Get more outrageous.

"I'm a guy who thinks a great professor who devoted a huge chunk of his life to teaching peasants like me might find an ounce of idealism left in his heart and maybe even a couple of thou in his back pocket for a good cause." He saw shocked faces all around him. "A damn good cause."

Kieron laughed nastily. "Don't try to close the sale too quickly, my boy. I'm only here to observe today. But if I like what I see, I may be back. Auf wiedersehen." He started away, but stopped and turned around.

"May I ask you a question?"

Billy's skin burned. "Shoot."

Kieron struck a pose, hands atop his cane. "What does this farm mean to you? I mean, personally. Why do you want it used for farming rather than, say, affordable homes for residents currently priced out of the market?"

Billy's mind turned to concrete. He couldn't speak. Last time it had happened was when he'd admitted to his father he'd dropped out of Burke, and his dad had said, "What can you do without a college education?" Like then, he couldn't think of a single thing to say now. A voice from far off spoke. Ira.

"Farming will insure this town retains its individual character and . . ."

"I am asking *him*."

Words whirled. *Earth has a right to be . . . intrinsic value . . . repository of souls*. But he couldn't say them. They weren't his. His old teacher was glaring at him.

"I thought I knew you there for a second, my boy, but I don't. I taught my students to speak their minds." He smiled grimly. "With feeling."

Then he was gone, sliding out the door behind them without having stepped more than a few feet inside. When Billy turned, he found Seth staring up at Ira with wide, wet eyes.

"He was such a bastard to you," she said.

"But it's true," Ira said. "I was busted."

"Did you go to jail?" she asked softly. Billy didn't think she'd even looked at him yet.

"No. Because I knew somebody. But if I had it to do again, I'd do the time."

An awkward silence ensued.

"That crack about parenthood was a low blow," Billy said. "I'm sure you still have the respect of your students and Amber."

Seth perked up. "*Amber?*"

Ira smiled thinly. "My little girl. Lives with her mother in Florida. Since my arrest, I've lost visitation privileges, and my ex wants sole custody. But I'm fighting it, keeping my nose clean."

"Oh, Ira." She looked like she was on the verge of hugging him. The guy hadn't even stood up for himself, and he was the hero just 'cause he had a kid? Billy felt his face heating up again.

"That wasn't really him, you know," Ira said softly.

"Huh?" Billy was feeling a little out of control. "Sure it was: The Little Corporal himself."

Ira shook his head. "Dr. Kieron really loved his Alex. And she died."

Seth was nodding her head sympathetically. Billy stared at them both incredulously. The man had publicly flogged him, and Ira felt sorry for him!

"She really suffered. Cancer. It's changed him."

*Yeh, made him a bully without a cause*, Billy almost said, but something stopped him, a sudden memory of Kieron standing behind the microphone, wavy salt-and-pepper hair flying in the wind as he blasted Sylco Cement and the eco-destruction it stood for, replacing it with his utopian vision of a future world where nature flowered, where folks simply reduced their wants, their need for so much power. Dr. Kieron always clapped his student on the back after Billy followed with a speech of his own, whether it sucked or not (it usually did), just like a cool dad would. But then, come Monday, back in the classroom Kieron was his old fascist self. Was he changed that much by his wife's death? Seemed like a rationalization to Billy.

He was about to say as much when Seth, stepping forward, stood on tiptoe and put both arms around Ira. Billy realized he was hugging himself, freezing inside his old man's jacket. When she finally stepped back, Ira's head drooped on his shoulders, his eyes on the floor.

"Better pay for this stuff," he mumbled.

"Me, too," Seth said.

About to follow them toward the cashier, Billy glanced down and saw Newton's face smiling back at him. He pitched the record on the table as if it contained anthrax and headed for the door Kieron had disappeared behind. King Kieron, the Conqueror, with historical inevitability on his side. He imagined the panzers rolling through the empty streets of Warsaw. But Polish resistance, crushed today, might rise again. The war had just begun.

Glancing behind him, he saw Seth smiling at the rangy giant beside her. He decided to make like horse-shit and hit the trail.

◯

Meredith's Pond was frozen over, all the ducks who stayed year-round huddled on the bank. Though he'd thought to just cruise past, he pulled the Dakota over, turned off the engine and got out. There was little tree protection, and the wind raked his cheeks. He hunched further down into his pea coat, glad he'd worn the John Deere cap Fred Pennington had given him. Since it was early on a Saturday, there was no traffic on the road. As he stood at the white-railed fence with the Keep-Out sign, he heard nothing but the breeze riffling the few remaining leaves.

This was the farm, too, the southern edge of it. The original owners had built a small summer home for a wealthy cousin who'd used it until he died. He'd named the pond for his daughter, and what a pond it was. Thoreau's Walden couldn't be cooler, Billy thought, watching the water flow beneath the ice over the small dam into Shawnee Springs Creek that wound through town eventually ending up in The Little Miami.

*What does this farm mean . . . personally?*

Why couldn't he answer? He truly did not know – just that it did mean something to him, a lot, in fact. Would he be hanging around fighting for it if it didn't? But he knew that Ira and Seth and anyone who'd listened in must think him a fool now. He was their leader, for God's sake, and hadn't been able to answer the easiest of questions! He'd been bushwhacked by the father of all bushwhackers.

The worst had been Kieron's not "knowing" him. Who did the bastard think he was? The guy recognized him all right but needed a scapegoat for the shitty way the town had treated him after he married the chicken queen.

*Damn.* He shifted his position on the fence, his legs beginning to go numb. Better get going soon, though he had no idea where he'd go. Library closed early on Saturday.

Wait a minute – he suddenly recalled something. What was all the whispering between the old man and Seth about? He recalled Kieron's face reddening, as Seth had leaned in close. What had she said? And why had the guy come looking for her? He watched his breath congeal as if the answer might materialize like the great blue heron he'd seen standing in the spillway last December.

That was something. After rubbing his eyes to clear the sleep that day, Billy found the slate-grey bird still standing as nonchalantly as if it were the first of May, not the week after Christmas. He gave it a wide berth, crossing the road to pass, and it never moved.

What the hell was it doing in Ohio in the winter? An omen that the world was about to be turned upside-down? Two weeks later, the auction signs went up.

What was that noise? At first he thought it must be an approaching car's radio, but, straining to hear, he decided it was closer to conversation. Looking behind him, he half-expected to see a group of hyped-up urchins approaching from Lucky Duck Day Care. Identifying the direction, if not the source, of the sound, he gazed up into the southern sky to see a wide V of Canada geese. Deep inside his funk, he hadn't noticed that the geese were missing, that the huddled bodies on the bank were all ducks.

While he watched them approach, their voices grew louder, never merging into one unified sound like other birds, but remaining individuals braying like filibustering senators. And finally as they flew right above him, the din was so loud Billy wanted to cover his ears but didn't. Unlike squabbling humans – the farmers the other night came to mind – the voices of the geese were so absurdly loud and nonsensical that they made a giggle rise up in his chest. He could never hear them without grinning. Reversing their engines to brake, wings outspread, they landed, one by one, on the bank, avoiding the frozen pond where he'd admired their hydroplane landings last summer, churning the green water into glittering rainbows as they plowed the surface.

He watched the geese climb onto the bank and plop down, some curling their long necks around to tuck their ink-black heads into their feathers – for warmth, he guessed. This fight was for them, too. What would happen to their numbers with houses every few yards, with the pond drained or, worse, polluted? Many folks considered geese overpopulous pests, but they had their place, too. (And where would the herons feed without friendly waters?)

Herons, he'd tell Kieron. Ducks and geese. We feed them; they feed us.

Suddenly freezing, he hopped off the fence, lifted his cap in salute to the birds, got back in the truck and turned the ignition, feeling energized.

○

Of course Seth and Ira were gone when he got back to the church, along with most of the crowd. Before he could flee, he was staring into the deep hazel eyes of Bonnie Gershowitz.

"Sorry, Bilbo," she said, fingering the jewelry that had so recently shielded him, "she left with Ira 'bout ten minutes ago."

"So," he said, "the loyal opposition has come looking for bargains."

She stuck her tongue out at him. Though her hair was wild and unruly, she looked and smelled fresh from the shower. He got a quick memory of her tanned, naked body.

"Said she had to get home to the kid," Bonnie continued. "Is he all right?"

"Why wouldn't he be?"

"Oh, Leta Hargrove – works in the school office? – she told me he's getting bullied pretty bad. Plus, he's hanging with geeky Matt Plummer. Who I also hear killed his precious gerbil the other day."

"Hamster," Billy growled. "Hamster, not gerbil. And Matt didn't kill it, Paul did."

"You know all about it, of course."

And before he'd really decided to, Billy told her the whole story.

"Wow. Poor, kid," she said, shaking her head. "Do you think she'll get him some help?"

"She has. Me."

"And where does your degree in psychology come from?" She smiled sweetly. "The School of Lost Causes?"

The pond, the geese, his sense that all would be well – fled. It was time to get out of here before his head exploded, as it was threatening to do. As he tried to frame a withering last remark, Bonnie's features softened.

"I'm sorry I made that 'pretty face' crack at the Bean last Saturday."

He stood amazed. For the last year and a half, she'd never apologized for anything. And now she'd handed him the perfect exit line. Looking at her now, appearing so vulnerable in her sad black shawl, he almost didn't say it. Almost.

"But you were right, y'know."

"'Bout what?"

"She does have a pretty face. And I *am* a sucker for it."

Bonnie's eyes narrowed. But before she could speak, he got out. Fast.

# Chapter Eleven

Kanawha County, West Virginia
March 13, 1999

All the way to Charleston, Billy had been in mourning, not only for what Aunt Della had told him over breakfast, the results of which had screamed at him as he'd passed the damn blue cow, Wally's World and the dragstrip hovering like a sci-fi nightmare that would all disappear as soon as the sun burned off the fog. (On principle he would not drive the new beltway.) But what he'd left back in Ohio dogged him like a bad hangover. What were Seth, Ira, Woody and the others doing right now with only a week left before the auction?

He was glad he'd left the check lying on the dresser at Grand-dad's. He sure wasn't going to cash it today. Maybe not tomorrow, either.

By the time he got to Winfield and saw the signs to I-64, the sun was blazing away. Spirits lifting slightly, his hand fluttered toward the stereo – the drug of choice for forgetting – but he let it drop. He was going to do whatever he was going to do today – and his idea was a vague one – fully sober. By the time he began passing factories on the east side, he hardly noticed them. His jaw set, he headed toward the heart of the city.

He remembered a bookstore near the Capitol – a place where he'd find a good cup of sludge, pastry and a phone book. He and his dad had discovered it while Ma was dying in the hospital. When he saw an exit for Capitol Street, he took it and – voila – there it still was, Taylor Books, and even open at this ungodly hour of 9:07.

Once his brain was eased by caffeine and pecan roll (compliments of Blue Jacket), he got the phone book (no internet here) from the boy behind the counter and went to work. He'd figured the squeaky oak floor and smell of cinnamon and fresh-ground dark roast would comfort him, but they made him even lonelier. Face to the page, he didn't look around even when he raised his head to sip, lest he might find himself searching for the garish, glittering bean tree. And the long-blonde-haired siren he'd seen sitting near the rear. Next thing you knew he'd be crying. *Concentrate, fuckhead.*

But after an hour, he'd tried every key word he could think of, from land to rural to county to preservation – hell, he'd looked at the yellow pages so long he figured he smelled like sulfur and his eyes were the color of dog piss. His mug of brew long empty, he staggered to the café counter blearily, his legs wobbly, feeling hopeless and helpless, far, far from home. Like every other man when lost, you drive a zillion miles out of your way, waste hours of time and wait till your nerves are raw – then when all hope is gone, you ask someone for directions. It was past time to hit the internet at the library, and even though the Asian kid at the counter looked like the last person to ask about land trusts, he decided to take a shot.

"Good sludge," Billy said by way of introduction.

The kid peered at him, curiously. "That's what my girlfriend calls Italian roast, at least the best stuff."

Billy stood up straighter. Well, by God, these West Virginians were all right! "Your girlfriend is a scholar and a gentleperson."

In the customerless café, all the capitol patrons long-ago fled to their desks, the kid leaned his weight on his palms and smiled.

"I was wondering if you could help me. By the way," he said, thrusting his hand forward. "Billy Acorn."

"Ezra Blankenship. Friends call me Ez."

Oriental mom, hillbilly dad, Billy decided. The boy's grip was firm.

"Look, Ez, I'm from Ohio, and I'm trying to find something, anything having to do with what's called a land trust, which is . . ." He cast about him as if Woody could be conjured out of the woodwork to explain. He'd suddenly contracted a caffeine-induced case of the stupids.

"Oh, sure." Ez had grabbed a clean rag and begun wiping the spot where Billy'd laid his cup. "Private entities that acquire land, often for the purpose of keeping it agricultural as opposed to placing it on the free market for commercial development."

Billy gripped the counter. Good thing he'd only had one cup or he might've had to sit down. Ez was rubbing hard at a bit of encrusted donut. "I'm a civic administration major at UC – University of Charleston."

There *was* a God. "That's great! Do you know if there's any . . . "

"The man to talk to is Dan Fountain. He's one of my profs at UC. But he's also head of Kanawha Land Trust."

"There's a land trust here?" He gazed around at dollops of sun spilled like gold coins on the hardwood floor. "I've been all over that phone book . . ."

"Guess you didn't look under 'Kanawha County.'" Ezra gazed out the window in the direction of the capitol. "Most people are against it." He shook his head, returned to polishing the glass. "Appalachians are strange. We all think we're Daniel Boone." He looked up. "Or Jesus Christ."

"Tell me about it."

"If you want to meet Dr. Fountain, I'll call him for you."

Billy no longer felt unsteady. When would his good luck end? (Then he imagined flaming houses in uninhabited new housing developments and cringed – good luck, hell.)

○

Despite the couple of pots of coffee he'd consumed, Billy found his brain remarkably resilient. It no doubt had something to do with the man across from him. Dan Fountain wore a tweed jacket, black suede vest and jeans. Though he looked about thirty, he was fifty if a day, the longer you looked – and Billy looked hard as he plied him with questions. After briefly describing Shawnee Springs' farm fight, Billy'd been listening – with mouth mostly open. Dan told him how fledgling, controversial Kanawha Land Trust, founded only five years ago, had bought up over 10,000 acres in three counties.

"What's your membership like?" Billy said, amazed.

Dan laughed. "A dirty dozen ex-hippies, rad lawyers, college professors and one Episcopalian priest." Sobering he sipped his sludge. "Actually, that's not true anymore. Started out that way, but we've got some regular folks on board, hell, even a few Republicans!" Another laugh. Billy grinned. There was no rushing a guy like Fountain, and Billy didn't exactly have an itinerary. Plus, it was a little like having Grand-daddy back. A native West Virginian who'd gone to Harvard, Dan had never meant to do anything else but return to his state and transform it, "pull it kicking and screaming" into the twentieth century ("even if it is the twenty-first," he'd drawled.)

"Most important, we've got farmers. So those that're fighting us out in the provinces as well as in the legislature have a little more trouble now that we're the people."

"Grassroots, that's good. What I have trouble with is the idea that people in such a beautiful state would not be eager to preserve land."

Dan sighed. "Economics, as always. West Virginia's always been like a third-world country, a colony to the rest of America to exploit for its resources – first timber, then coal, natural gas – so anything that's going to possibly interfere with a land-owner's God-given right to be exploited by outside interests to the maximum degree allowed by law (or even not allowed by law) is heresy, fightin' words!"

Billy thought of Garth Erickson: "Every Tom, Dick and Harvey tellin' us what to do" – he imagined all the Garths there must be up every holler – with a shotgun, the Lord and the legislature on his side. Environmentalism was a lot easier in Ohio, where there was at least an economy.

"And beautiful, you say?" Dan raised his mug, started to sip but had to put it down. His hand was suddenly trembling. "You shoulda seen this state when I was growing up down around Cabin Creek – gorgeous, old-growth forests. Now . . . a wasteland."

Billy sat quietly, waiting to hear the worst.

"Son, you ever hear of mountaintop removal?"

"Vaguely. That where they circle the mountain with one of those big drills, and cut the coal out as quick as possible?"

Dan laced his fingers on his stomach. "That's auguring," he said, gazing into the middle distance as if hearing the roar. "That was bad enough: gouging it out without even tunneling, leaving a helluva mess behind to pollute rivers and streams, throwing coal into trucks and hauling it out of state faster'n hell. Mountain-top removal is even worse. They literally blast the tops of the mountains off, leaving nothing but stubs where those beautiful appendages were. And then after exposing the mountains' marrow and bone to the punishing light of day, they just throw the 'over-burden' into the valleys, destroying the streams that feed right into New River, Kanawha, Ohio and Monongahela."

Suddenly Dan bent forward as if he'd been kidney-punched.

"And rendering the waters that have nourished us since the great glaciers retreated with their pristine beauty into . . . " He gripped his cup, waited for his fingers to settle down, lifted and poured slowly a thin, steaming stream onto the table top. It pooled like mercury, silvered in the light. "What's that word you like, son? For coffee?"

"Sludge," Billy whispered. Morning had waned into late afternoon and with the loss of light – it was actually quite dark in the empty café since the lunch crowd had fled – had come an increasing weight Billy was feeling in his limbs. Each trip up to the counter had found his legs heavier, his face even sagging. The longer Dan talked – and he talked as if Billy were the most important person in the world, as if he had all day – the more Billy began to dimly sense what he was doing here. He might be able to answer Kieron's question now. He waited what he considered a respectful length of time.

"But your work . . . it's borne great fruit."

It took a moment for Dan to come back off the mountain. "Yes, it has." He nodded. "Not nearly enough, but some."

Billy sat forward eagerly. "Do you know anything about the situation in Putnam County?"

Dan's bushy white eyebrows merged as he nodded slowly. "A desecration what's been done. I wish we'd had KLT when all that got started."

"Have you heard of Beck's Dairy?"

"Growing like a damn tumor. We tried to stop 'em. But no interest from the natives."

"Ever heard of Della Sizemore?"

He scratched his head. "Can't say I have, son."

It hurt, but no use blaming Dan. Beating the bushes was hard work. Billy took a deep breath. While Dan listened, body bent forward, arms balanced on thighs, staring off, occasionally nodding, Billy described what he'd seen, striving for objective accuracy. He liked Dan too much to bullshit him. When Billy repeated what Della had told him about their own land, Dan sat up straighter than he had since Billy'd begun the depressing litany. By the time he'd finished, the man's eyes were glowing like seasoned oak in a stove.

"Theme park, you say? We can get 'em on public nuisance, lack of infrastructure or public safety."

"Zoning?" Billy suggested helpfully.

When Dan stood up, he looked well over six feet, a fact Billy hadn't noticed before, also that the paunch and neck wattles were much more visible when the man stood. He imagined the figure the man cut before his classes – Dr. Kieron with an Appalachian accent.

"This ain't Ohio," he said, shaking his head. "No zoning."

Billy stood up, found his legs solid. "You're right," he said. "West Virginia is a third-world country."

"Colony, son. Colony."

"Then I guess it needs a Charleston Tea Party."

"Sludge Party."

During the pause, as the blender behind the counter loudly decimated fruit into atoms, Billy imagined the murderous machines on the mountaintops. Then he saw the valleys far below where the mess all wound up . . .

Dan turned toward him. "You tell your Aunt Della not to give an inch." He pulled out his wallet, handed Billy a card. "Call me anytime. Sam Houston's coming, and we're gonna kick Santa Anna's butt." Then he pulled out a twenty. "Here's for the sludge and my salad."

Billy raised his hands in protest. "Too much."

"Then the rest is a contribution to Bluebird or whatever the hell your land trust is called."

Billy sighed and took the bill, only because Grand-daddy said you never, ever refuse a gift from a West Virginian.

# Chapter Twelve

Shawnee Springs, Ohio
Sunday, February 26, 1999

From the pulpit of the Presbyterian Church, Billy surveyed the arriving crowd, standing beside Woody with his hands clasped before him, trying to feel good about this town meeting. Reverend Judith Wilson had been kind enough to lend them the church between Sunday morning and evening services, and he hoped the spirit would soon be moving. After yesterday's Kieron fiasco, he'd lapsed into a depression the likes of which he hadn't seen since the Sylco cement debacle. It had taken gargantuan effort to finally call Seth, who was terse and business-like. But at least she agreed to speak today. Thank God. Without someone who could show a little passion, they were doomed. (*What does the farm mean to you personally?* – he'd heard variations on that theme all night in his dreams: *What does your life mean to you, personally?*)

So today he'd showed up fifteen minutes early, huddled with Woody, who'd apparently made another thousand phone calls, and set an agenda. Then, everyone had started arriving. Everyone, it seemed, but the one he most wanted to see.

Then, lo and behold, there she was!

As he watched Seth walk into the sanctuary hugging herself, he had to force his face back to humble solemnity. She excited him in a way no woman had in a long time. Seth seemed so real – something even Freeman and probably Ira had picked up on – and was absolutely unaware of her ability to make other people feel her passion, whereas Bonnie had been obsessed with getting a rise out of every male who came into her sights.

Stepping to the microphone, Billy paused for several seconds before speaking.

"All right, folks, we have a few speakers who're going to give us a *brief* synopsis of the problem, leading to what we can do about it. First is Professor Haywood Freeman, who's lived here for 40 years and who's now president of Blue Jacket Land Trust. Woody can give us a little historical perspective."

While Channels' Six and Twenty-five's cameras rolled in the rear, Freeman described how the farm was older than the town; how, in his lifetime, it had been the homeplace for Edith Louise Brattenmyer, the oldest and only one of the six children who'd stayed; and how, in the seventies, when far-seeing town fathers had contacted her about perhaps the possibility of the town's purchasing the farmland, she'd responded.

"Edith Louise could sometimes be a colorful talker," Woody said, enjoying himself, " and though I hate to swear inside sacred walls, she responded in the following manner."

The crowd hunkered forward. Leave it to Freeman the charismatic to know what folks wanted to hear.

"Tell 'em I'll do whatever the hell I want to with my farm!"

Murmurs and some laughter. "Well, we gathered she didn't want to be bothered with us pesky mosquitoes at that time, and since the village had successfully dealt with her in the past on issues, we figured we'd continue to get along in Edith Louise's lifetime, at least. But after we formed the land trust, we did appeal to the younger sisters and found them not hostile to our entreaties to keep the farm a farm." He sighed. "But that changed after Edith's death last August. After that, our letters to the three living sisters, scattered all over the country, were referred to a Manhattan attorney. Then, as you know, in January the auction signs went up and we freaked." He sighed. "The attorney told us that the heirs wanted to sell for as much as they could get. It became not an issue of history or tradition or environmental preservation. It became an issue of money. As it usually does."

Billy could feel the weight settling onto their shoulders as if crows had come to roost there. He could practically see people locking up their wallets in safety deposit boxes.

"Which leads us to the financial side of our dilemma. If you know of any earth-minded angels, please coax them down out of the heavens for us. Here's William, treasurer of Blue Jacket Land Trust, to bring us up to date on fund-raising efforts so far."

*William.* Well, it beat Bilbo.

"Thanks, Woody. Before we get down to talking solutions, here's the bottom line. The heirs refused to sell the farm to the land trust at agricultural prices – otherwise, we could buy it and re-sell to farmers, no problem. *That* we could afford, but it'll be worth a lot more to developers at auction. How much more? Well, whatever that figure is will be the amount of money we need to raise. Here's our village manager Ken Littlejohn to tell us more."

Stepping aside, Billy allowed his eyes to stray past the pulpit to where the offering plates were stashed. Timing was everything.

"Thanks, Billy. Well, I hope you're as reassured as I am about this whole thing. I know I'll sleep great tonight!"

His levity was greeted with absolute silence.

"Well. What we have to do to buy this farm is come up with the difference between what that farm will likely sell for to developers at the auction and what it would sell for as farmland. That difference is the price of the easement, which we could put on it, if we had the money. An easement is added to the deed and says the land can't be used for anything else in perpetuity. That means forever, folks. Then whoever buys it can re-sell the land to farmers – and Billy tells me there should be some waiting in the wings to add it to their tillable land."

Billy nodded solemnly when the manager looked his way again. Thank God Ira had performed his miracle. Even if they didn't have all the farmers on board, they at least had them thinking about it.

"If we wanted," Littlejohn continued, "we could make a *portion* of it available to some small development: a house or two here and there . . ."

A shifting of folks in their seats. Billy understood: if the farm was worth saving, it was *all* worth saving.

"Of course that's up to us. With Blue Jacket Land Trust acting as agent, we can write an easement to do whatever we want to do. *If* we have the money to do it."

"How much?" a loud voice asked, destroying the silence, rattling around the ceiling's four corners.

"Well, when we compared what land had sold for in Cedarton" – the mention of the name seemed to send a cold chill around the room as folks imagined the rampant development that had left that once mainly farming town sprouting houses like weeds – "as opposed to recent sales of land for farming only in the county, plus . . ."

"HOW MUCH, LITTLEJOHN?" It was editor Cyrus Harmon, pen poised above his notepad.

"One million . . . at least."

After the initial shock, they began to clamor like stock in the chute smelling the slaughterhouse up ahead.

"I know, I know." Ken was shaking his head. "The auctioneer who'll do the job for the estate was quoted in yesterday's *Dayton Daily* as saying he's never seen a single community do what he's heard we're trying to do. Not one."

Now it was as if buckets of ice-water suspended from the ceiling had let go, splashing straight-down, plastering people's hair to their skulls. They'd given up Sunday afternoon for this?

When Ken cast him an imploring look, Billy lunged back behind the mic. "But think about it, folks. If everybody in this town of five thousand gave only a few hundred dollars, we'd have half of it right there. And there are other sources, too." Quick, he thought, before things veer out of control.

"Before Ms. Brattenmyer passed away, the village was considering its options, and we've learned that there may be funds available to help us – not *carry* the thing for us, but help us. And here's what may be available."

And, sweating only a little, he summarized how the village had already applied for a grant from the Federal Highway Administration for $500,000 and to Shawnee County Commissioners for a like amount. They expected replies any day, since the urgency, given the auction announcement, had been emphasized. If these villagers were going to unlock their purses, they desperately needed hope somebody else was going to, as well, and who better than *government?*

"Three weeks, folks. We've got twenty-two days left to do this. And what Ken didn't say . . . " Billy broadly gestured toward the nervously grinning town manager. " . . . is that the village has already voted to commit all of its greenspace fund – $187,000 – toward the farm's purchase. Plus, we've asked the township trustees to consider kicking in. So, folks, it's started happening already. And . . . " Before he could say more, they burst into applause. Billy waited impatiently. As it finally began to fade, he felt Woody beside him, bending toward the mic.

"Shawnee Springs, you're a truly amazing community!"

And they erupted all over again, applauding themselves. Well, all right. Whether he wanted to admit it or not, Billy needed them – and not just their money. For the first time he realized the difference between this and the cement plant struggle. They'd been entirely against something there; this farm fight suddenly seemed more about being *for* something. One thing was certain: this time, the village had bought in, big time. Pulling his hair back with both hands, he felt the sweat on his forehead. Now for the coup de grace.

"If you were at our protest last week," Billy said after Woody had stepped aside, "you heard and saw what so many of us feel. Eloquent voices were raised, and they spoke to our hearts. New villager Seth Abel's a believer in the power of community. Listen to her say a word or two about *why* we should do this."

He watched her rise, squeeze out of the pew and walk up the aisle. Finally she stood behind the mic.

"I don't know why people keep asking me to do this." Her quivery voice echoed in the big room. "It's not like you don't have your own people to do this so that you have to ask newcomers to get up in front of you and tell you what you need to do."

Billy inwardly groaned. *Too honest.*

"And I am new here. I've been told that . . . many times."

Damn, she was chastising them. But so far they were taking it.

"But if it takes a newcomer to tell you what you already know you should do, then I'll do it. Because Wood Thrush Farm is worth it."

Now she was standing up straighter. "I live there; I mean, not exactly *on* the farm, but entirely surrounded by it. You wouldn't believe the sunsets you see there, and because I'm kind of cut off from the town, I see them in total silence, with complete peace. And let me tell you, there's nothing on earth like it."

Billy let his body relax, realizing that his spine ached.

"It's like God's own blood poured across that sky. And the geese – you know, that flock that lives on the farm?" Nods of knowingness. Tight smiles. Billy saw the hands clutching purses closed ease up a bit. He tried to keep his eyes off the offering plates.

"Well, those geese . . ." She tossed her hair, and it had the effect on him of rainbow trout leaping from Tecumseh Lake.

"They . . . well, they *talk* – quarrel is a better word. I'll be watching the western horizon when they appear right out of nowhere, like out of a dream, and I go from silence to the sound of screeching, and they always make me laugh – at first. But then . . ."

You could've heard somebody crack a smile. Billy could hardly contain his jubilation. This would be all over the *News* next week. And TV tonight.

"Then I always feel some sadness. I can imagine them gone. And that makes me think: humans are not the only creatures on this planet. We need each other." She chuckled. "Oh, I ask myself: 'What do geese need from me?' They need me as witness, to see and hear them. And they need me to protect the land they live on. It's also for future generations that we should save the land. Geese can live with farmers. But when ponds are drained – and developers will do that – there is a huge loss of life. The geese. Ourselves. The land is the intersection where geese and people meet."

The same message he'd received at the pond yesterday.

It had gotten so quiet, he thought he heard someone wheezing. He thought he could hear snow falling outside. At last he allowed himself to glance at the stack of offering plates. When he returned his gaze to the pulpit, she had turned, was looking at him, waiting. It came to him exactly what he should do. A step or two, and he hugged her, closed his eyes and smiled. It would make a great visual for the six o'clock news. Without a weekend murder, this story might even lead. At last he released her, and Seth practically ran down the steps to her seat.

"Folks, if Wood Thrush is worth fighting for, then it's worth *paying* for. So I'm going to ask you, as the plates are passed, to dig deep. We're in a holy place here, and I mean no sacrilege, but I'd like to suggest that saving this land for our children is sacred, too. And the eyes of our neighbors elsewhere in the Miami Valley are upon us, to see what we do with this issue. Let's show we're committed."

He felt someone behind him, a hand on his shoulder. He glanced toward Freeman, smiling broadly. Beside him stood a beautiful black girl he'd seen in a play at *The Stage Door*. The old man leaned into the mic.

"While the plates are being passed, let's make this a real church service. I've talked Joan Newsome into playing the organ for us."

And as Joan played "Let It Be," volunteers moved among the gathering. Watching the plates fill and the snow fall (he could tell the sky outside had darkened, huge flakes were swirling earthward), he felt the warmth begin in his feet and climb. By the end of the song, he was sweating again, and his eyes were closed. When he opened them, he immediately fixed them on the pew where Seth had been sitting. It was empty.

Fifteen minutes later, Fellowship Hall buzzed with the voices of newly-formed CitFarm subcommittees: political strategies, signs and visuals, rallies and fund-raising. It *had* become a community affair – fine with Billy as long as Blue Jacket's inner circle remained in charge: him, treasurer; Woody, negotiator; Seth, poster-girl; and Ira, salt of the earth, if he'd get off the dime. Billy found his funk entirely lifted.

For an hour, his group of about five had brainstormed fund-raising schemes, including yard sales, a plea to local merchants to donate a percentage of sales and an information table at the Cedarton Mall. He'd just smiled and recorded them all, knowing such ideas would probably produce a drop in the bucket compared against the million they needed. But his mind never left the huge wad of greenbacks and checks that had been collected. He couldn't wait to count the take, and now that his group had broken up, he stepped out into the hall, ducked into the restroom, saw that no one occupied the single stall and went in.

He sat down on the lid and stared at the money. That's when he saw it: the check on top. It was the amount that first caught his eye. He nearly whooped aloud. Until his eyes saw the signature, and everything went blurry so that he had to wipe his eyes. But he was right the first time. Elizabeth Abel had written that check for two grand.

He looked around at lime-green walls as if they could explain.

He had her figured for Foodstamp City. He'd seen the crummy old farmhouse she lived in, the ten-year-old rust-bucket she drove, her yard sale clothes. Unless she had a sugar daddy somewhere – which he greatly doubted – she'd gone insane. That was it. Under his influence . . . He stopped himself, even snorted an echoey laugh. In the heat of the moment, while Joan played and the spirit moved, she'd been driven to perform the material equivalent of getting saved. He'd seen it in Grand-dad's Baptist Church, folks storming into the aisle thinking it was Jesus calling. Even as a kid visiting from the city, he'd known it was only the preacher's mega-doses of sin and guilt that browbeat them into believing that they'd heard God. And now Seth had responded to his call.

He smiled grimly, grabbed handfuls of fives, tens and twenties, saw checks for a hundred, even one for five-hundred from banker Howard Kasslelbaum (rich bastard could afford a lot more). Even without Seth's two thou, the take was impressive. He held Seth's check up for a final inspection. Though the amount itself was written boldly, the rest of the writing was squiggly and child-like, not the hand of a woman in total possession of her faculties.

He would make her take it back. Not only was it the right thing to do, but she'd be so *grateful* when he made her listen to reason. Shoving the wad into the large pocket of his army jacket, he rose, realized someone had come in and was washing his hands. He flushed just to look legit, then fled the bathroom.

It wasn't hard to find her. There she sat in the political strategies group, chin cupped in palm, with several others, listening earnestly to Sasha Arden, Burke student, explaining her plan to get local bands to play at a benefit next Saturday. Even distracted as he was, he had to smile – it'd never happen. But why snow on the kid's parade? Billy snuck into the pew behind Seth, tapped her on the shoulder. When she looked back, he whispered, "Meet me in the hall."

She nodded, her eyes still on Sasha. "In a minute."

"No. Now."

◯

Pacing at the end of the corridor, he watched the snow softly falling as he pondered what he would say. When he turned she was right there, arms crossed, her face ashen. "Don't *ever* do that to me again."

She walked a few paces closer but stopped well short of close. "I came all the way across the country to get away from a man who didn't give me any space. I'm sure not going to take that from you."

Wincing, he quickly re-ran the tape inside his head, seeing how his impatience with Sasha had translated into impatience with *her*. Dropping his chin toward his chest, he gazed up with what he hoped were remorseful eyes. "Forgive me. I wigged out when I saw this." He reached into his jacket pocket, brought out the check, extended it toward her.

She looked at it, then at his face. He held his ground, knowing silence would work best. Silence and a hard, parental stare.

She sighed, stepped back and leaned against the wall. She started to speak, then closed her eyes, clutched her fist in front of her heart.

"This is a chunk of the money I saved in the last few years while living with James." She'd been looking out the door at the snow. Now her eyes came back to his. "My husband. He's made a fortune marketing the natives' work." She hugged herself tightly.

Billy wanted to take her in his arms but figured she needed to vent this venom first.

"Want to step outside, get some air?" he offered.

She nodded.

◯

Outside late afternoon headed toward twilight. The falling flakes were big as half-dollars. In the schoolyard across the street, kids' Friday footprints were already half-covered. Further down the street in the large white colonial, lights were already on, their glow a warm counterpoint to the wind's freezing clutch as soon as they closed the door behind them.

She smiled up at him. "It's my fuck-you money. I mean, it's my half – I'd never spend Paul's. I've banked every birthday and Christmas gift of money his grandparents ever sent him."

He crossed his arms, nodded and waited.

"The first time I heard the term was at one of James's parties five or six years ago. Some yuppie gallery owner was talking about how he'd started saving fuck-you money the week after his wedding – and he'd needed it, since he got divorced within six months."

He allowed himself a tight smile.

"It's the secret stash that some men keep – all this guy's buddies admitted it," she continued, "to take off if their relationship turns sour."

"Their get-out-of-jail-free card," he added.

She nodded. "I thought it was awful, and I told them all the reasons that it was wrong: undermining one's marriage vows, betraying the other person, creating a self-fulfilling prophecy." She laughed harshly. "But the next day, I started mine. I knew I'd need to get away one day." She looked across the street, fought back the tears.

"So?" He flapped the check in the wind.

"It happened when you said 'committed.' I've never committed to anything in my life – not my marriage, not my friends, not to any cause – not really – though I've believed in things all my life." Her eyes shone fiercely green. "I've made some bad mistakes."

He said it very gently: "Like James?"

Her eyes flashed as green as he'd ever seen them before she lowered her head. When she looked up again, he saw the tears. With difficulty, he resisted embracing her, knew she'd take it as infringement. After wiping her eyes, she went on.

"My husband wouldn't give Burke a dime, as rich as he was. Whenever they'd call for an alumni contribution, he'd laugh and say, 'What the hell did Burke College ever do for me?' I hated him for that, Billy. Even though I screwed up here something awful, this place gave me a lot that's never left me. In ways, I was at my best here."

He longed to tear up the check, had wanted to ever since he'd discovered it. But tearing it up was what James would've done. He took a deep breath, watched a couple of cars crunch down the snow-covered, rutted street. Though he wanted to hug her – and more – he knew it wasn't going to happen tonight. The money was all she could give tonight.

"All right." He took a deep breath. "On behalf of the great Village of Shawnee Springs and Blue Jacket Land Trust, I thank you, Seth Abel, for making the ultimate sacrifice. For us."

And though he felt her repelling him, repelling *men*, with every cell of her body, and though God knew she needed space and time to sort things out for herself and for her son, his ancient instinct won and he pulled her against him, hard. When she began to tremble, it scared him, especially since she didn't cry or make a sound. But after a minute, she relaxed in his arms, small as a child. Holding her in the shelter of the doorway vestibule, he watched the snow grow ever whiter as the sky darkened. By the time she quit shaking, the sky was totally black, and he didn't feel cold at all.

# Chapter Thirteen

Shawnee Springs, Ohio
Wednesday, March 1, 1999

Billy appeared at Seth's promptly at five, as they'd agreed on the phone last night. For the first time since mid-January, a mild thaw had set in. By mid-day Monday, the sun had come out and melted most of the new snow. Leaving the Dakota, he saw them waiting for him in the back yard. When they asked Paul where he wanted to bury Data, he pointed toward the small woods about half a mile across the ruined cornfield.

Seth looked doubtful. "Don't you want him closer, like here in the backyard?"

Paul just shook his head and pointed. It was okay with Billy. Closer to the heart of things. "Okay," he said, "we can just about make it by sunset if we go now."

Seth retrieved the butter dish from the garage, and they crunched across the thin wafery snow-crust in silence. Finally they stood before the woods of slim cedars, maples and beeches. "Awesome," Paul murmured, looking them up and down as if the Enterprise lay secreted inside. By now, the sun barely hovered above the horizon, and the lower sky had become a blazing kiln.

Seth shaded her eyes. "Makes you want to know what's on the other side, where those geese go. I'll bet there's a pond."

Billy grinned. "We'll look for it. But not today."

The shovel worked well enough in the partly-thawed ground, and Billy easily carved out a small, shallow trench. After only a few minutes, Seth stepped back beside Paul, who looked up at Billy, as if for direction, but he waved it away.

"It's your gig, Paul."

The boy walked right over to where Seth had laid everything and picked up the butter dish.

"Can we leave him inside, Mom?"

"No." When they turned, Billy shook his head. "That plastic will take a million years to deteriorate. Your friend, on the other hand, will be soil in no time."

The sun was nearly gone, turning the boy and his mother into dark shapes. And though there was now a bite to the air, Billy felt warm enough inside Dad's pea coat. He thought he detected the tiniest scent of spring.

Paul held the butter dish against his puffy down jacket with one hand, and with the other lifted the lid. Pausing, he looked inside. Though Billy was tempted to lay a hand on the boy's shoulder, he stifled it. Let him find his own way. When Paul reached inside with his bare hand and brought the hamster out, Billy breathed a sigh of relief. Data's fur looked matted from all the touching Paul had done, but other than that, he seemed fine.

The boy didn't look up for at least a minute. Was he thinking? Praying? With the sun gone, it was getting colder. Still Paul stood silent before the grave for another fifteen point six seconds. Billy looked at Seth, who kept her lowered eyes on her son, who'd been almost erased by the dark. If he didn't act soon, they might disappear altogether in the growing dusk.

Paul dropped to his knees suddenly. When his small body began to shake, Billy felt every cell in Seth's body impel itself toward the boy, but she didn't budge. Every hair on Billy's head stood erect, as Paul's breath came huffing out in small staccato bursts. He watched Seth stand there and let her son silently weep. Then he looked down just in time to see Paul gently lower his palm toward the grave, tilt his hand sideways and drop the creature into the ground. When the boy looked up at Billy, he nodded.

◯

As soon as they entered the house, Billy felt the difference between the last time he'd been here. Out there, there'd been more room for the heaviness; in here, the solemnity was suffocating. While he and Seth sat down in the living room, Paul said he was going upstairs. His slow footfalls on the stairs sounded like sad drums.

Seth had done well at the graveside, but he had no idea where her head was now. Her long, lovely hair hanging off the back of the couch, her shapely bluejeaned legs hoisted onto the coffee table, she stared straight ahead, distant, remote. After seeing her son grapple with what he'd done, Billy figured she was probably in no condition to be wooed. He wondered if she really wanted to be upstairs with her kid and was just about to begin his goodbyes, when she spoke.

"Seeing Lloyd last Saturday took me back to what happened at Burke thirteen years ago."

He sat up straighter. "You seemed to be laying some heavy rap on him." Now she knew he'd been eavesdropping, but she gazed into the middle distance, her face grave.

"Lloyd Kieron and I go back a ways," she said.

"You said you were both involved at Pitney."

"It was a big deal."

"I don't know that much about it," he said. "Just that it was a monster nuke plant they built north of Cincinnati and never opened. Dr. Kieron used to brag that he and his students had shut it down."

She snorted. "Yeh, right. It didn't have anything to do with the fact that the Energy Commission eventually declared the design flawed."

"Didn't a bunch of celebrities go to jail protesting it? Martin Sheen, maybe?"

"Yes, but a lot of Burkers went to jail, too. Like Robin Warner and Emily Rubenstein."

"Friends of yours?" He was aware of loud footfalls above them. Was Paul raging?

She nodded. "In the fall of '86, Dr. Kieron took van-loads of students down every week. Robin and Emily finally got me to go. It was a real rush, facing off against the corporate polluters. After going only twice, I got up and made a speech. Dr. Kieron had asked me to, and . . . I wanted to please him."

Billy nodded. The guy had had that effect on him, too – until last Saturday.

"My father saw me on the news one night, and he called me. Boy, *did* he call me – every name under the sun, said I was shitting on everything his life had stood for and was pissing on my mother's grave."

He snorted. "My old man's the same."

She didn't answer, and it was all he could do not to get out of his chair, move to the couch and put his arm around her. But he could tell by the look in her eye that she was traveling solo for now. He realized it had grown quiet upstairs, maybe too quiet. He wished the boy would put on some tunes.

"So the Saturday that was to be our biggest rally yet, I didn't go. I didn't tell Emmy or Robin or anybody. I went to Glenora Wood, to the pine forest and hid while my friends went down there and . . . " She put her hand over her eyes.

He sat forward, spoke softly. "A father's anger is pretty damn hard to go against."

She shook her head. "Don't put me on a pedestal, Billy. I was a coward. I wasn't for the cause. I was out for one thing." She took her hand away. The tears seemed to have stopped as quickly as they'd started. "The praise of my teacher."

He considered telling her it was no big deal – we all want that. But in the heat of her glare, he thought he'd better skate slowly.

"Hey, he was a mentor to me, too."

She shook her head, wiped one eye before continuing. "So . . . I didn't go that day and there was a riot. Counter-protestors showed up – people the plant had already hired whose jobs would be lost if the plant never opened, unionists as well as believers like my dad in the Great Corporate Way, even a group of skin-heads who just saw it as an opportunity to kick some radical ass. Well, they did. Emily went to the hospital with a concussion and Robin went to jail. And I" – her voice broke – "I spent the night in Glenora Wood. I didn't want anyone on campus to know I didn't go."

Is this what she had confessed to Kieron at the flea market? Was he red-faced with anger? Nah, Kieron wouldn't give a shit about a student no-show at a no-nukes rally thirteen years ago.

But while he waited, wondering whether he should cross-examine, he found himself back at Sylco Cement, August '97, hotter'n the hinges of hell. And Mark and those stupid shits had made it even hotter with their fucking gasoline. Billy rubbed his suddenly-sweaty neck. The security guard had almost fried because of them – because of him.

"Well, you mighta had it worse than your friend who went to jail," he finally said. "I'm sure the cops knew they'd better take good care of the rich kids from the private college."

She sighed wearily. "What matters is I didn't show up. And Em and Robin let everyone know that I hadn't. I never went back to history class. The rest of my days at Burke were hell. I left before graduating – three months pregnant – to marry probably the only Republican on campus. James was *for* the plant!"

"I don't suppose you ever told Dr. Kieron about your dad calling."

She didn't answer, but he could tell the question inflicted pain. Eyes closed, she hung her head, hair hiding her face.

"Because he just might've understood, you know."

She shook her head again. He saw how she'd lived with the worst possible interpretation for so long, she wasn't going to give it up over anything he said. Only she could revise her own history – and he his. It was a perfect opportunity to 'fess up to what he'd almost allowed to happen to an innocent security guard, but something held his tongue. This was about *her*. For once, he knew it would be wrong to use someone else's pain for his own comfort. The sound of Neil Young wailing "The Needle and the Damage Done" from upstairs oddly reassured him.

"So," he said gently, "You think any good your activism accomplished was totally negated by your one no-show."

He didn't expect her reaction. She looked up immediately, tossing her loose hair backward out of her face.

"Billy. It was the show*down*. I put my personal need – to not embarrass Daddy – ahead of what was right. I was stupid enough to think I could still make him love me, that it was worth sacrificing the cause for."

Though her eyes were enshadowed, he imagined them flashing green fire. "So what's best for the masses always takes precedence over what's right for the individual?"

"If you're going to be political, you have to make sacrifices, just like anybody who's ever stood up for anything – from King to the Kennedys to . . ."

*To Kieron.* Or so the old bastard would have you believe. But she hadn't said anything about *him* being arrested. In, out. Slick as a whistle.

"For God's sake, Billy," she was saying, "you don't go to Burke and not learn that you have to sacrifice for a cause."

"Yeh, but how much?"

"Your life, if the cause is important enough."

"Or your child's?"

It stopped her. But only for one point eight seconds. She combed her hair back slowly with her fingers. "Hopefully it never gets to that. But I guess a truly worthy cause can demand everything. Think about the Chinese students in Tiananmen Square who put themselves and their families at risk."

He leveled his gaze at her. "I can't believe that you'd sell Paul out for any cause."

"I didn't say I was going to sell him out."

"But . . ."

"Theoretically." She smiled, tight-lipped, sitting back into the cushions.

Seth's words might've chilled him, except he was still pretty hot from the remembered blaze from last August. Plus, he didn't believe her; she would never sacrifice Paul. He sat forward, reducing the distance between them before he spoke.

"I know Burke's hallowed leader said the measure of a person's life is what he's done for others, but I happen to believe that what he – or she – does for, and to, himself is pretty goddamn important, too. For me, politics is always personal." Hearing himself, he knew instantly he'd stepped into a trap.

Her eyes narrowed. "So why couldn't you tell Lloyd what this farm fight means to you?"

*Damn.* Busted.

Before he could respond, a small voice came from the hallway behind them, startling them both. "Billy, you want to come upstairs and see the CDs I got from the library?"

He looked at Seth and found her looking at the floor, eyes averted. "All right?" Billy whispered.

She nodded without looking up.

O

The first thing Billy noticed in Paul's tiny upstairs room was the absence of Trek posters. Delighted, he looked toward the kid's unmade bed, but Captain Picard smirked at him from the faded, thousand-washed sheet. Ah, well, progress.

"So, kiddo, what you got?"

Paul handed him a postcard, his dark eyes gleaming. Glancing down, Billy saw the front of it was the Kit Carson Museum. That was in Taos. Uh oh. He lowered his weight to the kid's small bed. Paul sat beside him.

"I didn't really get any CDs. But I'm still listening to yours – every day, honest." He turned the card over in Billy's hand. "I wanted to tell you a secret."

He noticed the address: in care of Matt Plummer.

"I used Matt's address," he explained, "so Mom wouldn't find out. You promise not to tell?"

It's a little late for that, Buster, he wanted to say. But the kid had lost his home, his dad, his pet. The least Billy could do was keep a secret. Written in bold, cursive script, the message was terse: *Coming to get you Sunday the 19th, going home Monday the 20th – tell your mom. Love, Dad.*

"I asked him to come get me," Paul said softly. "If Mom found out, she'd kill me."

When Billy looked at Paul, the boy was literally glowing. And it was perfectly clear Paul wanted him to buy into it as much as his mother wanted Billy to buy into her guilt.

"He says to tell your mom, Paul. He's coming the day before the auction."

Paul shook his head. "It's the best part of the plan. She can't get ready to say no. She might even be nice to him."

"I wouldn't count on it."

The boy's mouth tightened stubbornly. "Well, if I don't tell her, she can't say no."

It would kill her. And here was this boy Billy had coaxed out of the closet asking him to keep the secret that would devastate the woman he still hoped to bed (and more? He realized it was true). Maybe he could somehow prepare her for it without actually telling her.

"So," he finally got out, "how do you like *Live Rust?*" Neil was banging away at "Cortez the Killer" on low volume.

Paul made a face. "Neil Young sings like a squeaky hinge. And his guitar is like jet planes crash-landing."

"Exactly," Billy said, mock-punching his arm. "Pretty awesome, huh?"

○

When he came back down, leaving the boy upstairs studying his dad's postcard as if it were holy writ, Billy found her still sitting on the couch.

"I'd better take off," he said.

She smiled, running her hand back through her hair again. "I'll see you out," she said, not moving. She looked as weary as if she'd just run a marathon.

"Don't get up. I'll find my own way out."

She wiggled three fingers at him. "Thank you for being here for Paul," she murmured. "And for me." And though he longed to join her on the couch and scoop her into his arms, he managed to stagger outside, his secrets for the moment intact. He had his hand on the Dakota's cold door handle before something she'd said ripped up his spine.

She'd called Kieron by his first name.

# Chapter Fourteen



Burke Hall looked like some sort of winter carnival, Billy thought, guiding Seth into the foyer. He'd taken her arm to help her out of his truck onto the ice and hadn't let go all the way across the parking lot. The huge SAVE THE FARM banner was strung on the wall just inside the glass doors, and as soon as they entered, their noses were assaulted by ginger, garlic and curry. She turned to him, smiling, her hair stringing across her glowing cheeks.

"I didn't imagine all this!"

He smiled back. "A lot of these vendors do the street fair in June and October, so the Chamber of Commerce had a list of 'em to call. They all agreed to donate thirty percent to Blue Jacket – some are giving everything they make."

He was hoping tonight was the night. After partying here for a few hours, he hoped to accompany Seth home to an empty nest. The kid was doing a sleep-over at Matt's, and though it hadn't been easy to talk her into letting her boy go so soon after his "crisis," Billy guilted her into it. "You can give more to him if you have a life, too," he'd said, calling her from Ira's. She'd finally agreed.

Inside the large, unheated foyer where they stood at the bottom of the stairs, Billy could see a booth selling some kind of ethnic sandwiches in pita bread, the line at least eight deep. Next to him, a young Burke female, clad only in tee-shirt and jeans, no doubt to show off her tattoos and navel ring, despite the chill, loudly hawked SAVE THE FARM grey tees with expressive, dancing figures and the names of the fifteen musical acts that had volunteered to perform. The atmosphere was as cheerful as a church pancake breakfast.

"Look," cried Seth, squeezing the arm she hung on to. A bearded, top-hatted young man in motley was blowing humongous bubbles through hand-crafted wooden wands. Pink and green orbs floated toward them, then caught a draft and sailed up high toward the chandelier.

"There go our dreams for Wood Thrush," a voice yelled beside them. Someone bumped his arm.

"Hi, Billy." It was Sasha Arden. A wisp of a girl in long brown curly locks, wearing a Wood Thrush Farm tee-shirt down to her frilly long skirt above shoes that looked to him like ballet slippers, Sasha was grinning all over herself.

"Awesome!" Seth breathed. "You did it!"

"Very impressive," Billy agreed. "I didn't think you could pull it off."

Seth punched his arm and gave him a look before asking, "How'd you get so many bands?"

Sasha's smile was diamonds in sunlight. "They're mostly my friends – I'm a musician, too. Plus, they believe in our cause."

Billy was reading the list of the twelve bands on her tee-shirt. "Day Tripper? No way!"

"Oh, yeh. Their lead singer's grandfather used to share-crop Wood Thrush back in the fifties. He said they wouldn't've missed this for anything."

"And the Miraculous Del-Mars," Seth said. "Aren't they the surfer guys?"

But Sasha had disappeared, swallowed up by the crowd surging up the steps.

"Did you imagine in your wildest dreams," Billy said, "that a college student could do all this?"

Seth frowned. "Of course. She's a *Burke* student."

He lifted his hands in surrender. "I was wrong to ever doubt that a Burke woman is as good as her word. Crucify me."

Though Seth didn't grant him the forgiving smile he'd wanted, she did take his arm that she'd let go of when Sasha had appeared. Her touch caused a ripple of warmth to travel the entire length of his right side. He could count on one hand the number of times a woman had taken his arm like that in public. He started to say something silly, but her eyes silenced him, filled him with a feeling so intense, he had to look away for a moment. Beyond the plate glass window, the last ragged streaks of sunset smoldered on the western horizon. By the time he looked back, Seth began dragging him up the steps.

Upstairs, on the landing outside the auditorium, vendors hunkered along the balustrade, selling home-made ginger, cacao and mixed fruit cookies, CDs for many of the slated bands, coffee and herbal teas. Billy gently removed Seth's arm, walked over and bought himself a large coffee and Seth a cup of Libido Lemon.

Seth examined her cup. "For God's sake, it's paper. No Styrofoam?"

"Nothing but organic and a thousand percent recycled and recyclable for these tree-hugging dirt-worshippers."

Seth's eyes narrowed. "Is that the way you see your fellow villagers?"

He had to yell to be heard above the din. "They think they're the loyal opposition to the reigning theocracy – capitalism – but *they're* yuppies, too. Look at real estate prices. Costs a fortune to live in Shameful Springs. Half of 'em don't even buy their groceries in town."

Her cheeks were flushed, her eyes glittering. "Lots of folks here break laws for their convictions: some don't pay income taxes for the government to build more bombs. Some demonstrate for peace in Central America. Some have gone to jail more than once for what they believe, for instance, over that School of the Americas place. I feel worthless beside them."

God, she was earnest, and though part of him loved that about her, it grated, too. Didn't she read the paper? She didn't seem to have a clue about their constant bickering about everything from the junk car ordinance to council's plan to attract light industry. Or affordable housing. But he could see she'd bought the standard mythology.

"Yep, they've got passion, all right," he finally said.

She sipped as if the tea he'd brought her were poisoned. "I guess passion isn't required, though, before you fuck someone."

His heart stuttered.

"I ran into Bonnie yesterday at Manic Organic." She smiled, but it was just for show. Her mouth was set in a tight line. "Is it true you've dated practically every woman in town?"

"Not hardly. As a matter of fact, it's more like five or . . ."

"Even married ones?"

"Only one, and she . . ."

"And is it true you love them and leave them?"

"I haven't found the one I want to marry yet, if that's what you mean."

She laid her cup on the window sill, folded her arms. "Just tell me right now if the only reason you've been helping my son is to fuck me."

Though the crowd roared on around them, it seemed to him as if things had grown quiet. With those twin emeralds on him full-beam, he couldn't lie. "Not the *only* reason." He knew better than to try to temper it with a grin.

Seth reached, took his hand in her surprisingly warm one and stared up at him. "Billy, did you tell her you'd fucked me?"

"No. But I guess I implied it. To piss her off."

She didn't drop her hand or let her eyes stray. She was incredibly beautiful, even outraged. "And why would you want to do that?"

He shrugged. "You've met her."

Turning, she steered them into the auditorium. He wasn't sure whether he'd passed the test – or only delayed it.

Inside, the Miraculous Del-Mars were finishing up their set. Looking around the auditorium, he was surprised to see nearly a full house. Out in the foyer he'd noticed the guy at the CitFarm table taking the suggested five-dollar donation had a bulging money box, including lots of checks. He thought of the donations that had shown up in the post office box this week – some of them a thousand dollars and more! – from Burke alumni all over the world, townsfolk, even college students. And some continued to send cash, a very good thing, since he frequently needed to exceed his revised thirty-dollar-a-day allowance – eating dinner out was what broke the bank, plus Ira didn't stock certain necessities like Starbucks and Ben and Jerry's. By his reckoning, along with the village's greenspace fund, they now had over four hundred K in the bank, with two weeks to go yet. He was just about to tell Seth they might make it after all, when she suddenly pointed.

"There goes Dr. Freeman."

Sure enough the man was doing his barnyard rooster strut up the aisle. He took the steps two at a time up to the stage.

"Good evening, everybody," he boomed into the mic. "Everyone having a good time?"

The response was deafening.

"Marvelous. Of course the reason we're here, besides enjoying ourselves, is to raise money to purchase the development rights to Wood Thrush Farm, and it is to that end that I've been given some good news today. I thought I'd share it before the next act starts."

The crowd quieted, grew expectant. Billy was instantly pissed. He'd given Woody Ira's number. If the old man had news, why hadn't he called him? He was the treasurer, after all.

Freeman plucked a piece of paper from his corduroy shirt pocket. "This is a cashier's check I received today from an anonymous donor. Now let's
see . . . " He held it at arm's length and squinted, pretending to read. "Could it really be twenty . . . five . . . *thousand* . . . dollars!"

The crowd went wild. Seth was on her feet, along with a good half of the house, screaming, cheering and yelling. Reluctantly, Billy stood up. Great news, but why the secrecy? Did it come from one of the town businesses or industries? But who among that group could afford so large a gift? Could be someone outside the community. God knows, there were a lot of rich Burke alumni. Could be anybody.

"If Billy Acorn is here, I'd like him to come forward and accept it, on behalf of Blue Jacket Land Trust."

Billy stood up. Seth made room for him to pass, squeezed his arm. As soon as he stood beside Woody, he said, into the mic, "Hey, this is almost enough for me to buy myself a farm in New Zealand."

He thought a momentary look of shock shadowed the old man's wrinkled face for a moment. "Don't worry, Woody. I don't like sheep."

After the audience howled, Woody presented the check. Out of the range of the mic, Billy whispered, "You know who it is?" When Woody shrugged, he knew it was a lie. Why did the old man want to protect someone who was so generous? Why did that someone want to be protected? Oh, well; another day, another twenty-five grand. He pulled out his wallet and slid it in with the five and two ones. Then he stood back behind the mic.

"You know, this is really great. With only sixteen days left till the auction, we've got a long way to go to raise the million we need. But we're getting there, and all of you are helping. By my calculations, this puts us over $500,000 – over halfway toward what we think we'll need."

The applause was a deafening wave. Billy decided to let them ride it for a few seconds before he gave them a reality check. Had to be done, if they were to keep up the fight, not see the thing as nearly done. "Woody, how are the efforts going to get the township and county to kick in some cash?"

Woody, who'd been beaming, instantly sobered. "Not so good. Though I have no official word – that should come after Monday's township trustees meeting – I have a reliable source who says the trustees are stalemated on the issue right now. Also, the Highway Administration turned down our grant request for half a mill – too many roads to build   and so did the County – seems like they have a very large prison to construct this year. But I'm an optimist, and today's gift increases our credibility as well as our coffers. We now really have a chance to do it. And I trust the township will see that they wouldn't be throwing their money away on a hopeless cause." He raised his fist. "Are we hopeless?"

*NOOOO.*

"Are we gonna raise a million?"

*YEEESSSS.*

Billy got back on fast. "As far as I know, CitFarm doesn't have any event planned before the auction, but a rally at the Holiday Inn, where the auction's going to be, on the day of the event, might be a good idea. We'll make plans at the next meeting, which will be here Tuesday downstairs in the meeting room. Please come. We'll need volunteers to do a million jobs before auction day. And if anybody knows any more angels like the one that just blessed us, please coax them down from the airy heights and tell them we're only halfway there."

When he paused, there was no applause this time. Good. Now if he could keep Woody away from leading any more cheers . . .

"And now, if they're ready . . . " He looked around at the guitar players who'd been tuning. Ricky Spain, his classic black Rickenbacker twelve-string at the ready, nodded. "Give it up for those masters of nostalgia, keepers of the sacred tunes . . . DAY TRIPPER!"

And before Billy was down the steps, the band ripped into a rave-up version of "Money." Grinning, he turned, halfway back to his seat, to see couples dancing in front of the stage. He obviously wasn't the only one who loved the old shit. Seth met him in the aisle, grabbed his arm.

"Well, come *on!*" she said urgently.

"Whoa," he teased, hanging back. "I thought you were strictly Mozart and Beethoven."

She grinned. "Roll over, Beethoven!"

And they crammed themselves into the sweaty mob and began to move. It didn't matter that Billy hated to dance unless he had a good buzz on; it didn't matter folks were smashing clumsily into each other like a senior citizens' mosh pit; what mattered was the smile on Seth's face and her writhing, sweaty body. And of course the twenty-five-thousand dollar check in his wallet.

O

By the time they wound up at the Trout, Billy was growing ever more certain that tonight would be the night. It was the first time he'd been in the tavern since celebrating his birthday with Ira. Seth seemed charmed by the orangish wood walls and the rough-hewn plank tables straight out of the nineteenth century. One-dollar bills with names on them were glued around the low ceiling, and Seth stared dumb-founded when Billy pointed to the fur-covered trout on the wall in the shadows beyond the bar.

"Man," she whispered, "Ohio winters used to be even colder than they are now."

He just grinned, squeezed her hand and led her through a low door into the dining room of William Davis's original cabin. Even darker, its walls pulsed with light from a huge fireplace in the rear large enough to hang huge pots in. Feeling her squeeze his hand back, he relaxed. Woody had said this would be a short planning session among the honchos about the group's next move, after which . . . well, the night was yet young.

Sitting at the rough-plank table in the low-ceilinged, dim darkness, drinking draft beer from a plastic pitcher, he watched Seth laugh at almost anything anyone said the least bit funny. And she'd hardly touched her beer. He wondered if she'd let herself have this much fun since she'd been a mom. Probably not. The Trips had played a non-stop ninety-minute set of sixties rock. By the time they slowed things down with "You've Lost That Lovin' Feeling," Seth felt like hand-warmed clay in his arms. Thank God she'd forgotten Bonnie's gossip.

"So. What next, Billy-man?" It was Mark Zamora – the punk had actually gotten out of bed before the concert was over. Necessary evil, Billy figured, since he was self-appointed leader of Burke's CitFarm volunteers. He glanced around the table at Vernon Baxter, local jeweler, and Sunni Sebastian-Masterson, manager of Manic Organic, who'd volunteered to head up publicity. Since Blue Jacket definitely needed CitFarm to do the grunt work, he didn't want any misfires.

"Well, first we go to the township trustees' meeting Monday night. John Schuyler's going to be there to plead his case for zoning concessions. We want to see who and what we're fighting. And be a presence."

"Why not just have another rally outside, raise some more hell?" Mark's eyes glittered.

"No," Billy said. "We don't want to jump the gun, act like it's a foregone conclusion that Schuyler's gonna try to twist arms. Then we lose points with the trustees, who may still help us out. We gotta play it cool until their cards are up. There shouldn't be too many of us there, and we mainly *listen*." He knew it was too lame a gig for Mark to show up.

"Yeh, but don't we gotta respond when – okay, *if* –Shyster starts trying to manipulate them into giving him his way."

"Excuse me," Baxter interrupted, crossing his arms and leveling his gaze. "Tell me again why Schuyler is the bad guy?"

Mark rolled his eyes, but Billy just smiled. Baxter was the only guy at the table wearing a tie, albeit a string tie with a silver and turquoise bolo. He didn't want to upset the chamber of commerce president, if possible. He looked at Woody. "Want to run it by us again, Professor?"

"All right," Woody began. "We've heard rumors that Schuyler wants to buy a big chunk of the farm to develop. And we know from what he's done in Cedarton how he builds: extremely high density. Since the land's currently zoned agricultural, he's going to try to get the board to approve re-zoning. Otherwise, why buy it? And he knows the current trustees will consider it. Affordable housing has been a huge issue in the last couple of years. Some trustees were elected specifically to do something about it. Since real estate in town's gone off the charts, many people inside and outside Shawnee Springs really want some affordable housing."

"And *we* want the goddamn farm," Mark put in, pounding the table suddenly with his fist. Billy noticed he'd drunk half of the first pitcher himself and had already drunk two glasses out of the second. First chance he got, Billy'd ask the waiter for their tab.

Woody gave Mark a stern look. "Yes, Mark. And if we can't buy the whole thing, the next best scenario is to buy as much as possible. That way, we reduce the amount that can be developed and hope that the developers who do buy it will build responsibly, with three-hundred foot frontages, with one or two-acre minimum lots . . ."

"Which is dreaming!" Mark interrupted. "Look at Gracious Acres – you could cut the front lawns with toenail clippers and still have time to smoke a joint."

Woody ignored Mark. "And the worst case scenario? The township votes to re-zone, and Schuyler buys the land on which to cram another of his cracker-box ghettoes. The size of the village could double in both area and population – we'd become a small city. It's fair to say the complexion of our community could change drastically."

Sunni spoke up for the first time. "Is that necessarily bad? I mean, gosh, new blood . . ."

"Cha-*ching*," Mark intoned. "Don't count your chickens yet, Sunni. Burbites want Big Macs, not tofu wrap-ups."

Woody set his jaw. "It's not that the new folks' values would necessarily be inferior to ours, but increased numbers mean increased pressure on, well, everything. We'd no longer be a village. We'd be a city – with city problems: infrastructure, need for more industry and commerce to provide tax base, need for . . . "

"How much do you figure the whole thing'll go for?" Mark interrupted, wiping foam off his upper lip with his sleeve.

Woody frowned. "Nobody knows."

"C'mon, Doc, your best guesstimate."

"Three and a half, maybe even four million dollars."

Baxter whistled. Billy thought Sunni blanched through her tan.

"So our one million – that's only for the easement thing, right?" Baxter asked. "How do we get the rest?"

"Farmers," Billy injected. "Fred Pennington tells me he knows about five who already would like to buddy with us to buy some of Wood Thrush."

Woody nodded. "Fred's a fine man. If he says he and others want to buy, I believe him. But does he have the money? Do the others? Have they applied for loans? They're wild cards until they commit."

"We're working on it," Billy said. He gave Seth a significant glance but she just stared straight ahead, grimly, probably remembering Garth Erickson in the gym: *Money talks; the farmer walks.* He hoped this talk wouldn't put a damper on his plans for later.

Mark leaned forward, spraying spit as he spoke. "Shit, maybe if we just blow up something, Schuyler'll back off. We could do some fucking damage at his Cedarton developments."

"Eco-terrorism?" said Baxter, appalled. "I think not."

"I'm not talking about burning down houses or killing people," Mark said before gulping the rest of the beer in his glass. "But we could do a whole lot less than that and still make a powerful statement. And if we do it before the auction, maybe Schuyler won't even show. We could scare him off."

"If violence ever enters the picture," Woody said, "I'm done."

"Me, too," Sunni said, hugging herself as if freezing.

"Goes triple for me," Baxter said, looking straight at Mark.

"Same here," Seth said. Billy felt Seth's eyes on him and wanted to agree, but God knew what Mark might say then about certain security guards. Again he looked to Woody. The old man folded his arms and looked straight at Mark.

"*And* I report the actions of any I suspect of being eco-terrorists. To the proper authorities."

The air sizzled for a moment as Mark met Woody's gaze. Finally the older man spoke.

"I understand your impatience with working the system, Mark, but history has proven time and time again the devastating consequences of behind-the-scenes violence. From Vietnam to – "

"Whatever." Mark studied his empty beer glass.

"Listen," said Baxter, dividing his gaze between Billy and Woody, studiously avoiding Mark, "who's really in charge here?"

As Billy and Woody pointed at each other, Woody laughed. "Cyrus Harmon has called us a 'benevolent anarchy.' Yes, we could've micromanaged everything from the beginning, brought in more of the village movers and shakers, county commissioners and so forth, but it's been better to just let people do their own thing. It's been the most democratic project the town's ever undertaken – folks see something they can do – like tonight's fabulous concert – and they just go do it. Blue Jacket, CitFarm: two sides of the same coin."

"My, my." Baxter was shaking his head. "Well," he said at last, "just like a fine watch somebody brings me after it's been through the washer, if a little shake makes it run, I'm not about to mess with it."

Billy squeezed Seth's leg beneath the table.

"Speaking of time." Woody looked at his watch. "Holy Toledo, I told Matilda I'd be home by nine."

"I need to go, too," said Baxter.

"Seven A.M. opening comes earlier every morning," chimed in Sunni.

Billy bit his tongue. Eight-thirty or nine was more like it, but he knew she couldn't wait to get away from Mark. And if Baxter lingered much longer, he'd probably wind up strangling the punk.

"See you at the meeting on Monday!" Woody flashed one last grin, threw a five down on the table, though he'd drunk only water, and fled, the two merchants right behind him. Mark stared at Billy for several more awkward moments, then slid out of the booth and stood. "It worked before, Billy-man," Mark rasped. "It could work again." And he was gone without leaving a dime for the beer he'd drunk. In the wake of the departures, the atmosphere – so bright before – seemed dark, ominous. Well, now he could tell Seth what he thought of violence, but before he could speak, someone else did.

"Well, look what the damn cat dragged in."

Billy looked up. Bonnie swayed as she stood, one hand on her hip, the other clutching a mug of beer. She was the absolute last person in the world Billy wanted to see. But he wasn't about to let her know that – or that what she'd told Seth had gotten to him.

"Yo, Bonnie." Billy grinned.

"Yo yourself, yo-yo-brain."

"Have a seat." When Billy gestured to Mark and Woody's empty side of the table, he felt Seth's thigh tense.

She looked straight at Seth. "Guess you didn't take my advice, huh?"

Seth didn't answer. After taking a huge swallow of beer, Bonnie said, "How's your son?"

"He's fine."

"I heard about the gerbil."

Seth blushed. Bonnie's sudden appearance seemed to have robbed her of speech, much the way Kieron had affected him last week.

"Poor kid," Bonnie muttered.

"It's late," Seth said, looking at Billy. "I need to be getting home."

"Well," Bonnie put in. "I hope he's not hurting too bad about killing his gerbil."

"It was a hamster," Billy said.

"You should consider getting the kid some help." She glared at Billy. "Some real help."

Billy was watching Seth's face when she said it, and though her head was lowered as she gathered her things, she took the hit. *Damn.* Why couldn't he douse this old flame and be done with it? He stood up, inches away from Bonnie.

"Paul's a great kid," Billy said. "He's got a lot to offer people of this town. Kids here lead a sheltered life. They need to learn a few things from" – he caught himself before saying outsider – "new blood."

Bonnie's mouth curled into a sneer. "Yeh. Like what?"

"Like compassion," he said, then louder, " not to be confused with self-pity."

Bonnie slumped as if the air had gone out of her.

"Good night, Bonnie," Seth said, patting the swaying woman's shoulder as they passed.

○

Inside the Dakota, they lapsed silent, holding hands while he drove the cold, dark village streets. Billy found himself calm after all that had happened. Nothing, it seemed, could be *really* good for very long. Something – or somebody – came along to fuck up whatever game you were playing.

"Sorry about that," he finally said.

"She was drunk."

"She can be like that even . . . "

"She's still madly in love with you, you know."

Billy felt his neck heating, despite the cold. Though he kept his eyes forward, he heard the smile in her voice. "She told me you won her heart with fresh veggies."

He snorted. "She had to have one hundred percent organic. Can you believe it, the way she drinks?"

He couldn't think of anything else to say. By the time he turned the truck down the ice-rutted road to her house, he wondered whether he'd go inside even if she invited him. When he pulled up and killed the engine, he glanced over at her. She stared straight ahead, her breath coming in great clouds. He knew better than to say a word. Words had almost cost him everything.

She touched his arm. "Good night, then." She squeezed his arm and got out. Meantime his heart had started racing again.

She thrust her head back inside. "Know what, Billy?"

He felt frozen as he looked up at her, loose hair falling around her face. She was gonna ask him in!

"You'll probably wind up marrying that woman."

Then she slammed the door hard.

# Chapter Fifteen

Putnam County, West Virginia
Monday, March 13, 1999

"Where in thunderation have you been?" Della hollered down the hallway as soon as Billy walked in the front door, assaulted by cooking smells. He remembered his aunt was extremely liberal with spices.

He threw his pea coat across the back of the couch and strode right into the kitchen where she stood holding a spoonful of gravy.

"It smells like Thanksgiving in here," he said.

"It is."

"What're we thankful for?"

She wrinkled her nose. "That they haven't paved over the graveyards yet, I reckon."

"And that Grand-daddy's farm might be saved for the future."

She froze. Billy stepped closer, leaned down, opened and closed his mouth around the spoon. The tart saltiness made his salivary glands ache. He'd bet Della was the only human in the universe who put cloves *and* soy sauce in her turkey gravy.

"What are you talking about, Billy Mike?"

Stepping back, he flopped down in one of the chairs at the table. "Damn, that's good. 'Scuse my french."

She sat weakly across the table. "Don't mess with an old woman."

"I drove to Charleston. I knew if there was any sort of land trust, that's where it would be." Her eyebrows lifted ever so slightly. "It took me half the day – but I found it." He reached into his hip pocket and handed her the card Dan Fountain had given him.

Della stared at it. "Kanawha Land Trust," she read in a near-whisper, "'Preserving the land today for tomorrow's children.'"

And while Billy repeated what Dan had told him about the land trust's efforts, he saw the flood gather like rising spring rivers in his aunt's aged, cataract-shadowed but still blazing-blue eyes – then stream down her red cheeks to drop onto the linen tablecloth.

"They know all about Beck's expansion, Aunt Della, and tried to slow it down. But they'd given up on it, since everyone out here had pretty much rolled over and played dead, Dan said."

She nodded, her head bowed for a moment before she spoke. "I remember a young fella with a beard coming to the door once, talking a blue streak about conserving farmland, using a lot of fancy words. I knew without really understanding a word he was saying that he was a good boy, even though he had that beard and, you know, that city look about him – and that he was right. But Don shoved him down the steps."

It was Billy's turn to be flabbergasted. "Uncle Don?"

Her chin touched her floral sweatshirt. Was this the woman who, according to his dad, had once roofed her whole house with the help of a couple of local kids, who tore out walls, hung drywall and plowed a hundred acres, who gave birth one day and canned a slew of tomatoes and pickles the next? Finally she raised her head. She was smiling but still crying.

"Honey, you've done what nobody around here could do, what your Aunt Della couldn't do 'cause she was too dern proud. You've brought us back the help we refused. Your Uncle Don . . ." She closed her eyes and shuddered. "He's totally against fighting this thing. He says that farming is done more efficient than it ever was – 'Agribusiness is good business,' he says all the time – and that the price we could get out of this land would set him and Al both up for life."

Now Billy knew why she was living here. "So if not for you . . . "

"No, honey, not me."

"Little Don? Claudia?"

"They're long gone from here. And they ain't ever coming back till one of us dies."

"Then who?"

"It's Al, honey. Your daddy won't agree to sell it – at least not yet."

The room tilted, and had he not caught himself, Billy would've fallen off his chair. "Al 'Money-Man' Acorn won't sell?"

She nodded. "Not yet, though Don keeps after him. I put off letting Don know how I felt as long as I could. I'd just say things kindly joking, hoping he might come around. But he got worse, bad-mouthing any of his neighbors for saying anything that questioned Hubert Harvey, the developer who did all this."

She waved her hand to take it all in. All Billy could see was that damn blue cow.

"So there was a meeting of the trustees. And I'd gotten a flyer up at the Big Bear in Winfield. I knew it was a showdown. If you had anything to say against the Beck's project – it was the beginning of their expansion, honey – then you had to come and say it." She glanced away for just a second, wiped another tear. "I fought all day with myself, but kept coming back to your grand-daddy and what this farm meant to him, how he said over and over, 'This land will return a hundred-fold what you give it.'"

Billy saw him, smoking his pipe, rocking in silence.

"So I went to that meeting and set beside Don. You know he's so shy, he wasn't there to speak but to show his support for the developers. And when they opened the floor, I squoze out of my seat, went right up to that microphone – I never looked his way once while I talked, and told 'em what I thought."

Billy could see it, and though he closed his eyes against the sight of soft-spoken Don Sizemore with his arms folded across his chest, his eyes murderous, the image became engrained, his aunt's wrinkled face juxtaposed atop his uncle's until finally she became Seth, looking so small, sounding so tentative, reaching way down inside herself for the courage to say the words.

He felt his aunt touch his arm, opened his eyes to see her hunkered forward, grinning ruefully. "They say I talked for twenty-five minutes, though it seemed about two to me. I gave 'em a history of the whole area, winding up with how we don't actually own the land, don't even own our own bodies – we're just on loan from God – and just ought to leave it alone for its own sake."

Billy stared. The same speech Ira had given the farmers. In Charleston, then all the way back, he'd patted himself on the back for what he'd done, how happy he was going to make Della. Now he knew, with the same conviction he'd felt after the fire that almost killed a man and the more recent fire whose damage he still did not know, that a man had no control, really, over much of anything in the world.

"Oh my savior!" Della yelled and jumped up.

Billy nearly flew off his chair. "What?"

"The turkey's burning. Help me, quick, Billy Mike."

◯

Billy carefully shoved his plate toward the center of the table and groaned. When had he eaten so sumptuously before this? Bonnie! She'd cooked huge, elaborate meals for him involving spices and even vegetables whose names he'd never heard and meats whose textures and tastes he no longer recognized when she was through with them. Across the table, Della, who'd touched hardly a bite but smiled and nodded while he gorged himself, read his mind.

"It's time you told me what you're running from," she said, locking her eyes on his.

He glanced up from where his gaze had landed in the middle of the table on the gravy boat.

She reared back in her chair and crossed her arms. "It's a woman, I bet."

He blushed in spite of himself. "We were great together, and then . . ."

"She wanted a baby. And you didn't."

He just stared.

"Darlin', 'No Kids' is written all over you." She cackled while Billy felt his neck heating.

"That obvious, huh?"

She nodded, still shaking with laughter. *You should see me with Paul*, he wanted to say. Instead he told her about his and Bonnie's breakup.

When he'd finished, they lapsed silent. "So Bonnie needs a baby?"

"Well, she wants one."

Della shook her head. "Huh uh. Some women need babies. Bonnie sounds like one."

"Maybe."

"Well," she said, looking up at last as if reaching some decision. "The only way to get over not wanting a baby is to get yourself one. That's what I did."

"Aunt Della, you always wanted kids."

She sat up straight in her chair, laid both hands on the table. "You don't know what I wanted, mister."

"But I've seen . . ."

"Claudia and Little Don? They're great, now they're grown. But I didn't want 'em. Both were accidents. I was trying really hard – well, times was different then – not to have kids before I got what I wanted."

"And what was that?"

Her shoulders sank. She looked away for a moment. When she looked at him again, her face was that of an applicant for a job she knows she'll never get.

"To go to college."

"I never knew that!"

She shrugged. "I only ever told my daddy."

"What'd he say?"

"He laughed and said, 'Did I go to college? Did your mama go to college?'"

"And that was it?"

She nodded. *Damn.* All this woman ever wanted was the thing he'd thrown away.

"Della, there's a college in Charleston."

She shook her head, tears streaming down her wind-and-age-burnt cheeks.

"I'll take you there."

She kept her head lowered. "I don't have the . . . requirements."

"You graduated high school – that's all you need. Registering is a piece of cake."

She glanced up. "But Don, he . . . "

"Don's not here." Billy laid his hand on top of hers. "I'll take you tomorrow."

She was silent for so long he feared he'd stepped on her pride. Finally she spoke.

"On one condition."

"Whatever you say."

"You go back and talk things over with Bonnie."

He nodded. "I will." The hardest lie he'd ever told.

# Chapter Sixteen

Shawnee Springs, Ohio
Monday, March 6, 1999

Billy was glad he got to the township meeting before Seth and
Woody. Sitting in the middle of two rows of chairs in back of the room,
he wanted to scope everyone out. Though he'd been to many a village
council meeting, this was his first trustees' meeting, and they were a
different-looking bunch. Anyone could see they weren't the best of
friends, since they neither spoke to nor looked at each other. Woody,
who'd attended a couple times, said it was the worst board in years,
with the trustees squabbling about every little diddling thing.

He recognized Sid Johnston, fierce-looking and red-faced president,
from photos in the *News*. Sitting next to him must be Marjory
Coleman, staring straight ahead, her lips pursed, as if to speak too soon
might spoil everything. Standing at opposite ends of the table were the
older council members. Dave Ekerd fit editor Harmon's description of
"a cherub with a beard." And Tess O'Neil's dark hair and eyes made her
the Irish beauty Woody said she was.

Almost invisible was the balding man with black glasses leaning
against the wall with his arms folded over his plaid sweater vest: Ray
Gershowitz looked totally aloof. It took all Billy's resistance not to
harden his heart against him. It had been apparent during Billy's fling
with Bonnie that she worshiped her brother. Professor of Cultural
Studies at Burke, he was everything she wasn't: tweedy Boston
College Ph.D. to her tie-dyed School of Hard Knocks. She had never
introduced them; she'd probably thought her intellectual bro wouldn't
approve of a college dropout and career volunteer who spent his time
waiting on the next Big Controversy. Gershowitz's would be the swing
vote, so they had to be hopeful, even though Woody had been skeptical
on the phone last night.

"It's perfectly apparent they hate each other," he had said.

"But they have an elected duty to do what the citizens want," Billy
shot back.

"That's the problem. Sid Johnston and Marjory Coleman were
elected last November, and they feel they have a mandate to deliver on
the affordable housing promise they made."

"But how can such a narrow agenda get someone elected in our
liberal little burg?"

"Well, the township is not the town. They're often at odds with each other. The farmers feel the village's bleeding hearts are clueless concerning their needs. Since available land for development inside the village is virtually nil, any growth, if there is to be any, has to occur in the township. Many farmers – for example, those ready to retire – are quite willing to see their land's value grow."

Depressed, he'd hung up and resisted calling Seth – she knew about the meeting. Right now these damn trustees looked like they'd just smelled pig shit. They wouldn't even look at each other. More than a tad anxious, Billy took a deep breath. It could be a long evening.

At 7:01, Johnston called the meeting to order, with no sign of Seth or Woody. Billy soon realized it didn't matter. It took forever for the minutes from the last meeting to be read and corrected, and it was a quarter of eight by the time a lengthy, tedious discussion of whether a cell phone tower should be allowed to be built had finally concluded. By the time Seth and Woody sat down beside him, Billy's brain felt like it was in a vise.

"Sorry," she whispered, looking wind-blown and flustered. "Paul had another skirmish with one of his tormentors."

"Did he kick the shit out of him?"

She glared.

"I'm kidding." He reached, squeezed her cold fingers. "Is he okay?"

But she just stared straight ahead.

"The next item," Johnston announced, looking as angry as if about to declare war on Dayton, "concerns whether to devote any of the township's greenspace preservation fund to this . . . " – Billy thought his voice rose sarcastically – "Wood Thrush Farm project."

"Yes, Mr. Johnston," put in Dave Ekerd, "the Citizens to Save the Farm need to know right away how much of the fund we'll devote to the purchase of development rights to . . . "

"Whoa." Johnston stuck out his hand like a traffic-cop. "The question is *if* we'll devote any of the fund."

Then Johnston, supported by Coleman, proceeded to harangue and legalize, often interrupting Ekerd and O'Neil with rude, insinuating comments. By eight-thirty, when Billy longed to choke them all, Ray Gershowitz spoke for the first time.

"Mr. Johnston, I think we may have the cart before the horse. Perhaps we ought to continue this after we've discussed the zoning issue. If we vote to rezone, it would seem contradictory to give greenspace preservation funds to CitFarm."

Johnston looked side to side. "Any opposed to temporarily delaying the greenspace issue? No? All right: zoning. Ms. Coleman?"

And with those words, it was as if the entire room took a huge gulp of air. This was the big enchilada. Beside him, Seth looked rapt.

"Thank you, Mr. Johnston. Today will be the second reading on a proposal that the land adjacent to Route 86, known as Wood Thrush Farm, be rezoned for greater residential density."

Instantly, Tess O'Neil started to speak, but Johnston cut her off with a quick karate chop of his right hand. "Before we vote, we'll hear a presentation by local developer John Schuyler."

To the front of the room strode the blonde, tanned man Billy had seen sipping cappuccino at the Sunset Café early in the morning before heading off to rape the land in Cedarton. Dressed in chinos and polo shirt, Schuyler had dressed down for laid-back Shallow Springs.

"Good evening, President Johnston, honorable trustees and fellow citizens. Knowing that the issue of rezoning is such a serious one in these times of economic upheaval, I asked, as a local businessman, to be allowed to share my views on how rezoning could at long last resolve the seemingly intractable problem of affordable housing that has bedeviled this community for decades."

Billy murmured near Seth's ear. "Slimy, ain't he?" But she seemed mesmerized, unable to take her eyes off the man. *Satan's many guises.* It was one of Grand-daddy's favorite phrases.

"As a developer and builder," he continued, "I know that some 1.3 million new households seek housing each year and that Ohioans purchase up to 40,000 new houses annually."

It squared with Billy's research.

"Now, how do we provide *affordable housing*? I know that Shawnee Springs, being the politically, racially and socially diverse community that it is, demands equitable housing. It doesn't view as desirable the large multi-roomed units in the $300,000 and up range that, say, Cedarton has built in the past few years. Don't misunderstand me – I simply build what a community wants. And it's been made clear to me by Mr. Johnston, by the many letters to the *News* over the past several years and the various forums held at this site and others, by the commission formally charged a year ago, then disbanded in frustrated disarray when zoning finally foiled them . . . "

Good God. The man's syntax had become rope with which he attempted to hog-tie his opposition. On his right, Seth was breathing so fast she almost panted, and her hands, when he looked, were clenched. Schuyler better watch his blind side.

"... that this town wants the type of housing that low-to middle-income folks can afford, to attract young families to enjoy and support its award-winning school system. Well, if it's going to be possible to deliver on this ideal of equity, this desire to make Shawnee Springs affordable to the type of clientele you hope to attract, something must change. That something is zoning."

During the dramatic pause, Billy realized he'd begun cracking his knuckles and quit when Seth glanced at him. Woody, hugging himself tightly and rocking in his chair, looked like a pretzel. Was anyone on the board going to object?

"All right," Schuyler continued. "If we all agree on the goal, here's how you achieve it in today's economy. If I am allowed to develop no more than one building per three-acre lot, it will be impossible for me or any other builder to deliver a house for less than $300,000. Therefore, if developers are to continue to make housing available and affordable to families who need it ..."

*Want it*, thought Billy grimly. Consumers *want*.

"... they must be able to obtain higher densities."

"Mr. Schuyler, density is what we do *not* want." It was Tess O'Neil, unable to hold herself back, her cheeks as flushed as if she'd sprinted a mile. "We're not Cedarton. And the village and township will be hard-pressed to provide the infrastructure such density would require."

"Not true," said Johnston flatly. "Mr. Littlejohn has done the study. Such services can be easily provided and paid for with the extended tax base."

"But they *don't* pay for themselves," put in O'Neil, her eyes flashing. "Ken's study also showed that the denser they are, the more pressure there is on services. Even cities, much less a village of 5,000, are hard-pressed to provide them."

"Plus," Eckerd injected, "farms require only thirty cents in service for each tax dollar they contribute, though residential subdivisions consume $1.25 for each tax dollar they pay."

Billy caught Seth's eye and gave her a thumbs-up, but she stared ahead grimly.

"Hear, hear," said Johnston. "This discussion should restrict itself to the one issue concerning the entire township, not just Wood Thrush Farm. And let's not forget that farmers want the option to sell some of their land for development, especially the older ones who're facing retirement without pension plans that most of us have. Rezoning would let them sell to developers for much more than what they could get selling it as farmland."

"That's why we need *easements*," pleaded O'Neil, looking clearly embattled.

The word seemed to ratchet up tension another notch or two. Even Cyrus Harmon, *News* editor, quit scribbling and looked up.

"Ms. O'Neil," said Schuyler, politely, "It's clear that many farmers in our township do not want easements. They want to dispose of the land they've worked for generations as they see fit."

Billy's chest hurt. *Dispose of land.* Couldn't the guy hear himself? And then he remembered Garth Erickson, who'd probably agree with the rooster preening his feathers in the front of the room. Maybe it was best none of the farmers had come (which angered him, until he remembered how early they rose).

"So: everyone ready?" interrupted Johnston. "I'm ready to vote."

"Mr. Johnston," Dave Eckerd said calmly, "we may have some present who have not yet been heard." He peered into the audience. "Would anyone like to speak to this issue?"

Billy was instantly on his feet. Johnston, head lowered as if ready to charge, and, with luck, gore Eckerd, stared at him above his half-glasses.

"Mr. President, my name's Billy Acorn, and I have a petition to present, sir."

"And what might be the nature of this petition, Mr. Acorn?"

"Sir, it contains the signatures of 1500 residents of Shawnee Springs and Shawnee Township who want Wood Thrush Farm's zoning to remain as it is."

Johnston glared at Coleman as if to say, *Why didn't you let me know this was going to happen?* before returning his glare to Billy, who spoke again.

"Also, I just want to say that Mr. Schuyler was right when he said rezoning is about the ideals of Shawnee Springs. And the ideal of the folks who signed this petition is not density, sir."

"And what do you think their ideal to be?" Johnston smirked.

"They like sunsets."

"Really."

"Yes, sir. And cows and pigs . . . even pig manure."

There were a few giggles. Cyrus Harmon was grinning.

"And smelling corn in August, and *buying* that corn at farmer's market."

"Mr. Acorn, everybody in Ohio likes corn."

"But the folks that signed this petition like Wood Thrush Farm enough to make sacrifices. Not only did they sign the petition but they came out and publicly declared their love . . . "

"Oh, yes, I saw your declaration of love."

"Sir, we've collected over $500,000 toward purchasing the easement. We just held a benefit concert, which raised seven thousand dollars." He felt Seth squeeze his arm. "And another five thousand showed up in the mailbox this morning from committed people all over the world."

"Very impressive, Mr. Acorn. But there are many more residents who did not sign your petition. We are considering *their* wishes, also. Is there anything else?"

"Just one more thing."

"Yes?"

"It's a fact that 3.2 million acres of farmland every year were gobbled up by development in this decade, sir. That's twice the rate of the eighties."

"Very educational, Mr. Acorn. Place your petition on the table. Does anyone else in the audience wish to speak?"

Billy heard Woody's joints popping as he strove to stand. But Seth beat him. Billy sat down for a better view.

"Mr. Johnston, I'm Seth Abel, and I'm new in town."

"Yes, Ms. Abel?"

"The land doesn't need density, Mr. Johnston. It needs responsible stewardship."

Tess O'Neil smiled. Ekerd raised a thumbs-up. Ray Gershowitz's face stayed absolutely blank.

"Those people Mr. Schuyler talked about, that . . . that 40,000 or however many . . . It's like in that movie: 'If you build it, they will come.' But they'll come not out of *need* but because you tell them to come. You create their desire by building. If we stop, maybe they'll stay where they are and put down roots."

"And you, Ms. Abel. Have you put down roots?"

She fidgeted from one foot to the other. Billy knew what she was thinking: Outsider.

"Yes, Mr. Johnston. I live on Wood Thrush Farm. I belong there. If it's developed, it'll die. And you and I will have killed it."

"Thank you for your opinion, Ms. Abel."

When she sat down, Billy squeezed her shoulder, but she wouldn't look at him. She was shaking. He wondered if she were partly responding to whatever abuse Paul had taken in school today. Woody stared straight ahead. Schuyler, hands folded before him like a deacon's, seemed to be working hard to suppress a smile.

"Mr. Johnston." It was Ray Gershowitz. His face was still blank. "I move that we table this motion until the next meeting."

"Second," said Tess O'Neil.

○

Out in the hallway, Billy accepted Seth's high-five and hug, but Woody, grim-faced, said, "This is only a temporary stay of execution. The motion's been tabled, not defeated."

Seth flared. "But this buys us more time. The board won't meet for two weeks: that means the day of the auction. If things go as well as they have, we'll have 1500 *more* names!"

"Plus a million dollars to show them," Billy added.

"They won't *dare* re-zone," she nearly shouted.

Woody looked doubtful. "Maybe." He cut his eyes toward the open door. "You saw how they're deadlocked."

"And I'm gonna shut up from now on," Billy said, punching her arm lightly. "All I do is recite facts, but you hit 'em square in the heart!" He knew, judging from Woody's non-expression, that the compliment was over the top, but what the hell. Woody didn't know what she'd been through today.

"Mr. Acorn, you guys really did your homework. I appreciate that," a voice boomed behind them. Turning, Billy saw the speaker was John Schuyler, wearing a coat made entirely from the fur of some animal from a very cold region and smiling like a preacher at altar call.

"I know you disagree with me," he continued, "but I've managed to obtain some facts, too."

"Do your facts tell you," Seth said through clenched teeth, "that overcrowded housing developments are more important than farms?"

His voice and smile never wavered. "More important than scenic views for comfortable suburbanites, yes."

"Farmland produces more than views, Mr. Schuyler," she said more calmly. "It produces *food*, not to mention nutrition for the spirit."

"Ms. Abel, most of our food is produced on commercial, not family, farms. If you're eating peaches and melons right now, you're supporting corporate, not family, farming."

He slipped on one black glove. Billy realized Ray Gershowitz was standing just behind the developer.

"What do you say, Ms. Abel, to those who argue – and it's said a lot these days, even in the hallowed corridors of Congress – 'Those anti-development people sure got their pretty views before shutting off the valve'?"

Though Seth stayed silent, Billy felt rage coming off her like heat from a boiler. He decided he'd better get her away before she decked the guy.

"But of course you're new here, as you said," Schuyler continued, "Maybe you've not yet met enough of your neighbors who might benefit from affordable housing in town. Like . . . " He turned slightly toward Gershowitz. "What's that teacher's name?"

"Adam Lett," the trustee said quietly. Billy couldn't tell if he were embarrassed to be standing beside the rooster or not.

"Ah, yes, Adam Lett, an English teacher at Shawnee Springs High for how many? – thirteen years – who has never been able to afford a home here, though he longs to end his commute, to enroll his own two children in the schools for which he labors. Only one example of the need that I – that responsible development – fulfills."

"There are plenty of other ways without developing the farm," Billy said, glad to find his voice calm. "The college owns a lot of land around it which it has no plans to use. Plus, there are quite a few homes, some of them abandoned, which could be bought for a song and rehabilitated with sweat equity."

When he paused, no one rushed to fill the gap, so he added, "Mr. Gershowitz, tell Adam I'd be pleased to help him build or refurbish a house inside the village. I'm no Jimmy Carter, but I can be had cheap."

Woody laughed, as did a few other rubber-neckers in the hallway, and Billy knew he'd said enough. He longed to squeeze Seth's hand to signal her to stay silent but couldn't bring himself to do it. He tensed when, after the laughter ceased, she spoke.

"And what do you think, Mr. Gershowitz? And, by the way, we thank you for your motion."

Billy, suddenly freezing, just folded his arms. *Don't back him into a corner.* It was too late now. Even Schuyler turned toward Gershowitz. Others standing around waited, too.

"I want to deliver on an issue of major concern to my constituency," the trustee replied. "And, yes, I'd like to see fine men like Adam Lett not only labor here but be able to reside here as well, coach tee-ball and serve on the Community Foundation board, if he wants to."

"Even if it means asphalting over the land that makes living here mean something?" Though Seth smiled as she said it, it was a horrible travesty of a smile. Billy couldn't help feeling whatever had happened to Paul today must've been the emotional equivalent of Desert Storm.

But Gershowitz was smiling. "I have to take everyone's concerns into consideration, Ms. Abel – and that's why I voted to table tonight:

to give us time to do that. If I'd voted tonight . . . " He paused to put one arm into a rumpled trench coat. "I'd've voted to rezone."

Then he was gone, his and Schuyler's heels clicking down the corridor toward the elevator. Woody's expression, when Billy glanced at him, told him everything he didn't want to know.

"Well, boys and girls, this old lumberjack needs to saw some wood if he's to fight another day. Ta!" And Woody disappeared into the exit stairwell behind them. Billy faced Seth.

"Hey," he said softly, "what happened to Paul today?"

Her face was the reddest he'd ever seen it, and her eyes so full of fire he couldn't tell what color they were. Her bottom lip barely quivering, she seemed to be considering many possible answers, selecting, discarding, revising. Finally, she took a deep breath.

"Okay, I'll tell you, but don't confuse my feelings about that with what I feel about this."

He opened his hands. "Would I do that?"

"Yes. *This* – " She pointed to the trustees' chambers. " – is about passion and commitment. This has nothing to do with Paul."

"All right." He put on his most agreeable face.

"Paul was suspended . . . . for fighting."

"No *way*." While a voice in his brain, yelled *Go, Paul,* another, quieter one whispered, *No. No*

"But he didn't fight, Billy. And after he told me what happened, I went up there and got him reinstated. It was either that or home-school him."

"So what did happen . . . if not a fight?"

"You remember Shawn and Lucas bullying him in the caf? Well, turns out they've kept the pressure on, and Paul's strategy was to avoid them, even staying in classes after the bell rings, to let them get to the end of the building before he leaves for the next class. Well, they waited outside English class till he came out. They stood there blocking the hall."

Closing his eyes, Billy saw it: Showdown at OK Corral.

"They started taunting as usual. Paul didn't answer, just waited for his chance, then bolted between them. Caught off-balance, Lucas fell on his butt, but Shawn got knocked backwards into an open locker, cutting his head. Well, when Mr. Hendrickson came out to see what was the matter and saw the blood, the bullies made up a very large lie."

"So only Paul got suspended?"

"No, they all three did. But only Paul got reinstated."

She sighed long and heavy. He longed to hug her as he had that night outside the church. Of course this had something to do with her going off on Schuyler. Personal, political: you can't separate them – nor should you try to. He tried to convey with his eyes what he could not with his body.

"And after I explained everything, going back to the cafeteria incident, Mr. Kincaid called the boys' parents right then and there – Shawn's dad was called out of a big meeting at Shawnee Springs Instruments to talk to us."

"Holey moley. Were the parents pissed?"

"Yes. At their children. And they're going to ground their sons for the rest of the year if there's even the tiniest repetition of their behavior. And Mr. Kincaid has assigned them to research hate crimes for a presentation to the whole school."

"Seth, I'm sorry as hell I told you not to go in the first time."

"And I'm sorry I listened to you, but there was one good thing to come out of it."

"I can't imagine what."

She smiled for the first time since Woody left. "Audio therapy."

"The boy was obviously born to rock."

"It's probably more the jock than the rock – I mean the time you've spent with him. Paul's growing up. When I told him about the boys' punishment, he said, 'They're who I really wanted to kill, not Data. Now I don't have to.'"

Billy relaxed against the wall. Things had worked out, no thanks to him. One thing was certain: he was not going to reveal the kid's secret, come hell or high water. He couldn't do him wrong again. But why was she glaring – did she already know?

"Billy Acorn, I can't believe you stood by and didn't say anything when we had that pompous horse's rear backed into a corner."

He laughed before he thought better of it. "That horse's rear was John Schuyler, who owns half the county. We hardly had him cornered."

"We could have, if you'd supported me."

"I ain't Lloyd Kieron."

Silence stretched like a winter horizon. Icy windswept plains with a tiny figure walking, bent by the gale. Him.

"Don't ever say that name to me again. Ever."

And before he could utter another syllable, she was through the door and down the stairs.

# Chapter Seventeen

Shawnee Springs, Ohio
Friday, March 10, 1999

As soon as Billy pulled up in front of Seth's house around eleven and saw one light burning in the kitchen, the full force of what he was about to do hit him. He hoped Ira was right, that the sleeping bags he'd borrowed from his pal were actually good to twenty below. According to the radio, it was only going to be in the upper twenties tonight. He'd camped pretty late into the fall; he knew what the thirties felt like, but he'd never done twenties.

And then there was the rising full moon overhead – Turkey Vulture Moon, Ira'd called it. When Billy had asked why, Ira had cocked an eyebrow. "'Cause the buzzards migrate this time every year. 'Fore you know it, the skys'll be full of them." He and Seth may get a little cold tonight, but at least with that moon, they wouldn't be stumbling around in total darkness.

He'd thought about calling, but it would be too easy for her to hang up. No, he'd been running his mouth about the land ever since he'd met her. It was time to walk, not talk. Striding up to the kitchen door, he could see her sitting at the table. For one second he wavered. Even if she consented to his crazy idea, wouldn't arrangements have to be made for Paul? Nah. The boy was growing up – she'd said so herself. He could stay by himself.

Billy knocked with authority but not, he hoped, loud enough to waken the boy, whose window was dark. He positioned himself so she couldn't look out the tiny window and see him. The Dakota was outside her range of vision.

"Who is it?"

"Name's Bruce Berry, ma'am. Hit a deer at the end of your driveway. Need to use your phone."

When she opened the door, he charged in and stood in the middle of the kitchen.

"Billy! You scared me to death."

From the looks of it, she'd been writing a letter. Man, did she look sexy in glasses.

"I'm spending the night out on the farm tonight. I'd like you to go with me."

She didn't laugh – but she did smile. "Like druids? Will there be a live sacrifice?"

"I've got two sleeping bags made out of Eskimoes' asses in the car, food, matches, candles, firesticks, flashlight, toilet paper . . . everything we'll need for a night beneath the moon. Passion, commitment, remember?"

She crossed her arms. "Last time I checked, mine was just fine."

"Touché. I was hoping you'd help me find mine. I did you and Paul a favor once." He hated himself for saying it, but it was the only good card he had.

She measured him with her eyes for several moments, then closed the door with her hip. "Give me ten minutes. Ginseng tea's on the stove."

By the time she came back, Billy'd downed two lukewarm cups of the vile brew. Her glasses were gone, and she wore what looked like a down parka, jeans and hiking boots, her long hair contained by the wool stocking cap on her head. Even dressed like a man, she was beautiful. Billy's chest glowed, though it could've been partly from the tea.

"Where's the gear?" she said, all business.

"In the truck."

"Get it. I'll leave Paul a note."

◯

He followed her through the gap in the fence and they began slowly crunching into sun-frozen snow above the ankle. Yellow moonglow reflected off the drifts. At first he liked the satisfying sound of their boots plowing forward, but soon he began to sweat, carrying both bags rolled up onto Ira's back-pack frame. He was having trouble keeping up with her, but he wasn't about to ask for a break. It couldn't be that far.

It felt like a mile before they got their first whiff of the woods wafting toward them as they made their even slower way forward, like army recruits on a midnight bivouac. Seth had never turned, never asked if he'd needed a break. Since leaving the yard, they hadn't spoken. Billy decided there was something about the moonlight, the hard, crystal snow and the shrouds of their breath that begged for silence. It was a long time till sunrise. And it was mighty cold.

When Seth stopped, he almost ran into her. He was about to speak when he saw her face, tilted upward, catching moonlight, her mouth open in wonderment as she stared into the darkness of the trees. He looked, too. Light penetrated the density for several yards. Beyond that lay a thick, solid black wall. The sweat on his brow began drying instantly. He felt a small prickle of fear in his heaving chest. But what was there to be afraid of here? Trees, snow, maybe an owl or two. Still . . .

When she turned, her eyes sparkled.

"We're here," she breathed. "Now let's see what's on the other side."

And though he wished she'd step closer and lock lips with him in a celebratory kiss, she turned, walked right past the first tall trees and disappeared into the woods, like a hobbit into Mirkwood.

If he'd thought the trek across the field was tough, navigating among the trees was like trying to walk in quicksand, unseen branches and brambles tearing at his legs and arms every few feet. Even with Seth guiding them with the flashlight, it was tough going, and every so often when Billy's feet got tangled, he'd crash into some huge, dark trunk or Seth would release some small sapling to whip his face.

Almost as soon as they'd entered, they'd disturbed a screech owl, whose blood-curdling cry sent Seth back-pedaling into him. "Owl," he'd said, and she'd stood, fascinated, till it had re-settled in another tree. And even though Billy knew there were no bobcats or mountain lions – at the most a coyote – on this land anymore, the intense darkness made him believe, if he didn't concentrate, that there *could* be, that this land was still wild.

Still wild. It seemed impossible. After all, if they really listened hard, they could hear the rare car on Route 86, which was, thankfully, invisible at this distance. But wild, yes, this wood was free to tangle any which way it wanted, to sink roots down to water and shoot branches up toward sun. Houses and streets could be built here – would be built here if John Schuyler got his way. It was impossible to imagine this living land becoming asphalt, brick, shingles and siding. Wildness was all there was here, and Billy liked it that way. Whatever happened tonight would be on this land's terms. But that was okay – he was here, he was accepted. As Ira had said, land has a right to *be*, independent of what humans think it should be used for.

Which didn't make him totally free of caution, though apparently Seth had no such inhibitions, or her desire to get to the other side was too great to give her pause. He was absolutely certain no woman he'd ever dated would've been in a dark forest in twenty-degree March snow on a dare. He was pretty certain now they'd have to zip their bags together for extra warmth, regardless of what Ira had said about their thermal qualities.

At last they came to what seemed the other side of the forest. Struggling through the last thicket, he half-fell forward to stand beside Seth, panting. She was looking straight and pointing.

"I knew a pond was here somewhere."

Beneath the moon, now directly overhead, lay a tiny glittering eye, their destination. They could've easily skirted the woods altogether, but somehow it had been important to go through, not around.

She turned to him, her eyes gleaming. "Don't you wish we'd brought skates?"

"It's enough just to see it."

"But where are the geese?"

"Someplace warmer, if they've got any sense."

She laughed her tinkling little-girl laugh. She'd become a kid at Christmas. He heaved the pack off his shoulders. It was good she'd softened toward him, amazing that she'd come at all.

"Let's dance," she whispered. And, taking his hands in each of hers, she waltzed him gracefully toward the pond. Giggling, her breath melding with his into one huge, glowing shroud, she let him lead. Suddenly she twirled away toward the bank of the pond. Arms outspread, a diva now on a grand stage, she pirouetted further onto the ice.

"Seth, we don't know whether . . ."

But she was skating now, or trying to, her arms windmilling as she yelled, "Come on, Billy. Don't be . . ."

The cracking was like a gunshot, and his ears began roaring as he watched her in slow motion, waver, stoop as if bending might reduce her weight and keep her above what waited below . . . And though he tried to yell, beg her not to move, stay there till he could do something, she looked at him, her face mirroring his panic and confusion, reached back to him with her red-mittened hand, took one step, two – then sank into blackness.

*It's not deep. She's not going to drown.* The voice prevented him from jumping in after her, which would've been a real bad decision. He ran back to the forest, grabbed a large branch, clambered back down and thrust it toward her, where she struggled to rise, then slipping, sat back down in the shallow black water. She grabbed the branch, steadied herself and let him pull her back to the bank where he let go the limb and took her, trembling, into his arms. She immediately thrust him away.

"No, w-we c-can't both be frozen. We'll c-c-catch our death."

Though he ached to clutch her soaked body and warm her, he knew she was right. He went to work, his nearly-frozen fingers still capable of doing his mind's bidding. They could hike back, but it would be a damned uncomfortable walk for her.

He threw down a ground cloth and unrolled one of the bags. "While I build the fire, you undress and get into the bag. But dry yourself as much as possible. Here" – he took off Ira's down jacket and threw it at her. "Leave your wet clothes in a pile." When she just stood looking at him dumbly, shaking, her mouth quivering, he smiled, though his face felt frozen. "I promise not to look."

She didn't respond. Was she in shock? He raised his voice, managing to keep all panic out. "NOW. You're gonna be fine, but we've got to get you dry, then warm."

He turned away. Was she in serious danger? He figured not but knew that staying calm was essential.

Finding more downed branches just inside the forest didn't take long, and inside the pack he found the matches and fire-sticks. As he got down on his knees to strike the match, he couldn't resist glancing around him. He couldn't have timed it more perfectly. Totally naked, she'd just begun drying herself on his jacket. Standing sideways on her own wet clothing, she looked for a moment as if she'd just stepped out of a warm bath as she bent, furiously wiping one long, moon-gleaming leg, her left breast a gathering teardrop, her hair, now free, spilling off her shoulder.

What thrilled him was how perfectly natural she seemed. Sure, they could run back to the house, but seeing her body in the firestick's glow convinced him that they belonged here, that she was really in no danger – not with a roaring fire and a thick bag. And whatever else he could provide.

Reassured, he returned to his task, not letting himself think too far beyond the immediate need. And as first one fire-stick, then another lit up, their red glow felt like his cheeks glowing – if they hadn't been numb, frozen slabs. He'd looked at her, even though he'd said he wasn't going to, and now here he was looking behind him again.

But she was in the bag, her shape now a small trusting child's, breathing heavily.

He had the fire blazing in no time, branches crackling, great blue-orange flames leaping skyward. He wondered if she could feel it yet, but her teeth were clattering like torn-loose shutters in a gale, and she appeared to be hugging her knees up to her chin, making herself an impenetrable closed circle. If nothing else, her clothes would eventually get dry. He had them dangling from branches of small downed trees he'd dragged over. God knew how long it would take.

"Can you feel the heat in there?" he finally asked.

"Yes," she rasped.

"We can go back, if you want, after you've had some time to . . . "

"NO."

"Okay." Her refusal didn't surprise him, though he wondered if he'd feel the same if *he* were the one wet and cold. Scanning the forest's edge for his next load of wood, he hardly heard her voice at first. Finally he turned back toward her. She seemed to be no longer in a ball. And the violent shivering had stopped.

"Billy, would you get in here with me?"

Her words ambushed him. While only hours ago, he'd've seen this as the whole point, he found himself hesitating.

For three point two seconds.

In no time, he had his boots unlaced, his jacket off and was unbuttoning his shirt. When he unzipped the bag a foot, he winced. He still felt warm as hell, but worried that the inrush of cold air on her bare flesh would burn. Even though she was so small, there was barely room for them both. Squeezing within the folds, he molded his body to hers, gently placing one of his arms beneath her neck, not uncomfortably, the other draped over her waist. He was careful not to let his hands, unspeakably cold, more than graze her skin.

"Billy," she whispered, "are you naked?"

"Yes. Doctors say skin to skin is the best way to stoke up the body's fire." He waited one point five seconds. "In medical emergencies of this nature."

He expected her to protest, but she didn't. And her body already seemed to be trembling less. Closing his eyes, Billy saw firelight imprinted on the backs of his eyelids, and other things too: snow-laden branches shuddering in harsh wind, Dad and Grand-dad walking ahead of him. He was in the mountains, it was Thanksgiving Day, and while his ma lay sick in the hospital at Charleston, the men were hunting on Grand-dad's land. The gun he carried was very heavy, and he didn't want to use it, but it was his twelfth birthday present.

Finally he lagged so far behind he wondered if he were lost. He'd given up and sat against a tree for a long time. Then he'd heard a distant shot, and he stood up, his guts on fire. Though dread made his feet drag even heavier, he finally caught up with them in a small clearing. The split-open carcass of a doe lay on the snow, and his father held its steaming heart in his hand as he looked around at his son.

"Come watch us field-dress it," Dad ordered, turning back to his work. Billy shook his head and stood his ground, while his grandfather watched him. "Get over here," his dad yelled. "Leave the boy alone," Grand-dad had said, and though Billy waited for a long time, his

father never said anything else. Finally Billy turned and walked back
to the truck. When they finally joined him after dark, no one spoke
a word the whole way back to Grand-dad's house. Neither man ever
mentioned the incident, and it was the last hunt Billy was invited to go
on. Years later, his father sold his gun, without even asking him, to buy
a ballet outfit for his step-sister Nerissa. He didn't care, so glad was he
to be free of the requirement to kill. His mother was dead by Christmas.

He woke from the reverie with a start. If he had disturbed Seth,
she made no sign. Billy realized she'd stopped shivering, that his skin
against hers was slick with sweat. And while he'd been counting the
days, the hours and minutes till the moment when he'd finally be skin
to skin with her, he now only wanted out of this suffocating heat as
badly as he'd wanted out of his body at his mother's funeral. Lying in
the coffin, blue satin surrounding her, she'd looked as she'd used to,
before she got sick. He longed for her to open her eyes, smile and call
him to her side. Heat like shame rose into his neck and face, watering
his eyes. His mouth opened, and he moaned.

"Are you all right?" she whispered.

He was surprised to find he could speak. "Yes, fine. Are you?"

"Yes."

He carefully unzipped the bag, got out, stood up and quickly
resealed. But before he could change his mind, he grabbed his clothes,
stuck bare feet into ice-cold boots and made his way toward the other
bag. When he turned away from the fire and the cold hit him, he began
to realize what he'd done. Caught between going back to her bag or
going to find his own, he saw a vision: three deer standing at the edge
of the woods. The longer he stared, the more clearly they came into
focus in the moonlight, two does and a yearling – like observing new
details in a painting that had always been there, simply obscured by the
act of looking.

Since Billy had left the second bag where he'd dropped everything
at the edge of the forest, he would have to approach the deer. Freezing
now, he didn't hesitate. As he walked up, bent and plucked up the
bag, they never moved, calmly appraising him with the dark eyes Billy
imagined he could see reflecting firelight and a naked man. Rather than
move away from the creatures and closer to the fire, Billy unrolled the
bag right where it lay, got in and was asleep within seconds.

○

He woke with a start, heart pounding. It took him several seconds
to remember where he was. Then it came to him: the fire, the pond, his
mother's face, the deer. While he waited for his heartbeat to return to
normal, he remembered what he'd done, or, rather, hadn't done, inside
Seth's bag. In, out, fast – good in theory, it was a lot more complicated
in practice.

He braced for anger, or at least regret, but, as he waited, nothing
came, not even self-pity. At the edge of memory flickered the doomed
hunting trip the week his ma died, but it was like looking at ancient
family photographs from childhood: there you are, but not really.
Burrowing deeper into his bag, he enjoyed the womblike warmth. Now
he saw again, as if on a VCR screen, his dad holding up the doe's heart.
It had felt obscene, but why? He knew his dad believed in harvesting
everything. He surfaced, gulping cold air.

Lifting his head above the lip of his bag, he saw darkness diluting
to grey light; also, the fire was out. Or down to a few embers among the
ashes. He could hear Seth snoring gently. It made him smile, reminding
him of Bonnie, the only woman he'd ever slept with who snored – not
always and not loud, just enough to let you know she was alive.

At last he reached an arm out and brought his clothes into the bag.
Unable to wait for them to warm before putting them on, his bladder
about to burst, he quickly got on jeans, underwear, socks, tee-shirt, then
flannel shirt, not without pain. After letting his body warm them only
for a minute, he felt ready to climb back into the world.

Standing, he realized the sky was growing pinkish-yellow in the
east. Hugging himself, he turned his back on Seth, faced the woods, sad
to find his deer family gone, and peed for a long time. When he turned
around, he saw reddish streaks in the east, a whitish-yellow glimmer at
the bottom of the sky beyond the pond. Tip-toeing forward, he glanced
at Seth. She was bunched up in her bag again, though she no longer
snored. An exhilarating standing-on-his toes feeling overcame him,
and he exhaled loudly, breath billowing like smoke. Looking around,
he saw only the pond's frozen surface. It had lost its moonlit luster and
now appeared a dull grey sheet, except near the bank where it was
broken, showing the dark water beneath.

Then he heard it. At first the screaming of a million insects, the
sound soon became the ronk ronk ronk of a thousand pissed-off dogs.
He grinned. The geese appeared like starships uncloaking as he looked
right above him. They'd flown in from the west, from Meredith's
Pond or maybe even Seth's own backyard, flying low, as if to strafe the
campsite, and Billy thought he could almost reach up and touch their

bellies. Their raucous squabbling that usually seemed to him, if not pain, then at least complaint, sounded now like insane laughter right out of the dark heart of winter, and he laughed out loud. If he'd had a deer's heart, he would've held it aloft.

# Chapter Eighteen

Kanawha County, West Virginia
March 14, 1999


As soon as he parked the truck in the university visitor's lot, Billy felt a sea change in Della. She'd kept up a brave front all the way to Charleston, facing forward, her short-blonde-and-grey-haired head tilted back so she could survey the latest desecration to the kingdom through her bifocals – all in silence. But now she was walking, head down, in the light drizzle.

"Honey, I might not have time for classes right now if we get a nest of copperheads stirred up out in Putnam County."

Billy recognized the delaying tactic. "Think of the possibilities for recruiting volunteers here. Nothing like a bunch of riled-up college students to hit the pavement – I mean, fields – in favor of saving land from more asphalt."

She walked a half-step behind him as he looked for the building housing the registrar's office. It was impossible to put himself in Della's place. His entire life of entitlement rose in him like finger-pointing shame. A Charlton Heston baritone boomed inside his head: "The measure of a man's life is what he's done for others."

*All right. Okay.*

When he looked behind him, Billy saw Della standing stockstill, her hands clutching her purse before her. His towering aunt who could roof a house in a thunderstorm now looked like a private facing court martial.

"Billy Mike, I just don't know if I can do it. It's like these old legs're trapped in cee-ment."

He wanted Seth or Ira here to say the right words. Hell, even Bonnie! But there wasn't anybody but him.

"Not a problem," he said. "I'll just bring them out here. Don't go anywhere." He took two steps.

"Darlin', wait a minute."

He waved jauntily. "Won't take a minute."

"Billy Mike, come back here. Give an old woman two seconds to get her wind, and we'll go in."

He stopped. "You sure? I'll be glad . . . "

She stamped her foot. "I said I was coming."

Starting up the steps, he didn't have to turn again to know she was behind him.

○

"You say you're a high school graduate?" The girl, about nineteen, clearly didn't believe it. Billy wanted to slap her but was trying hard not to intervene.

"I said I was, didn't I?" Della sat perched on the edge of the chair. "But you're gonna have to spit out that gum to talk to us." When she reached a tissue toward her, the girl's jaw stopped working, as she stared at the woman in the plaid coat before her.

"Spit it right here, honey."

Glaring at Billy, she took the tissue and did as she was told.

"I'm afraid," she said, "we'll definitely need a transcript."

Della glanced the question at Billy. "A paper from your high school proving you graduated."

"Honey, that school's long gone. They consolidated ever' one in the county into one big factory school back before you were even born."

"Is a transcript needed if she doesn't seek a degree?" Billy interjected.

"I don't know," the girl said, shaking her head. "Let me check. I'll be right back."

As soon as she'd flumped off, Della turned and slugged her nephew on the arm. "What'd you say that for? 'Course I want a degree. I ain't milking all day and not wind up with any cream."

Billy fingered his bicep. "It's just a way to get you in the door. After the first quarter. . ."

"Hello, folks. I'm Jewel Belcher. Can I help y'all?"

Billy looked up into blue-green eyes surrounded by wavy auburn hair. In one long, quick swallow of a glance, he absorbed her buxom figure with a tiny waist and long, stockinged legs. While he tried to remember how to speak, Della picked up the slack.

"Well, the young lady there said I need proof that I graduated high school to go to school here, and I don't think I can get it, at least not right away."

Billy tore his eyes away from Jewel's face long enough to glance at his aunt. Looked like she wanted to do more than punch him in the arm. He found his voice.

"Does she really need it if she doesn't seek a degree right away?"

"Billy Mike, I'm not signing up under false pretenses. I *want* a degree!"

"Of course you do." To Billy's delight, Jewel sat down in the gum-chewer's chair. "Miss Stiltner doesn't know about Eldercollege. She's new."

"I'm not elderly, " Della snapped.

"Nothing could be more obvious," Jewel said. "Eldercollege is a new program for more mature returning students whose significant life experiences qualify them for entry to college."

Della finally relaxed, laid her purse down on the floor and slid back into the chair. Billy could see Jewel talking to a governor's cabinet about sprawl – and making them listen. (A thought for later.)

"Huh," Della snorted. "I don't know about 'significant,' but I raised two younguns, three counting Don, my husband."

Jewel looked solemn. "Husbands definitely count. Mine is almost able to eat by himself."

Billy had forgotten to look for a ring. Sure enough, now that he looked, there it was, gleaming like a miner's lamp. (Checking in with himself, he was surprised not to find his heart falling – this gal was a jewel all right, but not because of her luscious hair – because she held the keys to his aunt's future.)

"Eldercollege students don't need transcripts. A quick placement test to determine your level of mastery in reading, math and English and you're on your way. Spring quarter starts in two weeks."

Della's face clouded. "Tests?"

"No one fails. The tests just determine whether you're in regular, advanced or *intense* courses."

Thank God she hadn't said remedial.

"Are all the elders herded into the same corral?"

"No. Though you have the option of attending special seminars only for elders, and elders certainly may take their classes together – the better to form study groups, for instance – your classes are heterogeneous."

Della again looked at Billy. "You're thrown in with the younguns," Billy translated.

In the silence that followed, Billy heard keyboards clicking, print-outs unspooling and distant bells chiming from a downtown church. The ball, it seemed, was in Della's court. Jewel folded her lovely hands and waited. Billy concentrated on the calendar above the registrar's left shoulder and imagined the struggle of the last several weeks. He found himself unable to look beyond March 20, only six days away. The future, it came into his head, never existed. Every moment was a new river to cross. Just close your eyes and dive. He liked it that way.

Della breathed a long breath. "Okay, sign me up," she said.

Jewel rose. "Let me get some forms. We're lucky to get you, Mrs. Sizemore. You won't be sorry."

And she was gone in a rustle of skirt. He was about to comment how lucky they'd been to speak to Jewel, when he turned toward Della. Glasses off, she was dabbing her eyes with a tissue. He quickly picked up a catalog and began riffling pages.

As if it were written on the pages, he saw in his mind's eye: *What if you'd never come?*

He shook his head at the circumstances leading them both here today. It warmed him until he remembered the check (now in his wallet) he'd brought in case they went by a bank. The page he was looking at blurred: grants management became grand larceny. His heart began tapping like a bad piston. How much did you have to steal before you did serious jail time?

He jumped when he felt something touch his arm. *No cuffs!*

"Sorry I hit you, Billy Mike."

"No problem." When he looked at her, her face had lost twenty years. "It probably won't be the last time."

◯

By noon, Della had been interviewed by the Eldercollege director, met several students, taken three placement tests, filled out mountains of paperwork and wowed everyone she'd met. She'd borne up well, Billy had noted, but her shoulders were sagging, her chin dipping toward her chest when they finally left the advisor's office where she'd signed up for two classes – Composition and Rhetoric and Intro to Political Science – beginning spring quarter.

"I haven't been this outta gas since Hurricane Hugo left me with all them trees to cut up," she declared. "Let's go home!"

Picking up the pace, they nearly collided with a white-haired man emerging from an office.

"Excuse . . . " Billy began.

The man's blue eyes sparkled. "It's Billy Appleseed."

Billy gripped Dan Fountain's outstretched hand. "Acorn."

"From acorns mighty oaks grow. Good to see you again, son." His eyes flashed merrily toward Billy's companion. "Good morning, ma'am, I'm Dan Fountain. You must be Della."

Billy watched their eyes appraise each other. Gorbachev and Reagan. Carter and Sadat. Dylan and Young. Each seemed to like what he/she saw.

"We just finished signing her up for classes next term," Billy explained.

Dan's eyes never left Della's face as he nodded. "Then you must be starving. I was just heading downstairs for a bite. Would you two visionaries like to be my honored guests?"

"Thanks, Dan, but I think Della's – "

"We'd love to."

When Billy looked at his aunt, her weariness had evaporated. Dan gestured grandly, Della stepped off down the hallway like she was on a runway and Billy traipsed behind, shaking his head.

○

Della seemed oblivious to the furtive stares from a few lingerers in the faculty dining room. "More private, plus I want to show off my new fellow land lovers," Dan said, leading the way. He'd insisted on treating them. Ravenous, Billy pigged out on the country-fried steak, gravy and mashed potatoes, but Della had hardly touched a thing.

"I understand you've been fighting the good fight out there in Putnam County."

Her eyes, which had been riveted on the older man's face ever since they'd run into him, lowered.

"I don't know about that."

"Come on, Aunt Della. I told him everything."

Dan was undeterred. "From what your nephew tells me, you've been pretty much the Lone Ranger out there." And he eloquently summarized what Billy had told him, including her impassioned speech while her husband and half the township watched – never exaggerating, getting the facts right without flattery or spin. Della's eyes grew brighter as he talked.

"Now," he concluded, "I'd like you to know that I'm putting at your disposal the resources of Kanawha Land Trust, modest though our organization is; unruly, outrageous, contentious and downright cantankerous as the membership can be. What can we do to help you win, Della?"

"We need volunteers to divide up into work groups – a bunch to organize peaceful protests in front of Beck's, a bunch to lobby legislators, another bunch to contact media and a bunch to contact folks door-to-door if possible but phone, if that's more feasible. And we need to raise money, piles of it."

Dan had removed a small pad from his pocket and was taking notes.

"And we need something to stand for what we believe – you know, they got that damn blue cow."

"Aunt Della!" Billy said, mouth full of steak. "Your language!"

She ignored him. "I been thinking. You want people to be fighting *for* something, not *against*. Something that gets to the heart of what farms are – most people think pigs and chickens and cows. But I think about what makes crops grow. Here, let me show y'all what I did the other night."

As she bent toward her purse, Dan's eyes shone at Billy – a lesser man might've winked. Della unfolded a piece of notebook paper and laid it on the table between them. With black marker, Della had drawn a sun in one corner. Jagged rays beamed toward low, rolling ground on which a figure walked, hand outstretched, sowing seed. Simple as a child's drawing, the lines were thick and bold. Holding his breath, Billy looked at Dan.

The older man picked it up, held it closer and studied it for five seconds. "Sun, seed and the circle of life. You've nailed it, Della."

Glancing peripherally, Billy saw her tight smile, remembered the earlier tears. Mouth still full of potatoes, he spoke.

"Maybe you don't need poli. sci. after all. Maybe you need to run for governor."

She looked at her plate. "I *have* considered it."

Dan nodded approvingly, handing the paper back. "This state desperately needs a woman's managerial skills. I've always thought that anyone who can placate crying children with their greedy mouths forever open and who absolutely lack the power to clean up after themselves could handle a legislature – and a public – with one hand tied behind her back."

"Damn right," Della declared. Billy marveled. She'd cussed more today than he'd heard from her in her whole life heretofore.

"And women *need* infants to clean up after. Fulfills 'em."

Dan raised his water glass. "Makes 'em tough."

"Oh, no. Having a young'un tenders your soul. Take a woman who's pretty feisty when she's young: what some young bucks might call bitchy."

Dan nodded enthusiastically, eating with abandon. Billy laid his fork down and looked at the glaring sun in the middle of the table. He could feel it heating his neck and shoulders.

"What she really wants to boss is *herself,* her own body, and it comes out as the mothering instinct. Don't tell me humans don't have it ever' bit as much as animals. A woman who is truly boss of herself, wants that child to complete the circle – triangle, really – between herself, her child and her mate. First, she looks for that perfect mate, and when she's found the one she instinctively knows has the right chemical *stuff* – what do you call it, Professor?"

"DNA," Dan said, voice muffled by biscuit.

"And let's say she's *past thirty*." Billy wasn't about to acknowledge her look, so he took his first gulp of unsweetened tea. *How'd people drink this crap?*

"She's likely to know exactly what she wants – and unlike when she was fifteen, it's what she *needs*. And him, too – her mate – if he's got the gumption to realize it."

Dan lifted his glass. "Women for Congress! For President!"

Billy couldn't help it. "Some women aren't so good at cleaning up others' shit. They're better at creating it."

"A lot of men would say so," Dan agreed. "Junior congressmen, for instance." He smiled conspiratorially at Della.

"Exactly. These juniors will find out what's what, eventually maybe, but why not save time, find a good woman and marry her?"

"And then." Fork clutched in his right hand, Dan rocked an invisible infant in his arms. "Happily ever after."

"What do you think, Billy Mike?" Finally, Della cut her steak and took a tiny bite.

Stomach sour, he turned toward his aunt. "I think you know enough about innuendo to get credit right now for Comp & Rhet."

Della looked at Dan mystified. "In-you-what?"

Dan shrugged, covering his two-thirds' eaten steak with his napkin. "Some egghead term for poetry, I think. Way too intellectual for me." Now he did wink at Billy. "So: who's the girl?"

Billy's stomach jumped. "Girl?"

"Who's gonna be governor or president or speaker of the house . . . after you bed and wed her – not in that order, of course."

"I don't know what you're talking about."

Billy found himself grateful the diningroom was virtually empty by now.

"Her name's Bonnie," Della mock-whispered. "And she's hot as a firecracker and mean as a snake."

"Della!" He found himself blushing like the time in third grade, when Tim Hussong outed him to Valerie Goins, to whom he'd given an anonymous valentine.

"And all she wants is one little senator."

Billy stood. "Dan, thank you for this tasty lunch, for your kind offer of help." He glared at Della. "And for this delightful conversation."

"Don't mention it. We'll do it any time you can squeeze in time from lobbying the legislature. You know what they say about politics, Della," Dan said.

She shook her head, chewing steak.

"Makes strange bedfellows of us all."

And while the new bosom buddies laughed, Billy heard Seth saying: "You'll marry that woman."

When hell freezes over.

He realized he was sweating inside his clothes.

# Chapter Nineteen

Shawnee Springs, Ohio
Saturday, March 11, 1999

Billy felt Seth walking behind him but didn't dare turn. As soon as he'd awakened her, he'd been ambushed by anger – it rose like her breath to envelope him. And she crawled out of the bag fully clothed. He hadn't noticed her things were no longer draped on the branch where he'd put them. She'd silently rolled up the bag and stood up. As she faced him in the gathering dawn, every wrinkle and line on her face stood out in bold relief. Her hair was tangled, her face yellow-grey, eyes transparently dull. He was too shocked for a moment to speak.

"Let's go," she said. "I want to get back before Paul gets up."

*Damn.* He'd absolutely forgotten the kid.

"You all right?" So lame. She was obviously terrible.

"Fine." It was nearly a growl.

He glanced around at the pond, then back to the woods. He wanted to tell her about the deer, the geese, his father and mother, but he didn't understand himself what had happened. Instead he turned his back and followed her into the woods.

It was much easier to navigate in daylight – just a little bunch of trees. Occasionally a cardinal or junco flitted from branch to branch. No turkey buzzards. No snow crocuses. Just trees and snow and unrelenting cold. He'd be glad to get back to the house. There'd be time later for figuring out what the hell had happened.

He believed he could now answer Kieron's question.

○

As soon as they walked through the gap in the fence and entered the yard, Billy felt weariness settle onto him like lead weights. And hunger. Before he thought better of it, he blurted, "Don't suppose you got any bacon and eggs in there?"

She shot him a sideways look. "You jumped out of my bed, now I'm supposed to feed you?"

His knees nearly buckled. Had she wanted him? He stopped, grabbed her arm. "Look, about last night . . . "

She tore her arm away and glared.

"All right," he muttered. "I'll just be leaving."

"Get in here." Turning, she stomped up the step to the kitchen door, unlocked it and disappeared inside. What could he do but follow? She'd left the door wide open.

After throwing the gear in the truck, he entered the kitchen, removed his boots and sat down at the table. Soon she padded back in wearing the slippers and robe he'd seen three weeks ago. "Paul's snoring like a baby," she said, her mouth, her entire face relaxed, the smaller lines smoothed away. Before he could answer, she turned and began banging pots and pans around.

◯

Bacon, eggs, toast and coffee had never tasted better. He wolfed it down, while she picked at her food, mostly drinking the coffee. Hell, yes – she was drinking coffee. Black. No herbal alternative in sight. He didn't take it for a good sign.

When he'd swallowed the last bite, she spoke. "I'm ready to tell you why I told you never to mention Lloyd Kieron."

She was gazing out the window, chewing at a fingernail – a gesture he'd never seen before. Even though the sun hadn't penetrated the clouds outside, the window was full of snow-reflected light. She waited several seconds.

"Lloyd Kieron is Paul's father."

He managed to get his cup down before spilling coffee all over him. She might as well have kicked him.

"I'd been to the college clinic and confirmed the worst. Then, when I couldn't stand being alone with it anymore, I went to Lloyd's office. He was reading student papers, and he never stopped the entire time I was there. I told him everything. He finally said, 'Elizabeth, you've got to be more careful.' Then he went on grading. I waited and waited for him to look at me, but that was it. Finally I left the office."

Billy inhaled, realized he'd been holding his breath. He sat back and stretched stiff legs. His hip still had a ghost of an ache from sleeping on the ground. Last night seemed eons ago. He couldn't even remember right now what the farm fight was about. The meal had become a rock in his gut.

"You saw him at the village building rally."

She nodded.

"And after I made you speak, you were telling him to go to hell, not me."

She didn't answer, chewing the nail again.

"But why are you telling me this . . . now?"

She finally looked at him hard. "You pedestaled me the same way you pedestaled him, Billy."

He grinned even though it felt wrong. "I've admired you, yes. I admired him until the day in the church when he treated you and Ira like shit."

"No," she interrupted, "you've never stopped. It's probably why you couldn't fuck me last night. You think I'm a saint. Well, now you know I'm not. I've made a ton of mistakes." When they heard running water, she glanced at the ceiling. "Like neglecting my son to run around protesting."

"Does Paul know . . ?"

She shook her head. "You know what I told Lloyd at the flea market?"

He waited.

"That I didn't want any of his fucking money. I only want him to know his son."

"Does James know?"

"That's why we're here. I finally told him. The week before we left." She closed both eyes a second before continuing. "He said he didn't think he could still be Paul's father." Her jaw clenched. "Can you imagine . . . after thirteen years?"

He could. Neither of the women his father had married after Ma died were ever mothers to him. But thirteen years of believing your son was biologically yours only to find out . . . Now Billy knew why James was coming.

"I've suffered for it – plenty. Now Lloyd Kieron is going to admit what he did to me."

"Paul is a wonderful kid, Seth."

She was staring outside again. She quit chewing the nail and thrust one hand into her dull, lifeless hair, combed it back, let it fall. Above them, a toilet flushed.

He lowered his voice. "So what're you gonna do about Paul? He may need more help than you and I can give him."

"Paul will be fine. He knows that all we've got is each other."

"Seth." His voice was raspy. "That's not true."

"And you. You've been a friend, Billy." She actually smiled. "To Paul."

"Thanks for breakfast."

He rose on shaky legs. If he didn't get out fast, he was going to say something he'd regret. He rose and staggered toward the door. She stayed silent while he laced his boots. At last, he stood at the door, his hand on the knob. "By the way, as of yesterday Blue Jacket has raised three quarters of a million dollars."

"Good for you."

They both heard footfalls on the stairs. *In, out, fast.*

# Chapter Twenty



Billy sat alone in the Trout sipping his fourth beer. Where the hell was Zamora, and what had he meant by "getting down and dirty with Schuyler" when he'd phoned this afternoon, gotten him up with a no-sleep hangover?

Sitting in the last booth in the rear near the fireplace, he was glad he could feel the heat. It reminded him of how cold he'd been last night. And though he tried to lose himself in the song playing on the jukebox, he couldn't keep his mind off Seth. He swallowed another gulp of the tasteless beer. Ever since the phone had rung like a summons to an execution, he'd been living in a hazy blur. What he was sure of, though, was that he could never go back to that moment when he'd decided not to make his move inside Seth's bag. But it didn't feel rational and conscious enough to constitute an actual decision – so then why was he worrying it like a loose tooth? And getting drunk, to boot – on CitFarm's money! He no longer made an effort to stick to his allowance, didn't want to know how much he was spending. Whatever it was, it wasn't worth the headache.

The longer he sat, the more beer he drank, the less he cared whether Mark showed or not. Despite the geese this morning, the whole farm thing tasted sour. Was his commitment that flimsy? Had he been after one thing, and one thing only, and when that had been denied him (by himself, for God's sake), was he left with nothing?

Just like with Bonnie?

He sure didn't want to go there. Where the hell was Zamora?

He wagged his head and swore, raised his glass to the waitress who frowned and ignored him, went back to chatting with the Burke students. Apparently he'd lost his ability with the younger ones, too.

He was getting drunk. Which made him think of Mark. Oh, well. If you can't beat 'em, join 'em. Closing his eyes, he dropped into an intense reverie. Deep inside his head, he began rewriting the sleeping bag scene, same setting and cast; totally different dialogue and action. Seth was whispering in his ear as they lay side by side in golden light, his warm hand cupping her breast . . .

"Yo, Billy-man."

When he looked up into Mark's leering face, the room seemed darker. How long had he been sitting here anyway?

"Looks like you got ahead of me. You look crocked."

Billy waved it off. "Just got to sleep when you called."

"Aha." Mark grinned. "You and Miss Seth doing the dance?"

Billy wanted to kill him right there. Beer mug to the bridge of his nose. He sat up straighter. "What's up?"

Mark looked over his shoulder. When he turned back, his eyes glittered in the firelight. All coked-up, as usual? At least he lowered his voice.

"The only reason I'm letting you in on this is because I respect you for what you did on the concrete company deal." The maniacal grin was back. "Brothers-in-arms, baby." He punched Billy's arm.

"Talk," Billy said, promising to himself as the waitress set the pitcher that Mark must've ordered down on the table: *No more beer.*

Mark sloshed the draft into a mug, gulped hugely before replying. "Since nothing's happening on Wood Thrush, we . . . "

"Something's happening. Freeman's meeting with trustees tomorrow – he would've today if he could've. If they come around and don't re-zone, most developers won't give a shit about buying that land."

"My sources say that ain't necessarily so." Mark wiped his mouth after emptying the glass, began pouring another. "Might be some who aim to purchase now and wait till the next board comes in. Or, hell, put up their own men and buy votes – anything's possible in America."

When the kid laughed his high-pitched squawk, the sound felt like a dentist's drill behind Billy's eyes. The dials on his uh-oh meter were twirling, and he had no idea, in his present condition, whether his instincts could be trusted or not.

"Drink up, Billy. You look like shit." He saw that Mark was halfway through another glass. Well, maybe it would be to his advantage to have the kid drunk.

"You go ahead. I'm a couple pitchers ahead," he lied.

Mark ducked his head. "So we need an *event*, you know." He looked around as if the cops might be closing in. "Something like slashing a few tires, fucking up a few trucks – *you* know." He grinned slyly.

Billy put on his best poker face. "So what do you have in mind?"

"Okay, but I don't care whether you're in or not, we're gonna do this. And don't tell Freeman. You heard him the other night." Mark's Adam's apple bobbed as he drank. "Fuckin' Ghandi-Martin Luther King motherfucker."

Uncertain how he might've reacted to this same scene even two weeks ago, he was now seeing Mark through Seth's eyes: *Machiavelli . . . cruel excuse for a political philosopher.* With the heat from the nearby fire flushing his cheeks, he realized that, like it or not, her eyes were now his. Mark shoved a full glass at him. "Come on, now. Drink up."

As Billy sipped, he knew he had to go along with everything for awhile or the jig was up. The kid looked at his watch. "In ten minutes, I'm driving to Cedarton. Know where Gooseflight Acres is?"

"Schuyler's latest development. West side of town."

"Yup. Grover and Howser scoped it last night: no security. Schuyler figures he owns Cedarton: no opposition *there*. It's Shallow Springs he's gotta worry about. And" – he slammed his fist down drunkenly, drawing a look or two – "he's goddamn right. We're gonna torch one of his works in progress, the half-finished one that sits way back. You can't see it at all from the road. We park a half-mile away at Burger King, cut through some trees that separate the strip mall from the development, throw some gas, light it and run. We'll be sleeping like babes by the time anyone reports it."

Billy asked as calmly as possible: "But how does this help CitFarm?"

"It lets Schuyler and all developers know we're a force to be reckoned with, that if we do it in Cedarton, we'll surely do it when and if building ever starts in Shawnee Springs."

Billy figured he'd done a good job of staying stone-faced, though his mind was racing. He wished to hell he hadn't had those beers, that he'd gotten about four hours' more sleep. Mark glanced at his watch again. "Five minutes till we gotta split. Grover and Howser are already there. You in?"

The kid had put all his chess pieces in place before moving his queen. The deed was going down, with Billy's approval or not. And there was no use trying to talk him out of it – at least not here, not now. Maybe Grover and Howser would be easier to talk down. It made him tired as hell.

Mark leered at him. "We gotta go."

Billy stood. "Let me recycle some of this beer. You finish the rest, I'll pay, then we're outta here."

He didn't wait for Mark's answer, hauled himself out of the booth and strode quickly through the doorway into the bar area. Thank God the phone was out of Mark's view from where he sat in the dining room. He dialed Woody and quickly filled him in.

"Don't go, Bilbo. I'll call the cops. They'll be at Gooseflight in minutes."

"Then it's bad press for CitFarm. Those guys won't keep their mouths shut. For all I know, they're gonna leave their signature at the site. It's better if we talk 'em down. Grab Fred Pennington or whoever else you can trust and haul ass over there. I'll stay with Mark." He hung up before hearing a reply, though he felt a tiny pang. Hadn't he railroaded his plan past Woody just the way Mark had bulldozed over him? Too late to worry about that now.

○

It was dark by the time they hit Cedarton's city limits. Though Billy had wanted to follow in the truck, Mark insisted he ride with him in the kid's ancient Monte Carlo.

"Too many cars could spoil the getaway."

He knew Mark already suspected him of making the phone call. They'd remained silent the entire six miles, Billy warring with himself over whether to intervene now or later. Finally he couldn't help himself: "You sure this is such a good idea, Zamora?"

"Guaranteed to get Shyster's attention."

"If this backfires, it could really hurt us."

"It worked at the cement plant. This is the same thing."

"Totally different. Getting mean worked because *they* were mean, releasing toxic chemicals into the air that made people sick. Also, we didn't burn down any houses."

"House: singular. And it's in a deserted development. Nobody lives there yet."

Billy shook his head. "It's still a house. Imagine photos in the *Cedarton Sun* of a burned-down house. Folks won't even hear that no one lived in it."

"You wussin' out on me, man?"

"It's strategy. With the township considering re-zoning and our need to raise more funds, we've got too much to lose right now by bad p.r."

"How much more can we raise in a week?"

"What if someone gets hurt?"

"That didn't bother you last time."

Billy closed his eyes. His headache raged.

"Remember what you said then, Billy-man?"

Billy looked out the window. Wasn't it time they were getting there?

"You said, 'What if King had thought about his followers whose heads were gonna get bashed every time . . . '"

Billy interrupted. "Where the hell are we?" But when he glanced at Mark, the punk's satisfied smirk told him everything. He'd gotten on his high horse and hadn't paid attention. Mark cut off the highway, slammed on his brakes and spewed gravel, his headlights shining on the sign: Sylco Cement. "Hey, Gooseflight is on the *other* side of town."

Mark looked at his watch. "Yup. 'Bout now, Grover's lighting the place up. If you step out of the car, you might be able to see the blaze on the skyline."

"Goddammit, Zamora," he yelled. When Billy's vision cleared, he saw the blade in Mark's hand reflecting light from the streetlamp above.

"Whoa, Bilbo. Maybe a walk back to Shawnee would cool you off." His evil grin seemed an extension of the knife. He was carving small circles in the air between them.

Billy grabbed for his wrist, but Mark sliced upward. Billy yelped, retracting his hand too late. His palm was flaming, but he didn't have time to look at the wound before Mark went crazy, bringing his leg up to kick violently. "GET OUTTA MY CAR, GODDAMMIT."

Paralyzed, Billy's brain shut down, and it was all he could do to find the door handle and open it. Before he could get out, Mark thrust his booted foot forward furiously and propelled Billy onto the pavement. Landing on all fours, he crawled as fast as he could toward the light, a mistake since it was the front of Mark's car. All Mark had to do was gun forward and it was all over. But he stayed where he was, panting, appreciating the joke of being killed in front of the company he'd brought to its knees.

Mark started the engine. Then he rammed it in reverse, gunned backwards, slammed it in drive and peeled out, scattering loose stone. One hit Billy right above the eye. When he lifted his hand toward the light, a jagged stream of blood flowed down his wrist, soaking his sleeve. It was too dark to see how deep the cut ran. Plus, he was afraid of passing out if he did know, so he stuck the injured hand under his other arm and applied pressure. He stood up, grateful to find he wasn't light-headed. He headed up the road back toward Shawnee Springs, certain it was too late to do anything about Mark's henchmen. He had to get somewhere and think.

○

Much later, Billy opened the door of Ira's house, grateful his friend wasn't there. He would not have entered if the Tercel had been parked outside, so he figured his roommate was at the school rehearsing that damn play for the eight-hundredth time. The first thing Billy did was wash and bandage the wound – not all that deep, and it hadn't bled that much on the old tee-shirt the farmer who had picked him up had given him. "Been in a fracas or two myself," the old guy said, grinning. Billy didn't contradict him.

"A scratch," he'd tell Seth when she saw the bandage. But would she ever see it? He didn't feel the usual surge in his groin when he thought of her, a sure sign it was over. Shit. It was *all* over now. Wait'll the media found out CitFarm had burned down one of Schuyler's crackerboxes. And Mark would make sure that Schuyler knew who'd done it.

He slumped into Ira's rocker and immediately felt the presence of his friend in the room – from the crumpled wad of bedding on the floor to the books on the table: Thoreau's *Maine Woods, Tao Te Ching* and Volume I of *The Chronicles of Narnia*. He'd tried to get Ira to read *Lord of the Rings* for years to no avail. "You're the only hobbit I need to know," he'd deadpan. And here the guy was reading C. S. Lewis. *Shit.*

Billy rocked harder, floorboards squeaking beneath him. For all his so-called activism, he'd had about as much effect on the life of this town as the crow whose complaint he could hear outside. Maybe his dad had been right: his education *had* made him unfit to work. He'd so far been able to fight off those words. He was working to save the farm, a sacrifice his dad, money man that he was, could never understand.

Billy's hand throbbed. He felt dizzy. Did he understand it himself? He'd been sure his activist days were over since that night. *Jeez Louise.* His hand was now sizzling with pain. It was somehow focusing his attention, taking him where he'd been careful not to go for the last two years.

Sylco Cement. Quarter moon. August twenty-seventh.

The name of the guy caught in the fire had been Andy Partridge, originally from Chicago, part-time Burke student and father of infant twins, Liam and Erin – which Billy had found out by calling the hospital daily till the guy's release. He'd even sent flowers to the guy, talked to his wife on the phone a coupla times.

He slowed the rocker, his head whirling. The pain was ebbing a bit, the dizziness and nausea passing. He kept the chair still, looking around him. Well, one thing was certain: he wasn't Ira. No, Ira was a better man than he. And Ira had a mission in life – two, actually: Amber, plus the Burke School kids. And he, Billy, had squat – not even a girlfriend. He began rocking again, remembering what had taken place earlier that hot August night.

"I just want you to consider," Bonnie had yelled at him, "the *possibility* of having a child with me someday, that's all."

He had laughed bitterly. They'd been about to make love, and after he'd unwrapped the condom, she touched his hand, shook her head.

"What kind of a mother would you make?" he said, both hands behind his head on the pillow in Bonnie's dark bedroom. "You're as needy as an infant yourself."

She slammed the pillow on his face. He jumped up and started dressing. "You're fucking crazy, Bonnie, you know that."

Then, as he was buttoning his shirt, he heard her gasping. The wild and crazy Bonnie, the only girl he'd ever met who could drink him under the table, whose sexual adventurousness exceeded even his, was crying over a hypothetical baby! She was just like all the others, who allegedly loved sex but really lived to have kids. (Seth, too; Seth, too.)

He had walked out that night without saying another word. Walked out and nearly killed a man and called it activism, called it doing good.

He watched blood flow down his arm. Springing up, he felt light-headed again and immediately sat back down, unmoving this time. He was ready to face facts.He caught a quick image of Seth's flashing green eyes. He would never be her equal; Dad was right. Unfit for work. Ruined by a life of free-lance activism.

Then out of the blue, he remembered the challenge Garth Erickson had flung at him in the gym after Seth had left: "There's a farmer in you, Acorn." He regretted he'd never get to try the thing he had absolutely no qualifications for.

He looked around him and saw the half-graded papers, Ira's mug with its thrice-used teabag, his taped-up reading glasses and garage-sale desk chair over which hung the awful robe Ira'd been wearing that Sunday morning nearly three weeks ago when Billy had been reduced to begging. It was time. It was past time.

He stood up. Whoa: a little dizzy. At Ira's desk, he sat down, plucked an envelope from the desk organizer. Then he pulled out his wallet. Tucked in a corner was the folded slip of blue paper, as pristine as the day she'd dropped it in the collection plate. He quickly copied her address from the check, his hand throbbing. He'd already licked the envelope before thinking about adding a note. What would he say? See you in another lifetime? He thought of Paul, saw the boy's shining face the night he'd shared his big secret. *Good luck, kiddo.* He was glad he'd left his stereo in the boy's room. He had enough CDs in the truck to get him to where he was going. (Wherever that was.)

One more envelope . . . Billy paused. He'd known all along the treasurer's job might provide more than living expenses. When the bank opened in the morning, he'd be there for a withdrawal: severance pay. Quickly, he scrawled Woody's name and address. He'd be long-gone by the time the checkbook reached Blue Jacket's president. Then he'd know, then they'd all know . . .

He had his gear packed and coat on when, without letting himself think, he picked up the phone and dialed the number he still had by heart.

"Bon, it's me."

"Uh huh."

"I'm taking off."

"Sayonara."

"Something went down today. You're gonna hear about it on the news, and I want you to know the truth."

"Your strong suit."

Why wasn't he slamming the phone down? But his hand hurt a lot worse than Bonnie's words did. He told her what had happened.

"So I was too idiotic, drunk or whatever, to prevent it. You know what it'll do to CitFarm."

"Shit."

Was that sadness he heard? He took a deep breath. "But that ain't why I'm calling."

He made it snow on skaters inside the little glass ball on Ira's desk, a Christmas present from one of his kids. He could imagine Ira staring into it beside some little girl who was not Amber.

"I'm calling to tell you I'm sorry."

"For what?"

"Being an asshole, not knowing I had a great thing when I had it, being selfish as hell."

She sniffled.

"Tell Ira . . . " He saw a shopping list in Ira's terrible scrawl: beets, tofu, Frosted Flakes. Ira didn't eat Frosted Flakes – *he* did. "Nothing, nothing. Look, I gotta go."

"Where?"

"Goodbye, Bonnie."

He laid the receiver carefully back in its cradle as if it might explode.

# Chapter Twenty-One



He slept fitfully, his dreams full of arguments with Bonnie, Seth, Ira and even Dan Fountain, as he fought to convince everyone he encountered to go to college (even in the dream, he suspected there wasn't really a college at all, that he was persuading them to do something that was impossible, or that they'd regret, that might, in fact, be harmful, but he couldn't stop himself). Finally Ira became his father, who just laughed at him. "You've been, and look at you!" He awoke in a sweat, filled with rage and shame, thinking of the bourbon bottle till he remembered he'd thrown it in a dumpster yesterday, half-full.

He rose and quickly dressed. Something about the light was drawing him outside. He managed to get downstairs without the floor squeaking too loudly. Finally, he got outside and drew a deep breath. Thaw was in the air: spring, possibility. He walked through the gate into the pasture, then into a little forest where he used to hide out when there were no cousins to play with and the adults were talking endlessly. It reminded him of the grove he and Seth had entered on their moonlit mission five days ago. He thought of Paul. Was James there yet? No, not till Sunday. But Billy wouldn't be there to . . . to what?

He snorted, scaring a red-winged blackbird into flight. Did he think he could make everything okay for everyone? *Yeh, dumbass, you do.* Whose voice was that? He walked even faster. Probably Bonnie. He laughed, and it rang among the pines. What bullshit. He was never going back, despite what he'd promised Della. Face Bonnie? He'd rather lose his left nut. And since Seth and the rest had no doubt labeled him Judas by now, he'd accommodate them. He'd kept enough money to take him somewhere south. Maybe he'd finally get that college degree and a job. He laughed again. No, the old man was right. He was unemployable.

And here Della was hungering for it. Well, some people made a lot more of a college education than he had, and he was glad she would get the chance.

Emerging from the forest, he found himself in a clearing which sloped gently downward to a meadow and creek flowing fast with snowmelt. Though unfamiliar, it resembled many another little sheltered cove on Grand-daddy's farm.

He heard the small, solemn lowing of a single cow. Unable to locate
the animal as he glanced left and right, shading his eyes against the
harsh sunlight, he walked a few paces forward and found her in front
of a downed ash tree, lying on her side. A beautiful brown Swiss, she
turned suffering eyes up at him. For some reason – why, he'd never
figure out – he knew instantly that she was in labor. And in trouble.

Slowly he approached her. She raised her head, but the rest of her
bulk clung like a rock to the hillside. He wondered how long she had
lain here. How often did the Janikowskis check on the tiny herd that
remained of Grand-dad's once-huge stock? No doubt Clyde Stevens'
bull had gotten into the pasture last fall and done the dirty deed for
which this old gal was paying the price.

He patted her head. She was obviously exhausted by what so far
must've been futile efforts. Pulling her tail aside, Billy saw no signs of
impending birth except the enlarged vaginal lips. He remembered how,
at ten, he'd watched his grandfather pull a calf. He'd been amazed at
the trusting eyes of the best milk cow in the herd as Grand-daddy drew
on a long plastic glove.

"Holy shit," Billy breathed aloud, starting to shake.

He replaced the tail and sat on the ground near the animal's head.
A great shudder seized her. Contractions. He looked toward the trees
from where he had come. Della probably knew something about animal
midwifery – she'd no doubt pulled one or two herself – or they could
call the vet. *No. You do it.* This time he knew whose voice it was.

You think I can't do it, old man?

*Well. You can't do much, despite all that college I paid for.*

Not everybody thinks so.

*Name somebody?*

Garth Erickson wants me to help him farm.

*You don't know a goddamn thing about farming.*

I can learn.

*All right. Pull this calf.*

His shakes had ceased. He rose and walked behind the creature.
Didn't want to startle her now. He took off his jacket, laid it aside
and rolled his shirt sleeve as far up his forearm as he could, feeling the
sun on his exposed flesh, thankful that Mark hadn't sliced his right
hand. Then, kneeling behind her, he relifted the tail, gently inserted
his fingers into the warm lips of her vulva. Her muscles were soft and
yielding. He paused only a moment before plunging his whole hand and
then arm upward, probing for the calf he knew was there, praying it was
still alive.

Billy thought of Ishmael in *Moby Dick*, who sank his bare hands into tubs of whale sperm, getting high on the rich, warm smell and feel of the lifestuff. He ran his arm further inside, feeling a body, then a pulse. The calf was alive, but it was twisted, stuck. No wonder the Swiss couldn't get it out.

Pulling his arm back a few inches, Billy found the forelegs. Grasping them, he pulled, gently at first, waiting to see the mother's reaction, but she was too either too tired to care or had decided to trust him. Spreading his knees farther apart for better traction, he heaved with all he had. But the head was jammed, probably against the mother's pelvic bone. He pushed the calf back. "Don't worry," he whispered. "I'll get you."

Billy stood on surprisingly sure legs. By this time the sun had moved higher into the sky, and sweat was streaming down his forehead. Though a breeze blew, it wasn't cooling him yet. Also, he realized his arm had grown numb, and his fingers were beginning to tingle. He ached to quit, knew that if he stopped to listen, he'd hear Al Acorn saying *failure, failure*. But he wouldn't listen – not this time. Gotta get that cow on her feet.

Striding around her, he tried grasping her head and shoulders and pulling her up. Nothing doing. Stepping back behind her, he bent down and with both hands pushed her great hind end. She moaned and then moved forward a bit. "All right, Bessie!" he shouted. Once more without thinking, he got down on one knee and pushed with both hands. Suddenly she lurched to her feet, and before she had time to sink down again, Billy re-inserted his hand just as her contractions kicked in again. Her muscles gripped his arm as a great wave of despair pulsed through him. He felt for the calf's head, his bandaged hand draped across the broad back, grasping flesh, trying to hang on.

Closing his eyes against the sun, he saw swirling stars, then flames, then darkness. This was it. The calf's head bumped his hand. Joyously, he grabbed hooves and pulled, grabbing onto a limb of the downed tree with his other hand. The Swiss gasped, and the calf was sucked back into the cavity from which it had come, but Billy pulled harder, teeth clenched, until both arms ached while the mother strained to help. The calf was halfway out, despite the great negative pressure to be drawn back inside.

"We're getting there, Mama," he yelled.

Letting go of the branch, Billy stood straight up, planted his feet firmly and pulled with everything he had, sweat pouring into his eyes. Suddenly his arm, shoulder, legs and feet were awash in birth fluid.

Ecstatic, he exhaled, ignoring the smell, realizing he'd been holding his breath, grunting and breathing out only when the Swiss did. The lips of the vulva were stretched thin around the dark head. A few more heaves, shudders and gentle pulls from him, and the calf was out to its chest.

In no time, the entire calf stood free, Billy had cut the umbilical as cleanly as he could with Grand-daddy's case knife, and the great beast stood licking her newborn from head to toe. Billy wanted to laugh, to dance. Instead he reared back his head and hollered as loud as he could, making sounds he'd never known he could make, sounds a newborn makes when forced into the light.

And as he stared through sun-stars whirling before his eyes, he thought he saw Grand-daddy and his dad bent down beside the calf, as if inspecting his work. Solemnly, Al Acorn extended his hand, and Billy saw it held the same doe's heart he'd offered his son a lifetime ago. This time, Billy understood – it was not a threat but a gift – and he reached out to take it. But their images faded, and he was left staring into the eyes of the brand-new calf shivering beside its mother on brittle-bendy legs.

# Chapter Twenty-Two

Shawnee Springs, Ohio
Saturday, March 18, 1999

The first thing Billy noticed when he pulled down Seth's driveway
was Ira's old beat-up Tercel. Good, he thought. Maybe he's softened her
up for me.

He couldn't help but notice the contrast between now and the
last time he'd been here, the morning after the night at the pond.
He patted his shirt pocket, felt the envelope containing the cashier's
check. What he didn't feel, though, was Dad's letter. Pieces of it were
floating in the muddy Kanawha, heading for the Ohio, the Mississippi,
then the sea.

It had been after eleven when he finally hit Shawnee Springs last
night, and he'd gotten a room at the Simon Kenton Motel, fell on the
bed and slept in his clothes. He didn't wake up until some kids started
screaming outside around ten.

It had taken him a few seconds to remember. Then he'd called Ira,
who'd told him there'd been no fire at Goose Run. Woody had got the
cops there in time to run off Mark's henchmen. However, photos of gas
cans, rags and CitFarm signs did appear in the papers.

"Jeez, you don't know how sorry . . . "

Ira cut in curtly, "We're meeting at Seth's tonight to plan the final
round. Best come on out and face the music."

Now, for the hundredth time, Billy patted the document like a hot
compress above his heart. A lot had happened since the morning Seth
made him bacon and eggs. Everything, in fact.

He cut the engine, peered at the house. He half-expected to
see them sitting at the kitchen table, but maybe they were in the
living room, talking as he had the first time he'd come over with the
Valentine candy. Thinking of the candy made him wince. *What an
asshole.*

By the time he stood on the porch, it was twilight, and he could
smell the earth. The thaw, along with day-long sunshine, had left the
fields steaming, and a light breeze was wafting the rich, black odor right
past him. Then the porch light snapped on, the door opened to reveal
Ira, an inscrutable expression on his face.

"Just got a call from Woody. Matilda's sister's sick. They had to go
up to Englewood, but he told me all we need to know."

Billy's heart lurched. *I'll bet.*

Ira stepped out onto the stoop and pulled the door shut behind him. When he turned around, he was smiling his shit-eatingest grin. "We did it, Bilbo. We raised a mill."

Billy's knees went soft.

"Woody said the last few days, the post office box was stuffed. Folks from everywhere: Burke alumni, farmers from as far away as California who'd read about us. School kids, environmental groups. The average donation was probably five hundred smackers."

"So we've got enough – "

" – To make a showing. But we still don't know if we have buyers to partner with."

Angels, Woody had said. Earth-minded angels.

Before Billy could respond further, the door flew open again. When Seth stepped into the light, her eyes were blazing.

"I've got a couple of things to say to you, Mr. Machiavelli."

"Whoa, whoa. I tried to stop Zamora."

"Well, you didn't try hard enough. And who had to explain the whole thing to the media? I did, Billy Acorn. Where were you when the hard questions were being asked?"

"Actually I was in West Virginia."

"You picked a helluva time to get in touch with your roots while we were doing damage control up here." Her green eyes smoked as she stepped closer. "Thanks so much for letting me face Wendy Small, the volunteers and farmers not knowing if we'd be ridden out of town on a rail." She stomped her foot. "Thanks for worrying us to death about you. Damn you, Billy."

He wanted to hug her to calm her down, but figured she'd really go off if he touched her. *Worried?* – he clutched it like a frayed rope.

"And you show up now, *after* the hard part's over." She was so close, she was spitting on him. "This is the most chickenshit example of copping out I've ever seen."

"Hey, folks." It was Ira, leaning in the doorway. "Wind's picking up. They say it's gonna snow again before midnight. Why don't we continue the reunion inside?"

○

Inside, the house had a different feel to it. There was something in the air – he could almost smell it. That's when it hit him: they were going to press charges. They'd made the decision sitting at this very table, where they'd pulled out chairs and were now sitting. Officer

Denny Newsome was on his way. Grand larceny. He'd go quietly, no handcuffs.

"Here's the money." He threw the cashier's check down on the table. "I see y'all have already tried and convicted me, but I never spent a dime."

Seth and Ira looked at the piece of paper – or what remained of it. It'd gotten sweat-soaked while he'd pulled the calf – might even have gotten a little blood on it. They looked blankly at each other. They hadn't known. That meant only one thing: Woody hadn't told them. The old man had gotten the checkbook in the mail all right (he'd sent it certified), seen the withdrawal, and hadn't said a word. Billy fell into the chair Seth had pulled out for him.

"Maybe you'd better tell us what this is about," Seth said softly.

Billy took a deep breath. "My dad said he wasn't going to bankroll me anymore. And I finally faced the fact that he was right, I was no damn good, and . . . " He could not find a safe direction in which to look, so he stared right back at her. " . . . I thought our cause was lost and I had let Zamora ruin us. I knew I would never be as good as you two, so I might as well be who I was, take some money and run."

Now she was shaking her head side to side. Ira picked up the check and, without looking at it, began tearing it into tiny pieces.

"I didn't run far – my grand-dad's farm in West Virginia. It took me six days until I knew I couldn't do it. I . . . " He saw the calf barely standing on spindle legs. He could never tell them, tell anybody.

"Billy, what's wrong with your hand?" She reached, touched the clean bandage.

"Just a scratch," he mumbled. He'd never tell her that, either. But what was this? Ira had reached and taken Seth's other hand, begun stroking her forearm. Then Billy knew. He couldn't speak, staring hard at the last man on the planet that he'd ever have imagined Seth – or any other woman he himself desired – would be attracted to.

"So you guys are, like . . . "

When they looked at each other, he could practically hear violins. Both spoke at once.

"It isn't what you think," she said, blushing.

"Nothing's really happened," Ira added.

Billy did his crowd-patting gesture. "You don't need to explain," he said. "I'm very happy for you both."

While they glanced at each other uncertainly, Billy took a deep breath.

"Look, it's perfect, yin and yang, ex-farmer and pro-farmer, Bluegrass and Buckeye." *Beauty and the beast*, he thought but didn't say, feeling mean even thinking it.

"Well," Seth said. "Maybe we should decide on our end-game strategy. If the media hype has done its job, there's going to be standing-room only in the Holiday Inn's ballroom tomorrow night for the auction. I'll notify Holiday that CitFarm's coming," she said. "And Cedarton police."

"Cops?!" Billy was horrified all over again. "They won't let us within a mile of the place."

"It's private property," Seth replied. "It's not up to them. It's up to the motel. Our notifying them will just be a courtesy."

"But," he sputtered, "calling Holiday gives 'em the chance to say no."

"They won't. Very bad p.r. The media are watching this like hawks. I won't tell them that we're going to hand out leaflets to everyone coming up the drive. They'll say yes. They're getting free advertising out of this. And you better believe I'll call the TV stations."

The tone of her voice – so like the voice that spoke to him that first day in the Bean – soothed him like a shot of warm brandy. "But, hey," he said, suddenly remembering, "we've got to contact the farmers, work out the purchase details."

"That's Woody's department," Ira said. "He's been holed up with Pennington and Erickson all week, making sure they understand everything."

Before Billy could respond, they all jumped at the sound of knocking on the back door.

"Who in the world . . ?" Seth began, but before she could stand up, the door was flung open.

"Sorry I'm late, but do you realize how long it takes to wash off clay after being ass-deep in it all day?"

Stepping inside, Bonnie filled the room, it seemed to Billy, so that there was no getting away from her accusing presence. She wasn't looking at any of them, seemed to be admiring the high ceiling, though there was nothing up there but a black water-stain, which was what he felt like.

"Join the party," Ira drawled, motioning to the last empty chair at the table. She quickly sat, gazing around at the walls before looking right at Billy. He read in her eyes that she hadn't said a word to anyone about his call to her the day he'd fled.

"So. You probably want to know what I'm doing here." She sighed. "Ira invited me. As much as I used to want to see the farm turned into affordable housing, I've decided – you guys convinced me, I mean . . ." She gazed directly at Seth – "*she* did, that it's best left alone. So even if I have to stay in my little hell-hole between the boozers and the losers, I'm with you."

Bonnie reached into a large ornately-beaded leather purse and pulled out a crumpled check and tossed it on the table. "I also know there's an admission ticket to join your little soiree. This was gonna be my down payment on one of those little pink houses."

Ira picked it up and handed it back to Bonnie. "We can't take your nest egg."

Bonnie's eyes hung fire. "You took *hers*, didn't you?" She turned her high beams on Billy. "At least that's what *he* said."

Billy swallowed hard. "I gave it back." She just stared. "Before I took off. I called you and I mailed back Seth's check. I think you should both keep your money. At least for now."

Seth was shaking her head. "Billy, I told you about men who don't give women space. I gave my check to Woody the day after I got it. It's part of the million he says we've now collected."

Bonnie whistled. "No shit? Well, here's a start on the next million." She laid her check beside the pieces of the one Ira had just torn up.

"Okay. All right." Billy slumped in his chair. "Y'all better get yourselves a treasurer with some sense."

"No, Billy." Seth's jaw finally relaxed. "We need you."

"Yeh, like a case of the clap."

"No one here can fill your shoes." She looked hard at Ira. "We tried."

Billy felt Bonnie's eyes burning his face. "So Seth," he said, "what'd you tell Wendy Small when she interviewed you."

"That anyone can put their name on a sign, that a bunch of gas cans and rags don't mean *we* did it, that, as far as CitFarm is concerned, if even one person gets hurt, it's not worth it."

Ira took her hand again. "She also said, 'Wood Thrush symbolizes the intersection of the human and natural worlds, and that just as you don't destroy the land in the name of human progress, you don't burn down houses to save a farm.'"

Billy nodded, rocking backward in his chair, grinning.

"Now," Seth repeated. "Let's discuss . . ."

The door flew open again, letting in a blast of cold air. Paul stood gasping in the middle of the floor, his eyes as big as pancakes. And right behind him, gently closing the door, was tall, gawky Matt Plummer, cheeks flushed.

"Mom, you've gotta come see . . ."

But Seth was out of her chair, her face a thunderhead. "James Paul Quaid, where've you been? You're supposed to be up in your room."

Paul cast a guilty look at the boy behind him.

"You can ground me for ten million years, but please, *please* just come outside for one second and look . . . "

Seth just stood there trembling, her face pale. Billy got a quick flash of the kid banging his brains out in the closet upstairs. Now he looked like the little man Billy had imagined he could be if he docked the Enterprise and sent the aliens home.

Ira rose. "Let's go look."

Seth seemed willing to be guided by her knight. When Ira led her outside, Bonnie looked at him.

"What the fuck. We wouldn't wanna miss the show."

Outside, the wind had kicked up considerably. Beside the steps was an old wooden apple crate. It was too dark to tell what was in it. About the time Billy strode up beside Ira, the kid had his flashlight on.

Holy shit. A humongous dead bird. A beautiful bird. Even in the dim glow of the flashlight, its hooked beak looked savage. No, the damn thing was alive!

"It's a hawk," Ira whispered, gazing up at them. "A red-tail."

That's when Billy noticed the tail, which he thought looked reddish even in the porchlight's dim glow. He'd seen huge red-tailed hawks soaring above fields, catching thermals, hunting mice. Its mottled wings looked torn all to shit.

"They shot it," Paul said, then louder, " . . . over on Rabbit Run Road . . . these two boys."

Seth's eyes were saying clearly *What the hell were you doing on Rabbit Run Road after dark?*

Sobbing now, Paul got out, "Why did they want to kill it, Mom?"

Seth knelt beside him, brushing back his sweaty hair. "I don't know, sweetie." She was trying not to cry, too.

The boy looked right into Billy's eyes. He wanted to but couldn't look away. "Boys do crazy things sometimes when they're hurt."

Paul nodded, cast his gaze back on the bird. Beside him, Seth kept looking at him. Finally Ira spoke.

"Have you got an old towel or a sheet or something?"

Within seconds she was back, handing Ira a tattered black blanket.

Ira knelt, carefully covered the motionless bird, including its head, and delicately lifted it as if it were an infant he'd just delivered. Hearing the rasping lungs of the boy practically clinging to Ira, Billy started to breathe again, a little dizzily, realizing he'd been holding his breath.

Ira stood up slowly, still holding the big bundle out from his body. Finally he spoke.

"Gotta get this big boy to the Raptor Center. Bilbo, call Sue Davenport. Tell her to meet me at the center. If she's not home, call Dave Bailey. We've gotta get this guy looked at tonight."

As he walked toward his car, Paul was on him like glue, Matt not far behind.

"Paul, where do you think you're going?" Seth hollered.

Ira barked back. "I'll need him to make sure the bird doesn't get out of the box. You come, too, Seth, and bring a blanket to put over it. If he gets feisty, we'll be a lot better off if he can't get out."

Billy rushed inside, found the phonebook and got Sue on the first ring. By the time he came out to tell them she was on her way, Ira's Tercel was at the head of the driveway. Bonnie turned toward him.

"Who would hurt such a beautiful creature?" she asked in a child's whisper.

It was the voice he used to hear after they'd made love and lay together holding each other until he'd get up and leave, always leave – now he couldn't remember why. He resisted the urge to get in the truck and, instead, walked up beside her. "Some mean son of a bitch," he said, "like me."

Then before he knew what was happening, she'd encircled him in a bear-hug, crying and gasping. His arms stayed at his sides until they suddenly remembered what to do. Then he embraced her, feeling an in-rush of something, like a genie going *back* into the bottle, like a hawk flying *into* the wind.

# Chapter Twenty-Three


Shawnee Springs, Ohio
Sunday, March 19, 1999


When Billy arrived to pick up Paul the next morning, he dreaded
what he might find. Had James arrived yet? But one look at her and
he knew. Opening the door, she smirked at him. "Well, well, aren't
we looking – " She waxed thoughtful, as if searching for a word. "
– chipper?"

He'd expected it. She'd watched him leave with Bonnie after they'd
all gotten back from the Raptor Center last night. "Lay off."

"Lay off what?" It was Paul crowding her out of the doorway as he
stuck his thin arms into a jacket.

"Let's go, my man." And Billy was leading Paul to the truck, arm
around the boy's shoulders. But before he ducked inside, he glanced
back at the doorway. Seth stood, arms crossed, watching them with a
huge smile. *Damn.*

"Pedal to the metal, Billy. Peel out."

He reached over and tousled the kid's hair – it was getting long.
"Cool your jets, dude. What's your hurry?"

"Ms. Davenport couldn't operate last night, with Geordi in shock.
So she said be here first thing in the morning and she'd see what she
could do."

Billy sighed. He guessed the kid's Trekkie days weren't quite over
yet. "Aye, aye, Cap'n. Warp speed . . . *engage.*"

He hoped Seth hadn't seen him throw gravel as he gunned onto the
blacktop.

○

An hour later, when they pulled back down the driveway, Billy
stared at the house as if he might penetrate its walls and know the
worst. It sat, he thought, a bit ominously in the late-morning snow-
glare. Beside him, Paul could hardly contain himself. As soon as Billy
pulled up to the kitchen door, the boy bounded out.

"Uh uh," Billy called. "Boots off first." Catching up, he quickly
doffed his old loafers. He'd worn them on purpose so he could make a
quick escape.

"Hey, Mom, we fixed the wing," Paul yelled to an empty kitchen,
kneeling, unlacing his boots. "Sue says Geordi's gonna fly again

someday. Then there'll be a raptor release. The whole town comes out to see it, if the weather's good!"

When there was no answer, Billy felt his stomach tighten. He followed, a few paces behind. By the time, he got to the livingroom, a silent tableau was in progress. In the chair sat Seth, her spine rigid. On the couch sat a compact-looking, dark-skinned guy with salt and pepper hair wearing a black leather jacket. In the moment before anyone spoke, Billy caught her eye, fiercely green. He quickly glanced back at the man, who stood up, faced Paul and smiled.

"Dad!"

Like a whirlwind, the boy swept into the room and clutched his father, nearly toppling him backwards onto the couch.

"Hey, *hey!*" James said, laughing, stroking Paul's back in smooth circles. The stroking went on for some seconds while Billy tried not to watch, tried to become invisible, avoided at all costs Seth's eyes which clearly said *You knew and didn't tell me*. When James lifted his chin, Billy saw his eyes were wet.

"Billy." Her voice was a harsh rasp. "I'll see you tomorrow."

He lost no time leaving through the kitchen.

○

Monday Billy awoke before Ira in pre-dawn darkness. His sleep had been thin, stressful, dream-filled: he and Paul chased an injured hawk that could barely fly, waiting for it to alight on a branch so that they could trap it in a net. Finally it flew into forest and was gone. Looking around for Paul, he found himself alone near darkening woods.

He'd slept in his clothes, as usual. Since returning from West Virginia, he hated to inconvenience Ira – the only way he could stay with his friend at all was knowing it would be over soon.

He rose, his senses totally alert, not the least foggy, as if he'd never slept (he hadn't, not really). He picked up his pea coat lying in a heap near the door, glanced behind him at Ira's motionless form against the back wall, eased the door open and stepped outside. Neither night nor morning, all lay still in a cold, grey pall. No bird sang. Sunlight seemed a distant memory. Realizing he'd been holding his breath, Billy let it out in a long white stream. A crow ripped the silence, calling from somewhere behind the house, *Auc*-tion. *Auc*-tion.

He hoped to catch Seth before she left for work. Sure enough, the Subaru was still parked by the kitchen door when he pulled in. Things looked quite a bit different from Saturday night. Desolate, though there was really nothing to make him think that. But the laughter, then the tears. And then he and Bonnie left alone. Not for the first time, he wondered if it were for the best he'd come back. What if they lost it all?

After knocking, he glimpsed her through the kitchen door sitting at the table, chin in hand, staring. He had to knock again, harder, before she finally looked over and hollered.

He stepped inside. It felt like the day after a funeral.

"He's gone, Billy."

He stood by the door, unsure whether to stay or leave. "I'm sorry."

She sighed, dropped her hand that had been holding her chin, let her head flop forward before she gazed back up. "He's gone back to Taos. With his father."

When she smiled, it was sad but beautiful. The beautiful woman that, empty nest or not, he would never have. It was better this way.

"We came all the way across the country to find Paul's father, and it turned out he'd been right there with us all the time." She waved him to a chair. "I know what you're thinking," she said, softly, "and I don't mind. You can't call me anything I haven't called myself. I dragged Paul away, because I couldn't handle my own guilt. I don't belong on anyone's pedestal."

He kept quiet. Had he put her on a pedestal? She was beautiful and unattainable. He couldn't take his eyes off her. She looked older than she had a mere month ago in the Bean Tree. You could miss a lot when all you ever thought about was getting laid.

"For how long?"

She came back from far away. "A week. This time." She laughed humorlessly. More silence. He knew she heard it, too, the sound of absence: no Star Wars or Jethro Tull.

"You and Ira?"

She shook her head. "I can't think about that. I've got to start thinking about being a better mother before I can be . . . with anyone."

He wouldn't argue with her. Until his trip south, could anyone have told him who or what he needed? This morning, he hadn't left Bonnie's till she'd gone to work. Seth's eyes said she was reading his mind. Before she could speak, he did.

"Ira and Woody counted the money. One million, two-hundred and fifty-two thousand." He let it soak in. "And contributions continue to pour in – from all over."

Her mouth corners quivered upward into a tentative smile. He hated what was coming next.

"Also, there's some bad news from the trustees. They met in executive session last night."

"And voted to re-zone."

He nodded. The lightning surge had become a throbbing behind his eyes as he waited. She closed her eyes, rubbed them with her palms.

"So a million isn't enough."

"Probably not."

"There is one thing left you guys could do."

*You guys.* He laughed, but it sounded like something dying's last rasp. "Rob a bank?"

She shook her head. "Call Lloyd."

They lapsed silent.

"Well." She just looked at him. "I'd better go to work."

"You could stay home."

"And listen to an empty house?"

He stood up and moved to the doorway. Her voice was small behind him.

"How do you do it, Billy? How do you do the hardest thing in the world?"

He saw the huge brown Swiss lying on the hillside. He imagined Della walking up the steps to the registrar's office, Ira watching Amber disappear into a taxi.

"You just do, that's all."

○

The pleasantries were over with quickly, and it was evident the professor wanted to get right down to business. Fine with Billy. It was freezing standing at the pay phone on Cedarton Avenue. The sky was as grey as a dirty tee-shirt.

"Let me ask you again, William. What does the farm mean to you? I mean, personally?"

Billy didn't hesitate. "It's about a way of life."

Silence. He imagined the jutting chin, the crossed arms, the iron stare.

"You get away from soil, you get away from what matters."

The professor laughed. "But have you considered what matters to the masses? Many enjoy high-rises and cineplexes more than rural sunsets."

"Because they've forgotten." Now he heard Ira's squeaky voice: *Man is not the measure of everything; the earth is.*

"To stop and smell the roses? Or the poison ivy?"

"Dr. Kieron, I called to ask you for money."

"I'll be darned."

"To buy Wood Thrush Farm," he finished.

"I already gave you folks twenty-five grand."

Billy went blank, then remembered: the anonymous donor. "That was extremely kind and generous of you, sir, but the trustees have re-zoned the farm residential. Now it'll sell for a lot more. We need more money, if we're to buy the farm tonight." Shifting from one foot to the other, he shivered. His mouth had begun quivering, his teeth rattling uncontrollably.

"Good luck, son. I've given all that I can."

"No," he said, "not even close."

"And I suppose you have?"

"Can't you do it for your son?"

"I have no son."

"Saving this farm could be saving him, too."

"Even if I had a son – which I don't – that's preposterous."

"Dr. Kieron, you could go anywhere in the world. And you've stayed right where, as you've said yourself, your wife was not well-loved. Why? Because this place is your home, your living history."

"Heaven help us, a Romantic. Do you also believe in crystal power?"

"Sir, if you believed half the things you taught me, you would help save this farm and . . . " He paused – what the hell. " . . . acknowledge your son."

The line went dead. Billy's mouth was so out of control, he knew he couldn't've said much more anyway. He cradled the phone gently, turned and nearly walked right into Bonnie.

"You okay?" she asked. "You look like shit."

He nodded, tried to smile but couldn't manage it.

"Come here." She opened her arms, and he let her embrace him. She smelled like ginger. Vanilla. Sage. Plus, her teal poncho tickled his nose. His hands rose, unbidden, and hovered at her waist, then clutched as he sagged into her.

"Whoa, sugar," she whispered so that no one passing could've overheard. "Lean on your Bon-Bon."

And he did.

# Chapter Twenty-Four

Shawnee Springs, Ohio
Monday, March 20, 1999

As Billy stood surveying the volunteers pounding in signs on the hill behind Holiday Inn, he could hardly contain his anxiety: where was she? He shook his head. Supposed to reach the twenties after dark. Who'd stay on the hill then?

He was carrying another check in his shirt pocket. Della had reached him at Ira's last night. She'd told him how Dan had called to say he'd gotten her moved into his section of Poli. Sci. next quarter and had scheduled a meeting of KLT to deal only with Putnam County. After Billy congratulated her, she paused. "Plus, me and your daddy talked on the phone" – she did not say she'd called him, Billy noted. "He's FedExed you something to that address you gave me."

"Hope it's a coupla million dollars," he'd joked while Della remained silent.

The package had arrived this afternoon, containing a check for ten grand. (Billy smiled – the exact amount of his severance pay upon graduation.) "Della told me what you're doing," his father had written. "Saving land is the right thing. Maybe this gift will help you help them. Good luck."

His first impulse was to put it in an envelope and fire it right back *too little too late, Al* – then he remembered the calf, how there'd be no "nest of copperheads" in Putnam County without his father's refusal to sell. So he'd tucked the check in his pocket; though Billy didn't believe in good-luck charms, it felt right to carry it inside with him.

Activity had staved off the cold when they'd first arrived and occupied a grassy hillside between the upper and lower parking lots which faced the entrance to the ballroom where the auction would soon begin. Billy had organized the volunteers like a drill sergeant, using a bullhorn he'd borrowed from the village police department. Within minutes folks were hammering in posts, hanging signs, tuning instruments and chattering like crazy. He *had* to see Bonnie before he went inside where he would aid Woody in any way possible to buy as much land as they could afford. Ira had absolutely refused to do it. "This is your baby, kemo sabe," he'd said. "I'm Tonto."

At least his buddy had agreed to report to the troops after his scouting trip inside. Here he came now, hunch-shouldered and grim as hell. Billy handed him the bullhorn.

"Now, people, the Holiday Inn folks have been really nice to us,"
Ira began. "They said we're welcome as long as we do not set foot
on the parking lot or harass anyone entering the door. Bidders have
to register and get their number to be inside the ballroom, which,
incidentally, holds five hundred, but they told us we can come into the
foyer, two or three at a time, to warm up."

Bidders. The word chilled Billy more than the dropping temps. It
made him see John Schuyler, wearing the smile that said You don't
have a chance. With or without seeing Bonnie, whom he'd left two
hours ago, Billy would have to walk through that door in a few minutes
and not come out until it was over. It warmed him a little to see Ira's
news being greeted with cheers from many of the fifteen or so setting
up the signs and portable P.A. system on the bank. Billy grinned back
at them. *Damn.* He sure wished Seth had not given up on Ira as well as
the farm. At least he had Della's words before she'd hung up: "I know
you'll do the right thing whether it's politics, babies or bedfellows."

Babies. *Damn.*

Accepting the bullhorn from his old friend, Billy punched him in
the shoulder. "Heard from Seth? She coming?"

Ira just rubbed his shoulder and shook his head. "I doubt it."

Billy was about to say something when a kid in a Shawnee Springs
Radicals jacket hollered.

"When will the auction start?"

"Six-thirty," Billy replied, "but there's plenty to keep us busy till
then. We need a couple volunteers to stand down at the bottom of the
drive and meet cars, as they turn in from the highway, greeting the
drivers very politely and handing our leaflet to anyone who rolls down
a window. Do not – I repeat *do not* be anything but polite. If we change
anyone's mind – and you never know – it'll be because of our firm,
friendly resolve, not intimidation."

"Come on, Billy!"

It was newspaper editor Cyrus Harmon's high school-senior son.

"I mean it, Bart. This is gonna be the sweetest protest the world's
ever seen. Look." His gloveless hand cupped something plastic. "Along
with each flyer comes a little bag of corn – candy corn, that is – to
remind anyone bidding what the best use of that land is."

Those listening cheered. It was Bonnie's idea from Saturday night,
when they'd finally gotten to plan over popcorn and hot chocolate.
Dammit, why wasn't she here? At her place, she'd sat him down on her
futon and held him for what seemed an eternity but was probably an
hour. They hadn't said a word, and finally he'd warmed up enough that

his mouth stopped quivering. Then she'd fixed him ginseng tea and gone to work. Dealer coming from Cincinnati. She was probably still with him. And where the hell was Woody? – though he cringed at the thought of facing him.

"I'll go with them." It was Sunni Sebastian-Masterson, stunning in a red poncho.

"Thanks, Sunni. Keep 'em in line."

After the corn-greeters departed, Ira asked for others to hammer in signs – Don't Pave Paradise! and You Can't Eat Houses! – as well as people to position the huge, six-foot-high letters Lamar Frazier had cut out with his jigsaw – NO SPRAWL – on the hill for maximum media effect.

Speaking of which, Billy noticed the Channel Twenty-Five van unloading in the upper parking lot. He smiled. Damn, if it weren't Wendy Small, reporter extraordinaire herself. He wandered on up the hill. He noticed approvingly some of the members of the folk group Spring Sounds had guitars and mandolins out of their cases and were tuning up – it wouldn't be easy to play in this cold, but it looked like they were going to try.

"Well, well," he said, approaching Small, who stood surveying the crowd in a black fur coat and jaunty red beret, "what brings y'all way out here on such a cool afternoon?"

Unspooling her microphone cord, she smiled her signature million-dollar smile. "We're here to see you get what you want."

"Good ol' unbiased American journalism," he replied, tempering it with a grin. "I don't reckon you'll say that on-camera, will you?"

She continued to smile at him, working on the cord while her cameraman practiced getting her in his sights.

Another cheer broke out, and Billy turned and looked below, hoping to see Bonnie or Seth, but it was Woody, wearing his knit cap with the big ball on it, looking like Santa in the Christmas parade. In the older man's lined face, Billy saw the burden he'd carried for them all, knowing for decades that such a day as this would come. Billy experienced a warm glow for a second that became a small, burning pain before he got down to where Woody stood in the parking lot facing the crowd on the hill. Grinning, he took Billy's frozen, ungloved hand in his red-mittened one: "Bilbo, my boy. I feel like we're going to get something tonight. I've been on the phone – sorry I'm late."

"Woody, I . . . " No words came. He couldn't believe it – he always had *something* in his bag of tricks. Woody waited, his face impassive.

Billy strove to get control of his mouth, his mind. For the hundredth time, he looked toward the parking lot: *Where the hell is she?*

Woody spoke softly. "I know: this is a tough day. Before you and I have our briefing, I want to inform everyone in general terms of how this is going to go. These fine folks are going to suffer more out here than we will in the comfort of the ballroom."

Billy wasn't so sure. He'd trade with any of the hill-folk in a second. They'd sing, speechify, stomp and holler while he and Woody watched prices shoot higher and higher, the property getting further and further beyond what they could afford. But, just as he wouldn't let his thoughts turn to fire, he forced himself not to look at his growing despair. She'd be here soon. She would.

"Bring that P.A. down here," he yelled up at the two women setting up the small battery-powered amplifier the size of a computer monitor. Once they had the mic stand adjusted for Woody, the P.A. as loud as it would go, Billy stepped behind him. "You're on," he whispered. And Woody stepped forward.

"Thank you, one and all, from the bottom of my heart for coming out on this inclement evening to see this dramatic conclusion to the events set in motion one month ago by the first meeting Citizens to Save the Farm called. And, thank you for that tremendous vote of confidence you gave me and Blue Jacket Land Trust a moment ago. I'd be less than honest if I didn't tell you that I'm scared to death about going in there." He let it soak in before adding, "But I also know in my heart that we'll come away from here tonight with something, perhaps even a lot, maybe even *everything!*"

That brought a cheer, even though it rang false to Billy. Still, Woody was right: no use leaving these troops with any other message than hope.

When Woody paused, Billy felt gloom settle onto his shoulders. No one had made them any promises. Independent as ever, the farmers hadn't committed a thing yet; and they might not. The sunsetting light almost seemed to fail, and he wouldn't have been at all surprised if the grey sky had opened and let huge flakes fly. Woody's amplified sigh came across like a chill wind.

"I'm not going to lie to you, friends. Mr. Hollinsworth, the auctioneer, has said repeatedly that in his twenty years in the business conducting thousands of auctions throughout the Midwest, he has never seen a single community accomplish what we're trying to do. Not one."

The effect was the same as it had been three weeks ago when Ken Littlejohn had uttered those words during the town meeting. The hush felt funereal. In the sudden quiet Billy heard the large banner flapping – the moment before the general's hand fell and the battle began. Dammit, he needed Bonnie punching him in the ribs. And where the hell was Seth – sitting at home worrying about a boy who was bonding with his dad? Stepping forward, he tapped Woody on the shoulder and motioned for the mic.

"Just because it's never been done before doesn't mean it can't be done," he heard himself say. "We'll just be the first ones to show the whole country that it *can* be the land first, before greed."

They instantly took up the chant just as they had at the first rally when Seth had so galvanized them.

FARMS FIRST. FARMS FIRST.

"This is a fight for our small-town way of life, for the soul of our village, for the soul of the earth. And just like an entire way of life can be lost one acre, one family, one farm at a time, it can be restored one acre, one family, one farm at a time. By folks like us."

ONE ACRE.

ONE FAMILY.

ONE FARM . . .

He tried his crowd-pat, but they were roaring now. What had he said? But when he turned to say something to Woody, he bumped into Seth. She had been standing there while he brayed! When he offered her the mic, she smiled and shook her head, chanting with the crowd.

Glancing behind him, he saw Wendy Small's cameraman panning the crowd, getting the visuals he needed for the news. Billy heard that celebrated voice in his head saying, "Shawnee Springs' valiant attempt to forestall the onslaught of urban sprawl in their community ended in defeat tonight when

. . ." *O ye of little faith*, he castigated himself, noticing, when he turned back to her, how the blood had risen in Seth's formerly pale cheeks. At that moment he was back in the bag with her freezing and shivering . . . What had he believed that night? – he couldn't remember.

"It's time," Woody whispered beside him.

For one panicked moment, he ached to run for the parking lot, get in the truck and gun it toward the interstate.

Instead he turned toward Seth. "How do I . . . ?" he began.

She patted his arm. "You just do, that's all."

And after one final look toward the parking lot, he let Woody lead him inside.

# Chapter Twenty-Five

Shawnee Springs, Ohio
March 20, 1999


As soon as he and Woody entered the hallway, Billy was ambushed
by a sense of doom even worse than he'd felt at Grand-dad's that night
the ghosts rose to confront him. Sure, this was important and all, but
*damn.*

They fought their way through the media and bystanders who lined
the hallway, and when they entered the ballroom and took their places
near the front, he couldn't keep from constantly gazing around him at
the gathering bidders, looking for evil-eyed developers – as if he'd know
them if he saw them. "Developers themselves probably won't be here,"
Woody had said. "They usually send their attorneys."

He gazed up at huge white dry-eraser boards with all the tract
numbers on them. A man and woman sat at computers, their backs to
the room. Woody began speaking calmly.

"During the first round, each of the thirty-six individual parcels,
ranging from three to one hundred and two acres, will be bid on, and
the highest bid for each will be recorded on those boards."

As he continued to explain, Billy nodded dully, unable to focus,
wondering what the hell he was doing here. But Woody had to have
someone by his side, Ira having bowed out, saying his skills were more
beneficial outdoors. Ants had begun crawling under his skin, and his
hands had begun sweating. He recognized the early stages of an anxiety
attack, which he hadn't experienced since the days he'd spent waiting
for Andy Partridge to get out of the hospital. Finally Woody shut up.

"So mostly we wait," Billy said.

"And watch. Until it's time to make our move. Between then and
now, I might need you to run messages for me."

Billy nodded. He figured he might have presence of mind enough to
do that.

Glancing behind him to look at faces seriously for the first time
since he'd entered, he saw Leigh Ann Roberts, waitress at the Sunset
Café, her face a study in tense anticipation; she was about to bid
every penny in her and her daughter's pocketbook on her dream. He
could tell she was terrified she would and terrified she wouldn't get
it. Wrenching himself away from such thoughts, he turned and gazed
forward once again.

"We'll need to differentiate hostiles from friendlies," Woody whispered. "I've spread the word through various channels that we'll partner with anyone who'll purchase more than 700 acres, that we'll use our million to purchase easement rights on some or all of it. Thus, a big-time investor could build some houses and let us help him out with the purchase price if he'll agree to leave a good chunk of it in farmland."

Billy found himself unable to even nod. Fixated on saving it all, he'd never seriously considered saving pieces. And though it seemed sacrilege even now, he knew Woody was right. Some was better than none.

From far away, Woody's voice returned, maddeningly. "So a *seemingly* hostile developer might actually be a friendly, willing to partner with us to save some or most of the farm. The only real hostiles are those developers – like our friend Mr. Schuyler over there swilling cappuccino – who want the prime parts of this farm paved and crammed with houses as thick as a late-game Monopoly board."

Billy stole a quick look at Schuyler, sitting with his lawyer, guzzling coffee, grinning and laughing. The image angered him just enough to restore his brain function. Making fists, he found his palms nearly dry.

The auctioneer, a red-faced man named Hollinsworth, strolled before the boards like a teacher greeting his favorite class.

"Good evening, ladies and gentlemen, and welcome. We're here to sell you a farm, and we'll be getting right down to business in a few minutes. But before we begin, Hollinsworth Auction and Realty has a lovely print to auction, the proceeds of which will benefit St. Jude's Hospital in Knoxville, Tennessee. Do I hear a hundred? One hundred dollars for . . . " And his voice lifted into the tongue-talking, syllable-mangling song carving silence into building blocks of desire. Billy felt warm waves traveling upward from his groin.

"Hi-yahh!"

He nearly jumped out of his seat when a man with a black handlebar mustache turned suddenly and yelled. Hollinsworth stopped chattering and identified the man, one of six or seven blue-blazered men standing throughout the mostly-seated crowd. "Two hundred," yelled the man, "Bidder one-eighteen."

Then Hollinsworth rattled on until he got two-fifty from another bush-beater, Earl, then three hundred from Carl. Within forty-five seconds the print – Meredith's Pond at sunrise, complete with geese – sold for four hundred, and Billy saw the "charity event" as the foreplay it was. Like tossed-back shots of tequila, fire had begun licking at the backs of tongues, loosening control, letting numbers larger and larger slip through lips unlocked by increasing desire. Billy sat back, breathing heavily, as repulsed as he was fascinated.

"Yes, prices will rise, and things will get a little intense," he recalled Hollinsworth saying in a newspaper interview. "But no one will be hurt by that except someone who wants to bid on the entire farm."

*Right, moron*, he'd wanted to scream when he'd read that. *Us.*

"And I expect, when all's said and done," he'd added, "the land will have been kept in the hands of local people."

But at what cost? he wondered, a bit dizzily, scanning the room again, noticing eyes growing glassy, mouths tightening or slackening. His own pulse quickening, he closed his eyes and concentrated, imagined Seth, who must feel she'd lost the child she'd fought so hard for, shivering outside in the cold, still believing. The thought was like drenching rain to the intoxication he felt spreading throughout the room. Opening his eyes at last, he realized bidding on Tract #1 was already over.

"You praying?" Woody whispered.

"Something like that."

○

At the end of an hour, Round One wound down. All tracts had been bid on, and no one responded anymore to Hollinsworth's machine-gun bursts followed by his preacherly croon: "If you're done, you're done, but if you haven't spent it all, get it up. You'll never have another chance to bid on Wood Thrush Farm. They just don't make 'em like this anymore. Come on! Carl's a-comin', Earl's a-runnin'. Loosen up, now!"

Looking behind him, Billy saw Leigh Ann drop her head, forced from the bidding, annihilated. Looked like she and Lucy'd go on living in the one-bedroom apartment over Deaver's. Someone might've told her a fortyish, single-parent, small-town waitress didn't have a chance in such a high-stakes poker game – but who could've? Billy saw the tear tracks running down Leigh Ann's lined face – a preview of what Seth and the others would look like when their ship sank? Billy let his head drop onto his arms folded on the table before him.

Beside him, Woody, working his lap-top, said, "The total's two and a half million right now. That's about where I thought it would be at this point – a little higher. Buck up, my boy. This farm may be saved yet!"

But the crowded, noisy, too-bright room felt suffocating. He'd begun thinking of how it would feel to walk out and face the hill-folk – face Seth, Bonnie and Ira – without the farm.

"My boy, you're looking a bit green." Woody placed his hand gently on Billy's arm. "Combined-parcel-bidding comes next – anybody can put together any tracts they want and beat out earlier bids. That's sure to go on for awhile. Why don't you get some air before the grand finale."

"Nah, I'm fine."

But Woody shook his head. "I'll need you soon. Go now. Fifteen or twenty minutes won't matter." He bent above his lap-top.

"Okay." Billy stood up. It was now or never. "Woody, I appreciate what you did for me. I took that money and you – " When he inhaled, it fueled the flames at the back of his throat. "Why didn't you turn me in?"

Woody never looked up from his numbers. "Because I know you, Billy." He smiled as he typed. "Our Bilbo."

Billy stood convicted, sweating. "There's something else."

Now Woody glanced up. *Jeez, he doesn't need this now.*

"I gave myself a salary." He was no longer aware of his surroundings. The room's uproar was vague static at the edge of his hearing. "Out of cash contributions as they came in."

Woody nodded. His expression didn't change.

"It was wrong, and I'm paying it back." With trembling fingers, he reached inside his shirt pocket and held his dad's check out to Woody. The back was signed, though Billy had no recollection of doing it. Woody's mouth opened as if he'd argue, but he didn't.

"It's not much, but . . . "

Woody accepted the check, turned it over and read its face.

"It's everything, Billy. Everything."

○

As soon as Billy stepped into freezing darkness, his senses revived. The scent of pine on the snow-tinged air made his blood race. Plus, the hill-folks were singing "My Farm" to the tune of "My Girl." His heart roused itself, and he looked above him to the cloudless night sky. He could almost make out a star or two through the light pollution. Traffic on the nearby interstate provided percussion on the hillfolks' last chorus. Walking toward them, he tried to stand up straighter. When he finally faced them, he knew it was more than the air energizing him. Almost everyone had stayed, and it was freezing. They'd probably missed dinner. He had no right to feel low, he decided as he stepped behind the mic. Besides, Woody's words still resonated inside his chest.

"You guys are the greatest," he said. "If we buy some land tonight, it's mostly because of you. You've never wavered. You've done everything without complaining, without even being asked – and you've done it with a ticking clock. Woody's always wondered if an earth-minded angel might come down and rescue us. Well, the only angels that have intervened in this gig are standing right here in front of me. "

They burst into applause, hooting and hollering, just as they had at that first rally. Only a month ago, though it seemed another century.

"He-ey, Billy!" Bart Harmon hollered. "We winning or what?"

Billy gave his report, putting the best spin on it he could.

"So what's it like in there?" a female voice shouted.

It was Sheila King, a young single mom who'd typed, duplicated and hung fliers; called everyone in town and even delivered a mass mailing door to door by herself. He did his best impersonation of Ira's shit-eating grin.

"To tell you the truth, Sheila, it's a helluva lot warmer out here."

They screamed and clapped, beating drums. He waved and turned away, almost walking into Sasha Arden standing behind him.

"Hey," he said, side-stepping. "You seen Bonnie G.?"

Sasha's smile took the place of the moon Billy couldn't see. "She went to get snacks for everybody at Kroger's."

He glanced at his watch, saw he'd only been outside for three minutes, and headed down the slope toward the strip mall. Hearing voices ahead of him, he stopped and stared hard into the darkness. When the group stepped beneath a streetlamp, Billy recognized Mark Zamora's loose-limbed swagger. It was the way he himself used to walk. And he knew exactly who the other two were.

"Hey, Billy-man!"

The punk and his buddies stopped in their tracks as Billy approached.

Remembering the knife, Billy kept his distance, though he was still close enough to see Mark's dilated pupils. "What are you guys doing here?"

"Same as you, my man. We wanna see J. Schuyler and company eat shit just like you do. If he loses, we win, but if he wins – " He made a slitting motion across his neck – "he loses."

Billy shook his head. "Over my dead body."

Mark glanced at his two cronies, then smiled. "Have it your way." The switchblade clicked open in his right hand.

"Reinforcements on the way!" someone yelled behind the punks. Bonnie smiled as she stepped into the light, carrying a large bag. When Mark half-turned, Billy saw his chance. Taking two steps forward, he swatted Mark's wrist hard, sending the knife flying.

Mark howled and bent double, grasping his hurt wrist with his good hand. Before Billy could follow up, Bonnie sprang forward, dropped her bag and grabbed Mark in a head-lock. "I've heard about you," she said. "The arsonist with the big, bad knife."

"Do something, goddammit," Mark yelled to his buddies, but they made no move. Retrieving the knife, Billy folded the blade closed and stuck it in his jacket pocket. Bonnie was now squeezing Mark's nose, garbling his instructions to Howser and Grover. Billy knew the two stooges weren't about to take on Bonnie, especially now that hill-folk were running down the path toward them.

Bonnie spoke calmly. "You prickless twerp. You're brave with a knife or a gas can in your hand, but take away your toys and you don't wanna play anymore."

Still grasping his disabled hand with the other, Mark began screaming. In no time, hill-folk surrounded them. It was a scene Billy would've enjoyed immensely anywhere else, but he had to do something fast before Holiday Inn security heard the disturbance and closed in.

"It's all right, folks. Just a misunderstanding. This man thinks brute force can bring us what the million dollars y'all raised can't. I suggest we escort him and his colleagues back to his vehicle."

When Bonnie released him, Mark glowered at her before turning and staggering back down the way he'd come, cursing, his cronies behind him.

"It's a parade!" Bonnie announced and they all got in line as Billy led the procession behind the thugs. Mark never looked back until he reached the Monte Carlo at the foot of the hill. When all three had gotten in, Billy sidled up close to the open window.

"Listen, Zamora," he hissed, reaching in and staying the hand that was about to turn the key. "Andy Partridge almost died because of you – and me. Andy was the security guard that night at the cement company, remember? If he'd died, it would've been more my fault than yours. And I'll never let that happen again. Never."

Mark opened his mouth to speak, but Billy spoke first. "I'm keeping your knife, and I highly recommend you don't get another. Because if you cut anyone else – and I include Mr. Schuyler – I won't stop until I cut you, too. I've got nothing to lose."

It was theater, Billy knew. He had a lot to lose – everything that Wood Thrush stood for, this woman standing beside him. But he knew Mark would understand none of that. Scowling, Mark fired up the engine, gave Billy the finger and peeled out.

"Okay, friends," he said, turning back to the half-dozen or so who'd followed. "Show's over. Back to work."

"Aw, man," whined Bart Harman, "I wanted to see Bonnie kick his ass."

As the group trudged back up the hill, Bonnie lifted her bag with one hand, took Billy's hand in her other. "So what'd you say to the little peckerwood?"

"Next time I'd let you claw his balls off."

Her arm snaked around his waist. "I love it when you talk dirty."

○

Back inside, Billy found a new ball-game. An eerie hush had settled onto the jam-packed ballroom and before Billy was even in his seat, he saw why. On the middle white board in huge black figures, he read: $3,200,000.

"What's that?" he asked Woody, breathlessly.

"A bid on the whole farm." The old man hardly looked up, his fingers flying over his keyboard. "Now combined-parcel people have to raise their bids to beat it."

This was it – the whole enchilada – but this time Billy didn't feel the sinking feeling. He thought of Bonnie with Mark's head locked, his arms helplessly flailing. He was in the mood to kick ass.

As soon as he sat down, Woody shoved a napkin toward him. Billy saw harsh black writing: "I'll bid on the whole if you'll pledge your million for the easement."

"Who?" Billy rasped, his tongue cemented to the roof of his mouth.

"A friendly."

Before Billy could reply, a bush-beater hollered: "I've got a new offer on tracts 27 through 36. Increased to one million, two hundred thousand. Same bidder, Number 105."

"That's Schuyler," Woody said. "He'll try to lead others to increase in order to exceed the whole-farm bid. All he wants is the land ideal for high residential. The hell with land-locked barns and outbuildings."

Billy could feel the room tightening. Foreplay was over. Hollinsworth, his arms raised in benediction, spoke.

"All right, folks. Bidder 155 is in the lead, but there's still time. Don't get in a hurry. Don't leave without doing your best. Don't blame me for not giving you time to make your best offer. I've given you a minute and a half to beat Number 155's offer of three million, *two* hundred thousand on the whole farm. There's still thirty seconds left."

Hollinsworth looked askance at the crowd, his head inclined.

"Mr. Hollinsworth, I've got an increase on Tracts 10 and 11 to $95,000, Bidder Number 332."

Within seconds, two other blue blazers reported increases. Gazing back, Billy saw Schuyler glancing around him as if his burning glare could prod people out of their torpor. But apparently his fellow bidders were maxed out.

Hollinsworth tented his fingers. "Cindy and Dave have done the math for you up here on their computers, my friends, and Number 155 is still in the lead. Is there no more action? We can go home pretty soon if that's what you want."

" Mr. Hollinsworth. A $100,000 increase on Tracts 27 through 36." Billy knew without looking it was Baldy representing the developer again.

"We have a new leader at . . . " The auctioneer waved toward the board. ". . . three million, *four* hundred thousand dollars. Is there anyone else?" And when Hollinsworth cast his gaze toward the rear of the room, Billy followed. He spotted a Russian fur hat in the middle of a furious consultation with two blue blazers.

Billy looked down at the napkin and saw the scrawled initials he'd missed earlier. "L.K." He half-lifted himself from his chair and gawked. When Shawnee Springs' most famous recluse at last nodded, Handlebar stepped forward, his face shiny with sweat.

"Mr. Hollinsworth, there's a new bid on the whole farm."

The room quieted. Billy held his breath.

"Three million, four hundred and *six* thousand."

"Bidder number?" Hollinsworth demanded.

"Same bidder, 155," said Handlebar, turning back to the fur hat. But all eyes, Billy saw, were turning back to the front. Schuyler stood, arms crossed as tightly as if strait-jacketed, his face impassive, his eyes murderous. He stared straight ahead at the board, ignoring the bush-beater who leaned toward him. Far behind the developer's table, Fred Pennington stood beside Professor Lloyd Kieron, hands clasped in front of him, as if surveying tall corn and finding it satisfactory.

"All right," said Hollinsworth. "If you want to stay in, you must raise your bid within one minute. Sixty seconds, folks, or we can all go home, and it's over. Don't let this wonderful opportunity slip away if you have the
means . . ."

Glancing in the other direction, Billy saw a crowd growing in the open doorway. There was Seth – and, beside her, cheeks as red as her hair, Bonnie. He caught her eye, gave her thumbs-up and she turned toward Seth, speaking near her ear. He couldn't bear to look back toward Schuyler's table.

"Forty seconds."

Woody, half-turned in his seat, punched Billy's arm. "Here we go."

Now Billy did look. Schuyler was sitting, staring at the table before him.

"Thirty seconds."

Billy glanced behind him again. In the rear to the right, Garth Erickson stood grinning. Council members Dave Eckerd and Tess O'Neil stood beside the farmers with Ken Littlejohn and Cyrus Harmon, their faces glowing. Leigh Ann Roberts, lines in her face gone, looked shell-shocked.

"Twelve . . . eleven . . . "

Then they took it up, loudly, the whole room, it seemed to Billy, on its feet, thundering:

"TEN . . . NINE . . . EIGHT . . . "

Standing tall, facing forward, chin upturned, stood his old history prof, looking as smug as if he'd just crushed an entire class of freshmen. *A devil of an angel.* Billy grimaced before taking up the chant with Woody.

"FIVE . . . FOUR . . ."

He watched Seth and Bonnie's faces freeze in awe.

"THREE . . . TWO – "

He thought his heart might melt in the center of his chest.

"ONE . . . *SOLD!*"

The explosion, when it came, almost lifted him off the ground. The room erupted into applause and screams. Many jumped to their feet, their arms raised in power salutes before they bellowed, hugged and kissed those standing next to them. Others, head hung, immediately stood and started putting on coats.

"I'm sorry I couldn't tell you sooner," yelled Woody at Billy's ear, "but Lloyd didn't want anyone to know until the very end, wanted to take Schuyler by surprise. He called me earlier today – that's why I was late – and said he was thinking about going for it, if the farmers were on board. Well, thanks to you and Seth, they were.”

“Just like the bastard,” Billy said as the crowd’s roar subsided. “Wouldn’t play at all unless he was sure he could win.”

“Ah, but he wasn’t.” Woody unfolded the napkin and Billy read Kieron’s neat script: “Not a dime higher than 3,000,200.”

Billy let it soak in. So he had given till it hurt. Maybe he’d given it all. But before Billy could say it, he realized Woody was being lifted off his feet by a grinning Garth Erickson. When he let Woody go, he pointed a beefy finger at Billy.

“Your butt’s mine now, Acorn!” he yelled.

Billy nodded and grinned.

“This time next month, we gonna be breaking ground. Give me your hand on it.”

Inside Erickson’s huge hand, Billy’s felt like a kitten’s paw. The farmer turned Billy’s palm up. “Damn, boy, we got to turn this sow’s belly into a slab o’ beef.” When he slapped his arm, Billy punched him back. The man’s blue eyes blazed. Then Erickson smiled and clasped him so close Billy could smell sweat and Skoal as the gruff voice spoke near his ear.

“Be proud to have you work beside me, son.”

Releasing Billy, the farmer turned to greet Pennington, who’d finally made his way over. After shaking Fred’s hand, Billy quickly put on his jacket and began shouldering through the crush. By the time he got to the doorway, Seth and Bonnie were gone, no doubt pushed backward into the hallway. Sure enough, when he squirted through, he glimpsed her flaming hair. She was standing beside Seth and Ira, who saw him approaching.

“Not too shabby for an unemployed white boy,” Ira drawled.

Billy’s eyes stung. Here was the guy who got the farmers on board, gave him a place to live, who covered his ass and never gave up on him. Who tore a blood-and-sweat-stained check into tiny pieces.

“Dammit, Ira, I . . . ”

“Look out!” Ira’s eyes widened. Bonnie blind-sided Billy, crushing him in a bear-hug. Over his shoulder, he saw Seth smiling and read her lips: You did it.

No, *we* did it, he wanted to correct her, but before he could, a familiar voice piped up beside him.

“Mom. *MOM!*”

Paul stood between them. Only a couple paces away stood James, arms folded and smiling.

"How . . ?" Seth managed to say.

"Dad said we could fly out tomorrow."

"But, James, your client . . . the show?"

James shrugged. "Paul wanted to see you win."

"But . . . where have you been all this time?"

"Everywhere," the boy said, grinning. "Dayton Art Institute, Paul Laurence Dunbar House, Air Force Museum, Glenora Wood, the raptor center – Dad even met Geordi!"

James' smile said: our son is amazing, isn't he?

But Seth was no longer looking at him. She'd clasped her boy to her furiously. Then, loosening one arm, she beckoned James. "Come on," she yelled. "Everybody!"

Bonnie pulled James into the circle, then motioned for Billy. Across from him Ira and Seth were sharing a kiss that looked more than merely celebratory. Suddenly he was on that hillside with the calf again – he wanted to sing and shout and dance. But not just yet . . .

"I'll be right back," he said to Bonnie and broke away, headed back into the ballroom where many still stood crushed together showing no signs of leaving. And, in slow motion, as in old newsreels of a crowded square the day Allied victory was declared, he saw the tall man in the fur hat standing near the back of the room. Kieron stopped not twenty feet away, his path blocked by rejoicing onlookers, and looked directly at Billy. Sounds became muted, and motion slowed further. The world fell away as Billy met his former mentor's naked stare. The man's impassive features did not change as he slowly brought his hand up to his forehead, then dropped it in a crisp salute. Billy felt a hand on his shoulder.

"Mom says you need to tell the hill people," Paul said as if from underwater. "Come on!"

Without breaking eye contact with the man across the room, Billy clutched the boy to his side. The man across the room took Paul's measure and nodded.

"Come on," Paul said, squirming away. "It's not fair to leave everybody outside in suspense. We gotta celebrate."

Billy finally looked down at the boy. "What's your hurry. We've got forever."

But the kid was gone. Billy started to follow, stopped and looked back at the crowd, but the fur hat was now nowhere to be seen. Sound rushed back in, like geese-laughter on the wind, while he stood in the middle of the sea of people.

He'd go out to the mansion before the week was out. Someone had to welcome Lloyd back to the community, back to life. It might as well be him, a man back from the dead himself. They'd talk about what came next after you'd saved a farm: endless closings, signings, deeds; plowing, planting, harvest. They'd talk about how hard it is to leave and how hard it is to come back.

# Acknowlegements

This book was truly a collaborative effort, and I owe immense debts to the following groups, individuals, authors and spiritual guides.

Basing a novel on an historical event is a daunting task, and the source of most of my factual information about the events surrounding the auction of Whitehall Farm outside Yellow Springs, Ohio in the winter of 1999 was drawn from intense, accurate coverage by the *Dayton Daily News, Springfield News-Sun* and *Yellow Springs News* as well as the many informational fliers produced by The Farmland Preservation Task Force, Community Service Inc., Tecumseh Land Trust and Patti Dallas's excellent video: *Yellow Springs and The Whitehall Farm: A Celebration of Community.*

The Tecumseh Land Trust, represented by Julia Cady, Al Denman and Krista Magaw, was extremely supportive when it became aware of this project, providing not only moral support and enthusiasm but also lending me valuable videotapes of the Whitehall auction itself, an event I mostly missed from my vantage point on the hill outside the Holiday Inn, where the auction occurred. My repeated viewings were crucial in helping me understand the process and the participants that produced such a miraculous outcome. Also, TLT generously lent me transcripts of audiotaped interviews with many of the major players in these events, providing valuable background and insight.

Although I had plenty of help, I accept full responsibility for any writing defects. I'm deeply grateful to the Oakey Dokes, a writing group that met for many years at Nancy Pinard's house in Oakwood, for listening to early drafts, steering me in right directions and keeping my wheels out of the ditch. Also, many individuals spent long hours reading and commenting on various drafts: Don Wallis, Rachel Moulton, Bill Vernon, Judy Hempfling, Kevin Stewart, Teri Piatt, Krista Magaw, Phyllis Wilson Moore, Katrina Kittle, Meredith Sue Willis,  and James Fountain. My wife, Viki Church, read every draft, held me accountable for all details, gave me excellent advice and never lost her passion for this book, helping me keep mine alive.

Thank you, Susan Bright, Plain View Press publisher/activist/poet, for believing this story might have an audience and helping me find it.

I've been influenced by numerous nature writers, but for me the essence is distilled in Henry David Thoreau and Wendell Berry. Thoreau's *Walden* began my love affair with nature; Berry's *The Unsettling of America: Culture and Agriculture* matured it. I also thank authors Kathleen Norris, Ann Lamott, Thomas Merton, Julia

Cameron, Natalie Goldberg, Wayne Dyer and the King James Bible for daily spiritual nurturance.

And, finally, thanks to my hometown, Yellow Springs, "the little community that could," for raising 1.2 million dollars in less than two months to purchase the easement insuring Whitehall Farm would remain forever agricultural. As Amy Harper wrote in the *Yellow Springs News* after the dust had settled following the auction on Monday, February 22, 1999 when Whitehall Farm was sold for $3.275 million: "We are the angels who saved Whitehall Farm."

# About the Author

West Virginia native Ed Davis has been a writing teacher at Sinclair Community College in Dayton, Ohio since 1978. He is the author of four poetry chapbooks, including *Healing Arts* (Pudding House, 2005); the novel, *I Was So Much Older Then* (Disc-Us Books, 2001); as well as many published stories and poems in anthologies and journals. His story "The Boys of Bradleytown" was awarded first place in The Best of Ohio Writer's 2005 annual contest. He lives with his wife and two cats in the village of Yellow Springs, Ohio. Please visit him at www.davised.com

# **About** *Measure of Everything*

" . . . the true heart of this book is its exploration of the relationship between people and the land. We see this realization through Billy's eyes as he
struggles to define why he has come to feel so strongly about this particular
cause. Beyond the desire to root for the underdog or rally against change,
there's a powerful life-connection between humanity and the earth, as well
as the animals we share it with, that draws people to such land disputes.  In
this Davis goes a long way toward explaining the question inherent in the
book's very title: What is the measure of everything? . . . Davis' rich and
poetic prose lends strength to the scenery, vividly capturing the land and
nature as well as the urban sprawl encroaching upon it. As in his first novel,
*I Was So Much Older Then*, Davis has a great turn of phrase. There are also
far more twists and turns to the plot than might be expected from a book
that's essentially about rescuing soil.  In some ways, it could be called an
agricultural thriller."
> **Eric Fritzius**, Greenbrier County (WV) Librarian

"Davis creates Billy Acorn, an unlikely and flawed hero who runs from
his mistakes only to find himself confronted by the very things he's trying
to escape. On his journey, he stumbles upon the connections between the
past, present and future that will ultimately drive him toward what he hasn't
known he's been seeking. ... Several compelling sub-plots emerge along
the way — a mother searching for a home and future for her son, a teacher
striving for redemption, and a once-prominent mentor struggling to reclaim
his place. Holding it all together is the small-town feel that Davis writes so
intimately about."
> **Scott Geisel**, *From Yellow Springs* (OH) *News*

"The story switches time lines and states throughout as the morose Billy
alternately works to save the farm, woo Seth, avoid his angry ex Bonnie,
keep the eco-terrorists at bay, and cope with guilty secrets. ...*The Measure
of Everything* looks at the disappearing farmland and countryside that urban
sprawl has created, asking the reader point-blank when it will end and what
will be left when and if it does."
> **Laura Merrell**, From *Dayton* (OH) *City Paper*

"Despite the plots and sub-plots as the story moves toward resolution, it moves so fast, that sometimes I felt like I was on a roller coaster ride and that's what I like.  It's a good thing to read a book that is so entertaining and also makes you think. This incredible story portrays how fragile the balance is of the preservation of the land, and how the destruction of our environment affects our society, the very way we live ... This story is one of the most heartfelt pleas I've ever read to stop, or at least, slow down the changes made to our society by business developers and big industry."
**Joy Lackey**, novelist, *Ghosts on Buffalo Creek*